Cowboys and Crowns Collection

PART 3

LACY WILLIAMS

The Other Princess

Prologue

"You're too nice."

Maggie Hale groaned and dropped her head into her hands. "Not this again."

She was seated across the nook table from her cousin Scarlett in the original Triple H ranch house, where Scarlett and her husband Miles lived. The remnants of breakfast—biscuit crumbs, the empty gravy bowl, a few scrambled egg curds, and a plate with a lone piece of bacon—were spread out between them.

Maggie needed more coffee if her cousin was going to keep spouting nonsense.

Scarlett pointed her fork. "Everyone knows the ranch house is the best place to live, but you and Uncle Gideon built that bungalow down by the stock pond. *Nice.*"

"You were here first." Maggie stood and went to the coffeepot. Thankfully, Scarlett made industrial-strength French Roast. Outside the window, dawn was lighting the sky with streaks of silver.

Maggie liked the bungalow. It was small. Cozy.

"Miles and I were here first," Scarlett said, "but you're royalty. You could've kicked us out."

As if Maggie needed to be reminded that she couldn't be just plain old Maggie. She was Princess Margaret, fifth in line for the throne of Glorvaird.

She would never think to kick Scarlett and Miles out of their home. An exclamation stating just that was on the tip of Maggie's tongue, but if she uttered it, she'd just prove her cousin was right. Scarlett and Miles and their toddler daughter Richelle lived in the ranch house with Scarlett's mom, Maggie's Aunt Carrie, and her stepdad Trey. It was a multi-generational household that worked for them.

Scarlett swiped the last piece of bacon as Maggie approached the table warily. She pointed it at Maggie. "Too nice." And crunched into the crispy goodness.

"Hey!" Maggie's protest was halfhearted. She knew better than to try and keep food from a pregnant woman. Scarlett's baby bump—this was her second child—was barely noticeable, and they hadn't announced anything yet, but Maggie had been around for Scarlett's first pregnancy and knew the signs. Frequent irritability, food cravings, know-it-all-ness. That one was pure Scarlett, though, pregnant or not.

"I am nice," Maggie admitted, because Scarlett was partly right. She was nice, but she wasn't *too* nice. "But that has nothing to do with getting the charity board to fund this riding program."

The therapeutic riding program was Maggie's heart-project. Getting it off the ground was the one thing she wanted to accomplish before she turned thirty in five years.

Horses had been her refuge when she'd needed one the most. And there were so many kids out there dealing with anxiety, abandonment, being bullied.

Her program could help.

She just needed the other board members to buy in.

"You need to throw your weight around," Scarlett said. "Wear your tiara to the next board meeting and remind those old geezers who you are. *You* started the foundation."

Technically, Maggie's dad had started it when she'd been

nineteen. He'd told her he wanted her to run it. And since he rarely asked her for anything, she'd agreed.

It had been her first time into Dallas since—

In the other room, the back door opened and closed. Probably one of the hands stomping into the mudroom to report to Scarlett, who acted as foreman for the cattle operation.

But it wasn't a cowboy who appeared.

It was Maggie's mirror-image. Her twin, who hadn't visited the Triple H Ranch in at least five years.

"Tirith. What are you doing here?"

Chapter One

THIS WAS NEVER GOING TO WORK.

Maggie wobbled across the carpeted expanse of her sister's living room, tilting and twisting on heels that felt like stilts. The palace walls were thick stone and would muffle any sounds she made.

She was no rodeo clown, but she'd probably get some laughs if she tried to wear these heels and pitched hiney over teakettle in front of the photographers who followed her family around any time they stepped foot out of the royal palace.

Muttering words that were certainly not suitable for her station, Maggie peeled off one torture device and then the other—otherwise known as Louboutins.

She retraced her steps back to her sister's bedroom. Before yesterday, she'd never been in this suite. It'd been well over a decade since she'd stepped foot on Glorvaird soil. Even the suite they'd shared as children would've felt foreign.

This morning, Tirith's personal assistant Elizabeth had laid out the plum-colored pantsuit, white silk blouse, and offending shoes while Maggie had been showering.

The clothes whispered along her skin, the softness almost

as foreign as having someone choose her outfit, down to the diamond cuff bracelet that felt like a shackle around her wrist.

And that was a drop in the bucket of discomfort after Maggie had been subjected to nearly an hour in a chair getting her hair, makeup and manicure done before she'd been allowed to dress.

The stylist had been aghast at the state of her hair. She hadn't had the heart to tell him that the highlights he was griping about were natural from being out in the sun all day. At least the manicurist had been silent in her judgment of Maggie's farm-girl hands.

Had they already figured it out? Would they go to the press?

Maybe she wouldn't even last the first morning of this charade.

She stomped back to the bedroom, shoes in hand. The crowd of *helpers*—more like handlers—had made themselves scarce after she'd been adequately groomed, and she now had the suite to herself.

She'd spent close to an hour last night practicing in the mirror, trying to get Tirith down. They might be twins, but Tirith was practically a stranger to her. How she stood, how she walked... if Maggie messed it up, this crazy plan would be over. She'd had deportment lessons from an instructor her mother had sent to the Triple H when Maggie was thirteen. That was twelve years ago, and she'd never had an occasion to use what she'd begrudgingly learned. She'd skipped senior prom in favor of going camping with her dad.

Now she went straight to the walk-in closet—bigger than her room back at home—and stepped inside. Flats. She just needed a pair of flats that matched this suit.

She blinked at the array of clothes in every color, each one with a designer label. Nothing like what filled her closet back home.

Even blinking felt wrong. Her eyelashes were Tirith's, not

hers. Curled with a wicked-looking silver tool, painted with mascara and lined with a pencil.

She should have probably been thankful the stylist hadn't given her false eyelashes.

Being Tirith was the whole point.

She sighed as she left the heels right in the middle of the closet floor and went to the set of shelves built into the very back of the space.

There. The ballet flats were plain black, and Maggie knew she could make it through the day without falling on her face if she wore them. She quickly slipped them on.

"Just be Tirith," she said under her breath as she went back through the bedroom and into the living area.

It was easier said than done. Her sister didn't even have a television, only bookshelves that lined one entire wall.

Maggie enjoyed curling up with a good book as much as anybody, but come on. Sometimes a girl needed a few hours of college football to unwind. There was something therapeutic about booing the referee when he made a terrible call. Dad kept several of last year's best games on the DVR for when they needed a fix during the off season.

The sleek orange cat tiptoed out of Tirith's bedroom door and into the bathroom. The second sighting Maggie had had of it. It must've slept under the bed. Or in the closet. Probably waiting to pounce.

Of course Tirith had a cat.

Maggie was a dog person.

She gritted her teeth.

She'd make do. It was only for two weeks.

She grimaced, then caught a glimpse of her face in the wall-mounted mirror across the room.

When was the last time Tirith had asked her for anything?

Never.

Not since they'd been taken—

Maggie couldn't let herself go there. Not when she was this close. There was a reason she'd stayed in Texas for so long.

But her twin needed her. And Tirith never needed anything. She was strong. So much stronger than Maggie.

The fact that Tirith had asked for help now meant she needed it desperately. How could Maggie say no?

She left the suite, forcing herself to walk with the same forbidding posture Tirith used. She wanted to run her fingers along the stone walls, remember their texture. Something else she'd forgotten in her long absence. She wanted to wander over to what had been the nursery when she and Tirith had been infants. Surely the cribs they'd slept in were gone by now. Or maybe not. The crown prince would be expected to produce an heir sometime in the future.

But there was no time for reminiscing. And she didn't want to make anyone suspicious.

Tirith's assistant had gone down a list of today's appearances while Maggie had been in the chair of doom, getting her makeup done.

First up, breakfast with Mother. Oh, sure. Run the gauntlet before the first cup of coffee.

Then again, if she could fool Mother, she could fool anybody.

As identical twins, Maggie and Tirith had switched places occasionally as children. But never for this long. And never when the stakes were this high.

For Tirith. It would be Maggie's mantra as she counted down the hours until she could return to Texas, where she belonged.

It had been more than a decade, but she still remembered the twisting path to the blue parlor, where Mother preferred to eat family meals.

Family.

They hadn't been a family since that terrible day.

Maggie breezed into the room. There was no room for emotion in a breakfast with Mother. Not if she wanted to pull this off.

Mother was already seated at the square table near the

window that overlooked a spit of sand that jutted out into the ocean.

There was a time when Maggie had been content to sit near that window for hours, watching the waves beat against the shore.

"Good morning, Mother," she murmured.

Alessandra reached out her hand, and Maggie squeezed it.

There were no bear hugs here, not like the kind Tirith would get from Dad two thousand miles away from here.

"You look tired, dear."

Maggie had to stifle a hysterical giggle as she sat on the opposite side of the table. Had it really only been yesterday morning that she'd sat across from Scarlett, arguing over whether she was too nice?

This breakfast was as different from that one as a Brahma bull was from a pasture of Holstein milk cows.

Fine white linen covered the table and fell halfway to the floor. Exquisite china and real silver tableware were a reminder that she had to be careful. Always be careful.

The staff hovered about, moving silently and efficiently. A young man in the dove-gray palace uniform put a plate of sliced fruit and baked ham and an egg over-easy on the table in front of Maggie.

A young woman poured tea into Mother's cup first, then Maggie's. Tea? Not coffee?

She might only be here for fourteen days, but she might die without her daily coffee fix.

Remembering Mother's comment, she made her lips form a serene smile. Tirith was always serene, wasn't she? "I'm fine."

Mother's eyes were on the spoon she was slowly stirring her tea with. "Your father called."

Maggie's stomach lurched as it had when she was fifteen and had climbed on the back of a steer to feel what it was like to ride a bull. Serenity was hard to fake. "Oh?"

She hadn't thought Gideon and Alessandra still spoke.

Everything between them was amicable and mostly handled through Mother's personal assistant.

But the divide was there, an impassable rift wider than the ocean between them. Maggie's fault.

She swallowed hard, but Mother didn't look up to see the emotion she couldn't quite hide.

"He wanted to know if he should come."

Mother's quiet words froze Maggie with that dang teacup at her lips.

But she didn't have time to freeze.

Her teacup rattled in its saucer as she set it down. She folded her hands in her lap, mind racing. Her first instinct had been a sharp *no!* but that would be a Maggie response, not a Tirith one.

She forced out a silent exhale. Tried for a smile, and, since they were talking about Tirith and what had happened two days ago, it was okay that her smile trembled.

"I hope you told him to stay in Texas."

Sorry, Daddy.

Mother's gaze flicked up and then back down. She set her spoon on the edge of the saucer. "That's what I told him."

Maggie was glad Mother wasn't looking at her too closely. She'd borne the guilt for so long that sometimes it lost its sharpness.

Until moments like just now, when she realized how much she'd cost her family. Once upon a time, Alessandra and Gideon had been passionately in love. And once upon another time, Gideon had chosen Texas, and Maggie, over staying in Glorvaird with his wife and two other daughters.

Although they remained married on paper, they hadn't seen each other in years.

Maggie didn't think she could stomach breakfast after all.

She was about to excuse herself when the door opened and a brunette peeked her head inside.

And then Maggie's baby sister Beatrix was ducking through the doorway.

"Good morning, Mother. Good morning, Tirith."

Bea. If Maggie had been free to do so, she'd have jumped up and embraced her sister. Bea was two years younger. They spoke on the phone weekly, sometimes more, and Bea had come to Texas for a visit during the summer.

Maggie missed her baby sister like a mama cow separated from its calf.

But Tirith saw Beatrix often. Jumping out of her chair like Maggie wanted to would be out of character.

So Maggie sat, even though she ached for that hug.

Her younger sister went to Mother first and got the same hand squeeze Maggie-as-Tirith had.

Maggie waited for the same treatment, but Bea leaned over and hugged her shoulders.

It brought hot moisture to Maggie's eyes, which she quickly blinked away.

"How are you holding up?" Bea asked.

That hysterical giggle bubbled up again, and again Maggie choked it down. "I'm..." She shrugged and then winced internally. Tirith probably didn't shrug.

Bea swiped a triangle of toast off her plate. "Do you want me to go to the ribbon cutting with you this morning? Or maybe you can get out of it...?"

"Not necessary," Maggie murmured coolly. "It won't take long, and I've got my army in place."

Tirith had promised that her personal assistant Elizabeth wouldn't question the request for a second bodyguard in addition to the one that usually followed Tirith around when she was out and about in the kingdom. Maggie wasn't sure she could function with just one. Another sign of Tirith's courage and Maggie's cowardice.

Maggie pushed back her chair from the table. "I should be going."

If she stayed much longer under Mother's watchful eyes, the game would be up.

But Bea followed her out into the corridor, linking their arms as Elizabeth fell in step two paces behind.

Mild panic coursed through Maggie. Did her sister know?

Before either woman could speak, a tall figure strode from a side hallway and toward them like some kind of heat-seeking missile.

"There you are. I'm glad I caught you."

Valentin!

Her cousin, the crown prince, swept both sisters into a hug that rivaled Dad's. And Maggie felt the hot prick of tears again.

Seriously? What was wrong with her?

Being back after all this time was making her off-kilter and over-emotional.

Or maybe it was that she'd always imagined Tirith an ice princess, shut off from real affection and warmth in the family castle.

But that didn't seem to be true. Bea had hugged her. And now Valentin, who walked beside them as they made their way toward the lower level of the castle and the garage, Maggie's destination.

"Annika is attending the naval base celebration with me," he said.

Annika. Annika. Maggie had to rack her brain before she remembered Annika was his current girlfriend. They must be serious if she was attending a royal event at his side.

Or maybe they'd been serious for a while and Maggie hadn't known it.

Tirith was also supposed to attend the recognition ceremony for a general who'd served in the Glorvaird service for three decades.

"She's a little nervous," Valentin said, "so I thought maybe you'd ride in the limo with us and... talk to her." He gave a shrug that Maggie had seen before when Miles was talking about Scarlett. The one that meant *women stuff*, as if he were baffled.

Bea still had her arm tucked through Maggie's and gave her side an unobtrusive nudge. Was that meant to be a *tee-hee* or a warning?

Maggie had to fight off that hysterical giggle again. Tirith would likely be great at dispensing advice about handling royal events. She participated often enough.

Maggie was hanging on to the distraction her cousin and sister presented. Every time she thought about this stupid ribbon cutting, she wanted to throw up. What was she going to tell Valetin's girlfriend that would ease her nerves?

"I'm sure that's fine," she murmured when it was clear Valentin was waiting for an answer.

He kissed her cheek and went on his way.

When she and Bea reached the garage door, a security guard in a suit and wired at the ear spoke softly into the air and held it open.

Bea let go.

Maggie froze.

Everything so far this morning, all the pretending, could be erased if she turned around now and confessed.

Once she stepped through that door, she was committed to this crazy charade.

Tirith needed her.

And Maggie hadn't come through once before. She'd let everyone down when it counted most.

She had to do this.

She stepped through the door alone.

Luc Moreno was a born politician. His mother had said so when he was a three-year-old standing front of a counter at the sweet shop. He'd cajoled her until she gave in and let him get a treat.

He knew how to get things done. A whisper in the right ear could pave the way when money and intent weren't enough.

And he also knew how to keep secrets.

He'd been a junior councilman for two years. And then after the bruhaha with Father he'd taken a hiatus from serving the public and spent the past two years working tirelessly with his brother Ernest's foundation. Trying to right what Father had done. If things went perfectly, all his work was about to come to fruition. All he needed was one princess to cooperate for another week. Seven days, and the deal would be done.

He stood just inside the sparkling atrium with its glass walls. Waiting for her arrival along with several other people. He'd greeted the hospital director, Nancy, and schmoozed with a parliament member and a photographer who happened to be an old friend from college. A couple other members of the press had been hand-selected and would accompany them inside. More press were gathered on the sidewalk outside, visible through the sparkling glass.

He'd been supposed to meet with Tirith for coffee before this ribbon cutting. She'd texted him early this morning to cancel, and she hadn't said why. His several follow-up texts had been ignored.

And then the royal limo arrived, pulling up to the sidewalk outside. Relief. If she pulled out of the polo match or the gala, he would be doomed.

As usual, the small knot of reporters swarmed the limo door even as the princess's bodyguard shouldered through them to make room for her to exit the car.

And there was Tirith.

Except it wasn't her.

The doppleganger looked like Tirith, but Tirith would never allow herself to be manhandled between the two hulking bodyguards. She'd own the space, even if she were sandwiched between them.

There was something off about her gait. Not a limp, but she didn't walk exactly like Tirith.

And she wore flats. He'd never seen Tirith in flats. Not once.

Which meant this was... Princess Margaret?

He'd never met the reclusive princess who resided in America. Not once in the two years he and Tirith had made plans to be seen together at public events.

Where was Tirith? After she'd ignored his texts this morning, he'd been concerned. Now that he saw this imposter, he was worried. He glanced at the limo but it was already pulling away from the curb.

What was the reclusive princess doing here?

The press shoved microphones in her direction, shouting questions.

"Princess Tirith! Princess—"

The clamor of voices was cut off by the swoosh of the hospital doors closing. The reporters knew better than to follow her inside without an invitation.

The bodyguards faded away, and the Administrator Nancy moved forward to shake the princess's hand. "Princess Tirith, thank you for joining us."

Luc waited for her to correct the woman, but the princess shook her hand with a smile that looked nothing like Tirith's.

How did no one else notice? The truth was as plan as the warm tan on her face, the crinkles of her eyes.

Maybe they only saw what they'd expected to see.

A loud noise from down the hall—a cart spilling over? A metal bedpan hitting the tile floor?—and the princess went from smiling to complete panic.

Her face went chalk-white, and her posture changed as she went from a forced calm into fight-or-flight mode.

Based on the way her gaze was darting about, seeking an escape, he guessed flight was going to win.

He didn't know why she was posing as her sister. Didn't know anything other than he couldn't let anyone get wind that this wasn't Tirith. His brother's foundation depended on it.

So he did think only thing he could think of. He stepped forward, close enough to slide his arm around her waist.

He murmured, "Hello, darling."

And he kissed her.

He felt the infinitesimal stiffening of her spine, and then she was all softness in his arms. She smelled like lavender and sunshine and tasted faintly like strawberries.

He pulled back quickly, aware of the camera snap behind them. He angled his body to shield her from prying eyes as much as possible. He told himself he was protecting her because if she lost her composure, her charade would be spoiled.

But he found himself gazing down into her ethereal blue eyes and realized he wanted to keep holding her.

Which is why he let his hands fall away from her waist.

He couldn't afford to be distracted, not when he was this close to achieving his goal.

There was a noticeable hush in the small group of doctors and administrators who surrounded them as they made their way down a quiet hallway and out to the hospital's central courtyard, where the new cardiac wing would be dedicated. Another horde of people and cameras would be waiting there.

He probably should've thought through that kiss better. *Probably?*

Because kissing her was going to make headlines for sure. He and Tirith were friends, nothing more. Friends who attended events together when having a plus-one was better than being besieged by posers and losers. They had always been careful to be circumspect in public, rarely holding hands. They'd let the public and the press speculate as wildly as they wanted, but they but knew there'd never be more than friendship between them. Luc had been happy with the arrangement, as had Tirith. He'd never kissed Tirith, never wanted to. He'd never felt more than the tiniest twinge of attraction toward the royal princess.

But kissing Margaret?

He'd had his share of first kisses.

And none of them compared to the thrill of that first brush of his hand against her waist.

Kissing her had been electric, pure emotion rising up inside him with no outlet, it was... everything.

What had he just done?

MAGGIE WAS BREATHLESS. And it was no longer thanks to the fear that had gripped her by the throat at the sudden clatter back in the lobby.

She tried the deep breathing techniques she'd learned as part of her recovery, but she could feel the heat of *him* right behind her, and every inhale brought the scent of his spicy cologne.

She'd just kissed her sister's boyfriend. And she'd felt... something.

Maybe she was confused. Her stomach was rumbling its complaints from her skipping breakfast. Maybe hunger had made her knees weak.

That was it. Had to be, right?

She could barely glance at him. But if she acted shy now, he'd figure it out. If he'd kissed her *hello* like that, in front of cameras, no less, he and Tirith must have been closer than Maggie had thought. She'd never asked Tirith outright, just made assumptions from the news articles and web videos the castle staff forwarded to her each week.

She should've quizzed Tirith a little better last night before she'd left Texas. Not that she'd had much time before the royal jet had been scheduled to depart.

Obviously, she needed to call her twin, but now wasn't the time. She was getting ready to step in front of that crowd of people with a giant pair of scissors and smile for the cameras. Shake hands. Be royal.

That was hard enough without worrying about a rogue boyfriend.

She, Luc, and her entourage waited off to the side as a

technician fiddled with a cordless microphone and then finally handed it to the hospital administrator.

And then Luc leaned in and spoke so that only she could hear. "Shall we go to lunch after this? Before the board meeting?"

Chapter Two

Luc did not, in fact, have the opportunity to spirit Tirith's doppelgänger away for lunch.

Her personal assistant insisted that Tirith had a previous engagement, which meant that Luc still didn't have the answers he needed. If Tirith pulled out of the gala, everyone who'd paid a premium donation toward his brother's foundation would demand a refund. It would be a complete disaster.

Luc saw the imposter again for the second time as she entered the luxurious boardroom that afternoon. He'd been waiting on her and was the second person to approach after Mrs. Teague, the chairperson.

He didn't miss the microsecond flare of panic in the widening of her eyes as he leaned in close.

But he only brushed a friendly kiss to her cheek the way he would've done for Tirith herself.

He did let his hand linger on her waist.

"Did you have a chance to eat?" he asked. *Where's your sister?*

She began to shrug but halted the movement, and her eyes flicked around the room. "Elizabeth had a salad sent over."

There was something behind what should've been a simple statement. Was she used to heartier food? Coming from a ranch, did she eat steak every day? Hamburgers?

"Your highness."

She glanced to where a gentleman Luc's father's age was approaching them.

She hesitated. It was slight but unmistakable.

"Mr. Hemry." Luc intercepted the man with an outstretched hand.

Hemry gave only a cursory shake, but it was long enough for Luc to note the quick look of appreciation Tirith's sister shot him.

Hemry wanted to update her on the status of the dog rescue they'd spoken about weeks ago. She was all smiles as she listened. Mr. Hemry had no clue that this wasn't Tirith.

He still didn't know why Margaret and Tirith had traded places, but it seemed the princesses wanted to keep it a secret. That he could do, at least until he discovered what was going on.

It was the work of a few minutes for Luc to guide her around the room, using the names of people Tirith had known for two years in natural conversation. He should've gotten an award for it. He wasn't even sure *she* noticed.

And then Mrs. Teague called the meeting to order, and he slipped into the seat next to Princess Margaret. They'd rounded the long, oval table and ended up on the curve, which meant his knee bumped hers beneath the smooth wooden surface.

The board meeting always kicked off with a discussion of old and new business. Luc's proposal was a line-item on the agenda and would be discussed later.

A delay which gave him too much time to wonder.

His curiosity had been piqued. He always did his research, and the twin princesses were no exception. He'd scoured both the internet and the Glorvaird public library archives before he'd officially met Tirith.

Everyone knew Tirith and Margaret were twins.

But no one knew what had happened when the girls had been twelve.

The two periods of their lives might have been drawn on a white board and bisected with a thick black line. Before twelve and after twelve.

Before twelve, the twins had both lived in the castle. They'd been in the news regularly, along with their younger sister Beatrix. Alessandra and Gideon had lived happily—or so it seemed—at the castle. When photographed, the twins were all smiles, often had their arms around each other, and appeared confident and carefree.

After the girls had turned twelve, Margaret disappeared from the media reports entirely. There was only a small clipping—a paragraph, literally—that mentioned Gideon relocating back to Texas with Margaret. There were no photos of Margaret after that. It was as if she'd disappeared.

And yet, here she was. Sitting next to Luc, so close that his knee was pressed to hers.

There was no mention whatsoever of what had happened when the girls were twelve, but it was obvious something had changed for the royal family.

There should've been rampant speculation in the media, but that was absent too. Had the royal family quashed it? Why? Why was all the secrecy necessary?

And the more important question: was Margaret's return going to interfere with his carefully-laid plans?

On the table before each chair was a blank notepad and pen. A few of the board members had laptops open in front of them.

No one paid Luc any mind as he slid the half-size notepad onto his thigh and wrote on it.

He slipped it on to Margaret's lap, and she jumped. She was nothing like Tirith, who was so cool he'd often wanted to check her pulse.

He couldn't even imagine kissing Tirith. They'd been

friends for too long, probably. And when he imagined finding the future Mrs. Moreno—eventually—he had no interest in an ice queen. He'd had enough deep freeze from his father before the man's death two years ago.

So why hadn't he been able to stop thinking about Margaret? Even now, watching her slender fingers pick up her pen from the table made him wonder if those fingers would feel cool against the back of his neck. Or warm, like the woman had felt in his arms.

Margaret was no ice queen.

Maybe like called to like. Maybe he'd recognized her intuitively. He hid his hotter nature—his temper, his passion, the fighting impulses that'd resulted in bloodied knuckles as a teenager—behind the cold politician. But the true nature that he hid had recognized her. Wanted her, even.

Talk about a distraction.

She added something to the notepad and slid it back onto his lap, her attention back on the long-winded Mrs. Devlin from across the table, who was speaking about an art exhibit.

He'd written, *I need to talk to you.*

Beneath his thick-lined scrawl, she'd written in small precise script. *We've just spent an hour together.*

He added another line. *In front of an audience.*

He gently gave the notepad back to her.

She glanced at it, then at him. Her gaze flicked from his eyes to his lips and then down at the paper. Her lips pursed. Oh ho. *She* was thinking about the kiss they'd shared, too.

MAGGIE HAD BEEN DOING her level best to think of everything but the kiss.

This man was Tirith's boyfriend, she reminded herself. Even though his knee was pressed against hers, sending fire along every nerve ending.

And yet, she didn't move away.

As the meeting dragged on, she'd forced her mind to wander to her sister instead of to the man beside her.

She needed to remember why she was here.

When Tirith had burst into the kitchen, her gaze had darted between Scarlett and Maggie.

There was no attempt made—by either twin—to hug each other. But Maggie had never seen her sister so rumpled. Her hair was escaping the clip at the back of her neck, and her taupe pantsuit looked as wrinkled as if she'd slept in it.

Maggie came out of her seat. "What's wrong?"

"I—" Tirith glanced at Scarlett. Stopped. Started again. "I need your help."

Scarlett stood from the table and toted her plate to the counter. "I'll leave you to it." She leveled a look at Maggie. "Think about what I said." About using her status to push the charity board around. Not likely.

Tirith had seemed to wilt once Scarlett was out of the room.

"Sit down." Maggie pulled out one of the kitchen chairs, and her sister stumbled into it.

"I've done something. Horrible." Was Tirith... crying?

Maggie lowered herself into the chair next to her as, sure enough, Tirith pressed a napkin to her eyes. She took a gasping inhale. "I was d-driving, and I was d-distracted. T-texting. And I..." She shook her head, pressing the napkin to her face again.

The sisters might not have been close, but Maggie couldn't stand by and see Tirith so upset and do nothing. She put her arm around her sister's shoulders.

She could guess what had happened if Tirith had been texting and driving. A wreck. Or worse.

Why hadn't Tirith had a driver? Her sister rarely drove herself. Or maybe that was Mother. Maggie didn't know enough of their day-to-day life to say for sure.

"I h-hit a pedestrian," Tirith burst out. "A l-little girl."

Oh no. *Oh, Tirith.*

Maggie squeezed her sister. She had no words of comfort. Tirith must have been drowning under the guilt.

Tirith cried into her napkin almost silently as Maggie sat with her.

Finally when Tirith seemed to be calming, Maggie let her arms fall away, resting them on the table in front of her.

"Did Mother send you here?" Maggie asked quietly. If there was a firestorm of media coverage back in Glorvaird, the ranch was as good a hiding place as any.

"I sent myself," Tirith said after a moment's hesitation. "It was very early, and there was no one else about. The palace staff jumped in to handle things and... no one knows, except for the girl's father and the first responders. He agreed to ... to keep things hushed up as long as the family pays for every expense for her."

Maggie's stomach was a knot of tension. "So the girl...?"

"She's alive." Tirith sniffled. She shook her head, pressing the napkin to her face again. "Every time I close my eyes, I see her little face. That moment just before, when I couldn't stop the car..." Her voice squeaked and broke on the last word.

She put down the napkin and grabbed Maggie's wrist on the table, her tear-splotched face fervent in its appeal. "I need you to go back. In my place."

"What?" Maggie's voice rose, the immediate emotional response surprising her more than Tirith had.

But Tirith didn't let go when Maggie tried to pull away. Her bulldog sister said, "No one knows that I'm here. I can't —can't stand and smile at every ribbon cutting and school visit like there's nothing wrong. I ruined a little girl's life. Forever!"

"So cancel the events." Maggie hadn't been back to Glorvaird since— "I can't."

"Please, Maggie. I've never asked you for anything." Tirith still had that grip on her, but Maggie pulled away and stood, agitation pushing her to pace to the kitchen island and back.

"I made a promise to a friend," Tirith said. "There's a

charity ball and polo match, and without my support, his fundraisers will fail. It's really important. I have to be at these events." She cleared her throat. "Or someone that the public thinks is me."

Maggie shuddered just thinking about it. There were reasons—important reasons—she hadn't been back to her homeland in over a decade.

But Tirith was right. She never asked Maggie for anything. Maggie had always been the weaker sister. What did she have that Tirith needed? Nothing.

Except for today. Today Tirith needed a stand-in. A mannequin. A prop.

Tirith played with her fingers, staring at them on the tabletop. "Please, Maggie. My personal assistant will prep you on everything. Mostly you just have to stand there and smile and nod."

Right. Tirith had made it sound so easy. Now, Maggie shifted in the uncomfortable boardroom seat. *Stand there and smile and nod.* She'd already managed to mess that up in spectacular fashion.

She should never have given in to Tirith's tearful pleas. But she had, and now she was stuck here. *I need to talk to you.* If Luc managed to get her alone, what exactly would she have to do to convince him that she was Tirith?

She hadn't worked out a way to put him off, what to write on the notepad, when he suddenly tensed beside her.

She snapped back to attention. She shouldn't have let her mind wander so far.

Mr. Gower—she thought—had clicked on a slide presentation and was going through the slides in rapid-fire succession. He was rushing so fast that she could barely process the information.

And beside her, Luc's shoulders drew tighter and tighter. Why? Was this a special project of his?

"Excuse me." Maggie was as surprised as Mr. Gower that she'd spoken out of turn. No help for it now. Everyone at the table was looking at her. Her face burned. "Could you please slow down a bit?"

Mr. Gower frowned. "We've seen this presentation before," he groused. But he did slow down as he went through the remaining slides.

The foundation asking for funds provided programs and scholarships for children with Down syndrome.

"As I mentioned, we've considered this charity before," Mr. Gower said as the last slide clicked off. "It is beyond the scope of our bylaws. We only make gifts to organizations that have been a going concern for three years or more. This foundation"—he tapped a finger on a sheaf of papers on the table in front of him—"has only been viable for eighteen months."

That didn't seem like a good enough reason to deny them. Not to Maggie. What would Tirith do? She didn't even know whether Tirith had commented on the proposal the first time it had been presented.

She cleared her throat delicately. "I'm sorry. I can't remember at the moment. Surely the board has made exceptions before."

Beside her, Luc shifted. His knee pressed against her thigh.

Mr. Hemry joined the conversation. "We have made an occasional exception in the past," he admitted, "but some of our members have expressed concerns about this foundation because of its connection to one of our board members." His eyes swept to Luc and then away. "It has always been important to this board to avoid the appearance of favoritism."

She glanced at the man beside her. His jaw was locked so tight, she wondered if he'd ever pry it open.

"I move to dismiss this proposal without funding," Mr. Gower said.

"But—" She cut off her words at the hot press of Luc's hand on her knee beneath the table.

She glanced at him, but his gaze was far off, somewhere across the room. He squeezed her leg once and then let go.

"We can review the proposal again in a few months," said a woman across the table. Maggie couldn't remember her name. There'd been too many names thrown at her today.

"I move to delay," Mr. Hemry said. It seemed as if he sent an apologetic glance her eway. Was she imagining it?

The motion to delay was seconded, and then a vote was called.

Maggie didn't know whether she should vote or not. She was silent as a chorus of "ayes" echoed around the table. And surprised when Luc joined them.

She ended up abstaining. She could only hope she hadn't messed things up for Tirith after she returned.

And she couldn't help the curiosity coursing through her. She grabbed her pen and wrote on the pad still on her lap.

Why did you vote to delay?

She slipped it to the man beside her.

It was only a moment before he sent it back to her. He'd written only two words.

Politics, darling.

She couldn't help glancing at him. He wore an air of grimness that he hadn't had before.

And she wanted to know why. But if she asked, he'd know she wasn't Tirith.

She had to slip out of this meeting before he cornered her.

Chapter Three

The next day, Maggie checked her phone once more before slipping it into the tiny clutch purse she carried. The phone and a tube of lipstick were about all that fit. Seriously? Who carried something so impractical? Tirith, obviously.

Tirith, who hadn't returned her call yesterday, or the barrage of texts she'd sent this morning.

She'd wanted to talk to her sister before any media photo of that kiss with Luc made it over the ocean to her sister.

Bea had slipped into her suite this morning as the stylists were torturing her in the chair. She'd brought an update on the girl who'd been injured by Tirith's reckless driving.

Since she'd been small, Bea had harbored dreams of being a nurse. She had contacts in the medical profession who'd been able to tell her that the girl was pulling through.

Maggie hadn't had to fake the tears that had sprung to her eyes. She'd been praying for the little girl ever since Tirith had told her what happened. Knowing that the girl would survive was wonderful, though Bea had cautioned there would be a long recovery.

Three hours later, Maggie smoothed the skirt of the

flowing pink-patterned dress she'd been tucked into this morning. How long had it been since she'd worn something like this? Maybe a church service, more than a year ago?

A dress like this wouldn't survive ten minutes on the ranch.

She needed to get out of the day limo and walk onto the grounds of the Glorvaird Botanical Society. She'd insisted Elizabeth stay at the castle, afraid she wouldn't be able to hide her terror.

A group of people waited for her, the men in suits and the women in knee-length dresses similar to the one she wore. And hats. She couldn't forget the fancy hats. Hers was on the seat next to her.

It was all too familiar. The trees, their leaves fluttering in the breeze, would close in on her if she stepped out there. The flowers, so pretty from here, would turn menacing. And those pretty dresses and day tuxedos... She hated to think what her mind would conjure with those.

The memories were too stark here. Too close.

She pulled in a deep breath, pushed it out.

Every few moments, someone glanced toward the limo.

Thank goodness they couldn't see through the dark-tinted windows to watch her try to control her panic.

Tirith had insisted this event couldn't be cancelled. Tirith would understand Maggie's fear. If it could have been cancelled, it would have been. Because as important as her sister had insisted it was, Maggie wasn't sure she could go through with it.

Behind the knot of people on the sidewalk, a green lawn was populated with colorfully-dressed patrons. A huge white tent had been erected at the back of the property. And flanking the lawn on both sides would be the carefully-tended gardens.

A garden party.

Nothing to be terrified of.

Unless you were Maggie.

"Just go," she muttered under her breath.

"Your highness?" the driver questioned politely. His gaze flashed to her in the rearview mirror.

He probably thought she was nuts.

He'd be right. She was crazy to have agreed to this.

"Do you want me to go?" he asked.

Yes!

But she answered, "No," on a sigh.

She got out, not waiting for him to come around and open her door. The midmorning heat hit her in the face like a torch. She forced her wobbly legs to carry her onto the sidewalk.

Thank goodness she'd opted for flats again.

Immediately, the knot of people surrounded her.

"Your highness."

"This way—"

She tried to keep her focus on the people, but her vision blurred at the edges. She started to sweat.

"Could I have a glass of water?" she asked no one in particular, but a man peeled off from the group, presumably to find it for her.

She was going to faint. She was going to embarrass herself. Tirith. The entire royal family.

She gasped, reaching out—

And Luc was there beside her, his arm sweeping around her waist.

"Thank you all for your attentiveness to the princess, but if you don't mind, I have to borrow her to say a private hello."

He left the innuendo right out there and received several chuckles even as he swept her away.

She would've been outraged if she'd had any energy for it. As it was, she couldn't catch her breath. Each inhale was a shallow burst of air that did nothing to fill her lungs.

He held her closely to his side, carrying most of her weight across the lawn. To where?

"Stay with me," he murmured into the hair just above her ear.

What else was she to do? She'd lost motor power over her entire body. Black spots danced in her vision.

And then they followed a flagstone path several paces into a secluded hedgerow. A lovely old tree with a gnarled trunk overhead provided a canopy of shade.

And Luc settled her onto a stone bench that was cold beneath her legs.

"Put your head down," he demanded. And it wasn't as if she could fight him as he nudged her shoulder down with his hand.

"Breathe in. Out. With me." He knelt beside her, inhaled and exhaled slowly until she was matching his rhythm, until the darkness in her vision had receded.

She started to sit up.

"Easy." He kept a hand beneath her elbow.

How was she going to explain her panic attack? She couldn't go back out onto the lawn. Couldn't face all of this. How could Tirith have asked this of her?

Tears pricked her eyes. Her breath rattled in her chest as she fought them off.

"I need a horse," she said on a soft laugh.

And then realized exactly what she'd done. She'd admitted she wasn't Tirith.

Maggie loved horses. Tirith tolerated them.

"I don't think there are any on the guest list."

She stared at him, stunned.

"I've been compared with an unflattering animal numerous times, so I'm probably the best you're going to get." He said it so gravely that it took her a moment—and the quirk of his lips—to realize he was joking.

"You aren't surprised."

He shook his head. "I made you out yesterday at the ribbon cutting."

"Before or after the kiss?" She hadn't meant to ask that, not really.

Something sparked in his eyes, but he looked away. "Perhaps I'll tell you another time." He brought a pointed stare back to her. "Would you like to tell me why I'm hiding in the hedgerow with Princess Margaret?"

"It's Maggie. And I...can't." The story was Tirith's to tell.

"Then perhaps you'll tell me why you suffered a panic attack just now?"

MAYBE LUC SHOULDN'T PUSH SO hard. She'd barely recovered her breath.

He'd reacted without thinking when he'd been walking to meet her and saw the panic clear as day on her face. But it was the tears after she'd calmed her breathing that had cracked something inside of him.

Unfortunately, there were five hundred people waiting on the lawn and among the rosebushes, each one eager to shake the princess's hand.

Each one with a pocketful of money to donate to the right cause.

He needed her to go back out there.

He glanced past the guards who'd faded back but stood under the shade tree several yards away.

"I don't suppose Tirith explained what was riding on the next few days?"

She shook her head.

"And she's not coming back?"

"Not for ten days."

He was doomed. Ernest would never forgive him.

But his mother had taught him to muddle through, so that's what he would do. "Can you tell me what happened?"

Her eyes were vulnerable, if slightly distrustful. "My sister knows you. But we've only just met."

He considered her. "True. You aren't certain if you can trust me. But I didn't betray your secret yesterday."

He'd even gone so far as to kiss her to keep it. Yes, that had been a real hardship.

Her eyes narrowed slightly. "And you have some reason for that, I assume."

He wanted to grin, but he didn't. She might've been out of the game, but she hadn't forgotten it. He could work with that.

"Fine. Here's something you can trust: leverage. I know your secret, and I can use it as leverage over you. But if I reciprocate, you'd have leverage, too."

It was a strategic move on his part. Maybe too risky, but he'd bet on her honesty. She wore her emotions too much on her sleeve.

Her blue gaze fixed on his face. Even that was different from Tirith's. Tirith only ever half-listened to him. Her intelligent mind was always a step ahead, always puzzling answers. He'd learned she didn't mean to offend. It's just how she was.

But he almost felt the intensity of Maggie's gaze like a touch.

"Tirith knows my story." Though not all of it. "After my father died, our family discovered he'd gambled everything away, including money he'd stolen from my brother. Money that Ernest had earmarked to start the foundation."

It still hurt saying it aloud. Now Maggie was one of a handful of people who knew. He'd spent the past four years smoothing over the family's reputation and trying to rebuild what his father had destroyed for Ernest and Katie and Guinevere. He'd catered to people he couldn't stand. Curried favors from too many.

And he'd gotten things back on track. Almost.

He needed a princess to walk out on the lawn with him.

He looked at her expectantly.

She exhaled softly. "I want to help you." When she raised her soft, sad eyes to him, he believed her.

"But...?"

"But." She looked away again. "When I was twelve, Tirith and I were kidnapped out of a garden party much like this one."

Everything around him seemed to grind to a halt.

Whatever he'd imagined, it wasn't this. None of the media speculation had even come close.

She must've read the shock on his face, because she laughed softly, sadly. "It was kept from the press."

"And that's why you've stayed in America."

She bit her lip, nodding slightly. "I came back for Tirith. She said she'd made a promise. She just didn't tell me it was to you." Something, some emotion flitted quickly over her expression and then was gone.

And he knew they were running out of time before someone came looking for her.

"Do you think you can face the crowd?"

She kept her eyes down. "I don't know." Those long lashes lifted and revealed the vulnerability beneath. "Would you stay with me?"

"I think I can suffer the hardship."

ONE OF THE first hurdles Maggie had overcome in therapy had been asking for help. She'd learned not to be ashamed to lean on her father, her biggest supporter during those dark days.

She'd grown up. Or so she'd thought.

There was something about asking Luc for help that made her feel sick to her stomach.

She'd promised she wouldn't let Tirith down. Neither would she let him down.

Her mouth felt as dry as a Texas summer day as she stood up from the bench on shaky legs.

She walked beside him, past the hedgerow, and out from the secluded shade into the morning sunlight.

"How's your kung fu?" she asked. Maybe if she kept talking, she'd be able to keep from throwing up.

"Never learned," he admitted cheerfully.

"Ju jitsu?" she asked. "I've taken a few classes but didn't stick with it. No?"

He shook his head.

"What about karate?"

"Sorry." His grin was quick and contagious. "You'll have to rely on your palace muscle men."

There'd been bodyguards that fateful morning, and it hadn't changed the outcome. Darkness and memories threatened to send her back into hiding.

"I can shriek like a little girl. I have it on good authority that it's terrifying."

His teasing voice intruded on the blackness that had begun to take over her thoughts.

He was here, and she wasn't twelve anymore. She was a resourceful, intelligent woman who could train a horse ten times her weight, who subdued rowdy cowhands with a single look.

She was a princess.

Once out in the sunlight, it was apparent she and Luc had been missed. Hordes of people were waiting for them, wanting a press of her handshake or a selfie with her or to mention to her that they didn't like the royal family's most recently policy on healthcare or tax reform or whatever.

As promised, Luc stayed by her side. When the press of the crowd should've separated them, he stepped close and kept a hand at her waist.

And when there was a slight break in the crowd, he leaned in and spoke into her ear. "Thank you for doing this. I know it must be difficult."

He couldn't know how difficult. Every time someone passed by in the edge of her vision, it brought back a flash of memory. Of *that* memory, of being grabbed and silenced with a hand over her mouth.

"You should know that my niece will be eternally grateful."

His words shook her out of the memory that threatened to suck her under. He seemed to know somehow that she was on a knife's edge, teetering between blind panic and hysterical, uncontrollable laughter. Neither was appropriate.

He kept talking.

"She was born with Down syndrome."

Oh. She hadn't known. "What's her name? Your niece?"

It took him a second to respond. "Guinevere. I'm afraid my sister-in-law was a lover of classic literature."

Maggie couldn't help smiling at that.

"The foundation is Guinevere's baby, really. She's seventeen now. My brother is quite a bit older" he added when he must've read the question on her face. "Ever since she was a toddler, she's always wanted to do what the children around her were doing. Whether that meant playing tag or drawing or, when she was older, taking riding lessons. My brother and sister-in-law could afford it, but they also made sure she realized how privileged she was. And Guinevere..." He huffed a half-laugh. "She can't stand for others to be left out. So the foundation was born to benefit other kids like her."

"She sounds like she has a kind heart." Maggie would love to meet her. "Is she here?"

"The kindest. And no. But she'll be at the polo match on Friday. It's a charity match, and the teams are a mix of Guinevere and her friends, professional players, and a few celebrities."

"It sounds delightful. I can't wait to meet her."

"She's amazing." But he was frowning. "Which is why what my father did was unconscionable." He stretched his frown into a semblance of a smile. "But that's not your concern."

Tirith had made it her concern. And Maggie couldn't help wondering why. How had her sister met Luc? How long had it taken her to fall for his charm? To discover the man's true heart beneath?

Maggie had seen enough to know he was someone she'd like to know more. Someone she could fall for—if he hadn't already been taken by her sister.

They were besieged by another large group of patrons, and Maggie kept shaking hands. Smiling. But her thoughts kept returning to Luc.

When she began to be overwhelmed by all of it, he smiled charmingly and joked that he didn't want her to get sunstroke, and then gently guided her to the most private corner beneath the huge canvas tent.

When she sat, he pressed a cold glass of lemonade into her hand. "Halfway there," he said. "Good job on not fainting."

She smiled a little just before she drank from the cup.

"So this is the big secret, hmm?" he said almost absently as he gazed around the area. He stood with the confident ease of someone accustomed to power. One hand rested in his pocket, the lapel of his jacket open to reveal a flat, toned belly beneath. "The reason you haven't been home in so long."

"Glorvaird isn't home anymore," she admitted softly, tearing her eyes away. He belonged to Tirith. Not her.

"How is it the public never found out?"

"There was no need. The ransom demand was made almost immediately and..." She suddenly had to focus on her breathing. In. Out. In. Out. When she could, she smiled for him. "And then it was over."

Such an understatement to encompass those forty-eight terrifying hours. But now wasn't the time or place to talk about such a sensitive subject. There were people circulating all around, though she and Luc been given a wide berth. What had she been thinking, confiding even this much in him?

She pressed the back of her wrist to her forehead. "I've been trying to get in touch with ... with her."

She'd almost slipped up and said her sister's name. Luc

was intelligent. He must know who she was talking about. "I thought I should explain to her that"—she dropped her voice —"the kiss meant nothing."

His eyes narrowed slightly, his gaze resting on her face for a moment that stretched a smidge too long. He clapped a hand to his chest. "I'm terribly wounded. Not sure I'll survive this critique on my romantic skills."

She attempted a smirk, but a reluctant smile pulled at the corners of her mouth. "I don't want any hint of scandal, or confusion, when she comes back."

There was something calculating behind his gaze, but it was quickly shuttered. "As much as it pains me to admit this, your—*she* and I have—"

"Excuse me. Your highness? The second receiving line is waiting." A staff member who looked suitably embarrassed to have interrupted them stood nearby, shifting his feet anxiously.

No more time for talking. Though Maggie wished he'd waited a few more seconds before interrupting.

She and I have ... what?

Chapter Four

"OH, YOU'RE A BEAUTIFUL ONE, AREN'T YOU?"

Maggie approached the regal palomino, and the groom holding its bridle gave her room to admire the marvelous beast.

"Well, I feel appropriately put in my place."

Luc's wry statement made her want to nuzzle her face against the horse's snout. To hide.

They'd never finished their conversation two days ago.

And as she hadn't been able to connect with Tirith, she was more unsettled than before about her feelings for the man.

Seeing him at today's polo match brought all the emotions from the garden party right back to the surface. Yesterday, she'd spent a hour on the phone with her therapist. Talking through the flashbacks and crazy emotional roller coaster had helped. Or at least she'd thought it had.

But today, as their eyes met across the horse's shoulders, the shared knowledge of what she'd been through was there in his eyes.

"All right?" he asked in little more than a whisper.

She smiled tightly. "I found a horse," she answered.

She'd come out today determined to show him that she wasn't weak. That maybe she wasn't as cool and collected as Tirith, but neither was she as weak as she'd seemed when she'd had the panic attack. She didn't want to admit to herself why his good opinion mattered so.

Across the lawn, tents had been set up for the spectators, who were now gathering. She supposed she was meant to be over there, smiling and politicking.

She didn't want to.

One of the uniformed polo players approached, and she realized for the first time that Luc was in uniform, the dark green checked shirt molding to the curves of his shoulders.

The other player nodded to her.

Luc made introductions. "Princess Tirith, may I present my friend Jean Marc? Jean Marc, her highness."

She accepted the quick handshake, didn't miss the speculative glance she received from the other man.

"I didn't know your highness had a fondness for horses," Jean Marc said, "or I'd have twisted Luc's arm for an introduction long before now."

Luc slid his friend a sideways glance. "Did I say friend? I meant associate... more of a passing acquaintance, really."

Jean Marc laughed, but then turned serious. "Luc, I have some bad news. Everett just called me from the ER. He had an unfortunate incident with a cake and a flight of stairs."

Luc's smile faded. "What about Roberts?"

"Out of the country," Jean Marc said. He looked to Maggie, making sure to include her. "He was our substitute."

"So we're short a player," Luc said.

"It appears so."

Maggie glanced to the tent where the younger players had gathered. She could see one of the teens speaking animatedly to a couple that might have been his parents.

"Perhaps we can play with seven," Jean Marc said.

"Or I could join," Maggie said.

Jean Marc's head snapped to her, but she couldn't look away from Luc, whose eyes had gone wide.

"Your highness, I did not know you could ride," Jean Marc said in the polite way that she was sure everyone used to mollify her sister.

"I've had lessons," she demurred. "It's a charity match—meant for fun. Correct?"

"I'll see if I can find an extra uniform." Jean Marc left them alone.

Luc frowned. He took her elbow and leaned in close. "Are you trying to be found out?" He smiled and waved at someone across the lawn, but his voice was low and almost furious when he continued. "Tirith isn't known for her riding."

"Our father is a rancher," she reminded him. "It can't be out of the question for her to ride."

He shook his head. "So you'll pretend to be a barely passable rider. Disaster averted."

His sarcasm was not lost on her. "Won't most of the spectators be focusing on the children? That's the focus of today's event, isn't it?"

He sighed. "Princess, it's impossible for anyone to focus on anything but you." He didn't sound happy about it.

"Is this about protecting your event? Or is it about protecting me? Because I don't need your protection." But how could he know that when she'd blubbered all over him at the garden party? Surely he thought she was a foolish, over-emotional woman.

He started to answer, then snapped his jaws closed when a young woman with a bundle of clothing in hand came and fetched Maggie to change.

In minutes, she had donned the uniform of the team that would play opposite Luc's. Good. Maybe a little distance would benefit them both.

Maggie met the green team, shaking hands all around and exchanging pleasantries. And then turned to her own.

A boy of about thirteen introduced himself as Franco. She wondered how he would reach the ball without falling from his horse. "Are you Luc's girlfriend?" Franco asked.

Maggie's mouth opened and closed. She imagined she resembled a fish in an aquarium.

"It's complicated."

They were the very words she'd been thinking, but Maggie wasn't the one who'd said them.

She glanced behind her to see a young woman approach. "That's what Uncle Luc always says when I ask him about it."

"You must be Guinevere."

The girl was smiling and wearing a uniform that matched Maggie's. Her handshake was quick and firm, and she kept on smiling even as the teams were announced to rousing cheers from the crowd.

The horse Maggie was introduced to was a pretty mare with a coat like lustrous chocolate. She let the horse get her scent, stroked its neck with a gentle hand.

The mare was intelligent, comfortable with all the noise and strangers around her.

When Maggie swung up into the saddle, she was almost herself again.

Be Tirith.

She could do this. She just had to pretend she couldn't ride.

"THAT'S IT!"

Luc turned at Maggie's cry, which was almost drowned out by the cheers of the crowd as Guinevere knocked the ball through the goalposts.

Jean Marc rode close as they wheeled their horses to the center of the field. "Moreno. Get your head in the game."

Luc glared at him, but he couldn't deny his friend was right.

It was impossible to concentrate with Princess Maggie

riding. She'd almost come unseated twice—he had never imagined she knew trick riding—and had fumbled her mallet at least three times. Each time she made an error, the crowd reacted. It was as if they were on the edge of their seats, unable to look away.

Luc knew how they felt.

And the blue team was winning.

Somehow, without seeming to do anything at all, Maggie was passing the ball to her teammates and setting them up for plays that led to points on the scoreboard. And it wasn't only Paul VanGardner, the professional player on her team, who was benefiting from her sneaky maneuvers. She'd diverted the ball to Guinevere and Franco more than double the times she'd sent it to VanGardner.

The game was playing out exactly how Luc had wanted it to. And Maggie was making it happen. *And* entertaining the crowd.

Maybe he owed her an apology.

The umpire blew his whistle to signal the end of the third chukkas. They'd take a four-minute break while grooms changed out the horses. Then, they'd play the last period.

Luc guzzled from a bottle of cold water, trying to ignore his buzzing thoughts. It was impossible.

Maggie was like no one he'd ever met.

She'd been through something traumatic and yet had braved the garden party. All for him and to benefit his brother's foundation. And now this, today, for Guinevere.

Who had abandoned her team and was skipping over to Luc. "Guess what?"

He never could guess. Guinevere might easily be thinking about unicorns and rainbows instead of the game they were currently playing.

"Tell me, Peanut."

"Princess Tirith invited me to the castle to see the horses there! Isn't that amazing?"

He raised his gaze to connect with Maggie, who stood

several yards away. She wasn't paying attention but laughing at something Franco had said. Her eyes shone with true joy.

He wanted that gaze pointed at him.

"Uncle Luc. Isn't it amazing?"

"Amazing," he repeated.

"So you'll take me there? To the royal stables?"

Behind him, Jean Marc was mounting up on his fresh horse and ordering his teammates to do the same. "Moreno!" he bellowed.

Luc brushed a kiss on Guinevere's cheek. "We'll see, Peanut."

For now, he had a match to finish.

Chapter Five

MAGGIE HAD BEEN TO THE GLORVAIRD NAVAL BASE once as a small girl. She could still remember being awed by the sailors marching in formation, thinking how ugly the squat, brown brick buildings were, smelling the salt even though the ocean was out of sight.

None of it had changed.

Today there was a crowd gathered on a wide expanse of runway. A portable stage had been set up for the ceremony, and several men in uniforms, their chests decorated with medals, stood in parade rest behind it.

Valentin and Annika were having some kind of fight. Maggie had noticed the tension between them in the limo. It had been impossible to miss. Annika had sat with arms crossed, her body angled away from the crown prince. She'd barely responded to the small talk Maggie had attempted. And Maggie thought it was more than the nerves Valentin had mentioned when he'd invited her to today's event.

Now the three of them stood awkwardly silent as the assembly was called to order. Several photographers flashed cameras from the back of the crowd.

A red sports car came screaming up the tarmac, squealing to a stop behind the royal limo with a screech of tires.

The general who was introducing the ceremony went on as if nothing had happened, but heads in the crowd turned to the commotion.

Max, Valentin's younger brother, who stood tall and sleek in a designer suit, got out of the sports car and strode toward them.

Valentin glared, but Max ignored him, offering a dazzling smile to Annika and then Maggie. He touched Maggie's elbow as he leaned in to brush a brotherly kiss against her cheek.

He did the same to Annika, and Valentin's tension went through the roof. He looked as if he wanted to punch his brother.

And then Valentin was called to the stage. A smattering of applause heralded him, and he had no choice but to make his way up the steps to the platform, leaving Max to stand between the two women.

"Who picked out his tie?" Max said under his breath. "He looks like an old geezer."

Maggie didn't think so. She knew nothing of men's fashion but thought Valentin looked sharp in a dark tie with the charcoal suit.

Annika giggled.

Maggie frowned, but neither Max or Annika was paying attention. Max had shifted closer to her and was leaning in to whisper in Annika's ear.

Maggie forced her eyes to the stage. Valentin was delivering his speech with poise and his natural charisma. But then he glanced over to them.

Annika giggled again at something Max had whispered in her ear.

"Shh." Maggie hushed the other woman. Annika hadn't grown up in the public eye. She didn't know how the press could spin something out of control, like her whispering and giggling with her fiancé's brother. It would turn into a wildfire of coverage if it looked like Valentin was jealous.

At least he'd focused again on the crowd, continuing his speech as if nothing had happened.

Max shot Maggie a look, his eyes sparkling with mischief. "Don't be a stick in the mud like my brother."

Annika sent her a haughty smile. Was she encouraging Max's flirtatious manner? It was difficult to tell.

Maggie sent what she hoped was a quelling look and forced her attention back to Valentin on stage.

He was wrapping up, and she clapped along with the crowd as he pinned a medal on the chest of an older sailor. They shook hands, and Valentin came down the steps as another man in uniform moved behind the microphone and began to speak.

Valentin strode to them, forcing his brother to shift out of the way as he moved to stand at Annika's side.

Valentin kept his focus on the stage, his expression blank. But a muscle ticked in his cheek.

Something was definitely wrong.

Max glanced at Maggie briefly. He wore a smirk, one that was entirely out of place. What was his game? Was he purposely antagonizing his brother?

And Annika. Today was Maggie's first interaction with the woman. Surely she and Valentin were in love. They were engaged! A wedding date had been set for next summer.

But wouldn't a woman in love avoid any hint of impropriety? Especially at such a public event?

It's politics. She heard Luc's whisper from several days ago tickle her memory banks. He'd been talking about the board meeting, the interplay she hadn't understood.

Was this politics, too? A power struggle between the two brothers? What was Max thinking?

On the ranch, things were simple. The family worked

together to keep the place running, to take care of the animals, to turn a profit. If Maggie had a problem with someone, she talked to that person and worked it out. There were no hidden agendas, no power plays.

If this was what it was like to be royalty in Glorvaird, she'd gladly leave it behind when she returned home.

Chapter Six

Two days before the gala, Luc found himself in a place he'd never been before. The castle stables.

Maggie had kept her promise. Luc had assumed it was one of those things adults said to placate a child. A promise they'd never keep.

But he was learning he shouldn't assume anything with Maggie. Of course she'd kept her word.

She'd called him last night to coordinate the visit, and they'd ended up talking for over an hour. She was funny and open and curious. And he was in trouble, because he liked her. Too much.

Now, she and Guinevere walked slightly ahead of him, talking easily as Maggie pointed to a dappled gray in one of the stalls. She'd worn jeans and a pale pink button-down shirt, which he was sure she hadn't found in Tirith's closet. The tails of her shirt were untucked, and her hair was down around her shoulders.

He could almost imagine her as she must be on her Texas ranch. Maybe add a cowboy hat and a smudge of dirt across her cheek, and the image would be complete.

She glanced over her shoulder at him, wrinkling her nose when she caught him staring.

She and Guinevere moved to the next stall. His phone dinged, and he fished it out of the pocket of his slacks. An email. From Ernest. He let the women pull away as he quickly scanned it.

Even with revenue from the gala, without the funding from the charity board, his brother's foundation wasn't going to make it through the year. It was clear from the text that Ernest was discouraged.

Bitter disappointment surged. Luc had worked tirelessly on the week's events and squeezed funding from every conceivable charity and grant he could think of.

And it wasn't enough.

Maybe he should give up. Ernest could go back to his job in the public sector, but Luc knew he didn't really want that.

A glance at Guinevere, animated as she talked horses with Maggie, was all it took for Luc to know he couldn't give up. His niece would be devastated.

He just needed to think of a stone he'd left unturned. Someone with deep pockets. They didn't need much to meet the foundation's first-year needs. Fifty thousand dollars. It was a drop in the bucket for some people.

"Uncle Luc!"

Guinevere's call pulled him out of his panic-induced brain fog. This wasn't the time to fix his brother's funding problem.

After he dropped off Guinevere, he'd seclude himself in his office and see what could be done.

He joined the two women outside a stall that held a striking ebony stallion with a white blaze down his face.

"Tirith says her father shipped this horse all the way across the ocean as a gift for Princess Alessandra. Isn't he beautiful?"

"He is." A horse like this one was an exceptional, valuable gift. But the rancher and Princess Alessandra remained estranged.

Now that he knew about the kidnapping, Luc couldn't help but wonder what part it had played in the separation.

"Was it a very important message?" Guinevere asked, nodding toward the phone he still held in his hand.

Ah. Guinevere never missed a thing. "Nothing that won't keep."

Maggie's eyes held a soft question, and he shook his head slightly. He'd tell her later about the funding problems. Or maybe not. She was leaving in a few days, and Ernest's foundation wasn't her responsibility. He and Tirith had cooked up the plan to save it together, and Maggie had been gracious enough by stepping in to handle the events in her sister's place.

"Are you and Tirith going to get married?"

MAGGIE WATCHED Luc react to the innocent question. He first appeared stunned, then his eyes cut to her and away. If she wasn't mistaken, a faint blush rose high on his cheeks.

"No, Guinny. No." He almost sounded choked up.

"But you kissed. I saw it on the telly."

Now the teen looked at Maggie, who grew uncomfortable under her probing gaze.

"Friends kiss sometimes," she murmured.

"Yes! Tirith and I are just friends," Luc said quickly. Their eyes met and held.

She could almost read what he'd left unsaid. *And this isn't Tirith, anyway.*

Maggie was well aware.

Her sister could attend a garden party without having a panic attack. Tirith was cool and unaffected by the social undercurrents that threatened to drive Maggie crazy. Why couldn't people just say what they meant?

Tirith... Tirith had captured Luc's attention from the beginning. They'd known each other for years.

Most of the time, Maggie was glad she'd gone to Texas,

glad she'd been spared the pressure of growing up in the public eye. Right now, though, she realized what she'd missed —the opportunity to meet this man years sooner.

Stupid.

Even if Luc had known them both for years, he'd have chosen Tirith. Calm, relaxed Tirith. Not scared-of-her-shadow Maggie.

She turned her attention back to the conversation in time to hear Guinevere say, "That didn't look like a friend kiss. I played it over three times." She glanced between the two adults. "It looked like a true love kiss."

If Luc had barely blushed before, now Maggie's face was on fire.

And it was only made worse when she caught Luc's intense, thoughtful stare.

"It was an act," he told his niece, almost idly. He didn't look away from Maggie. "For the cameras."

If anything, she blushed even harder. He knew that she wasn't the world's greatest actress. He'd seen it firsthand, though she seemed to have fooled the general public.

She broke the stare and turned to the horse. The stallion Dad had gifted Mother.

The last thing she needed was Luc focused on her feelings for him. Mostly because she still wasn't sure what those feelings were.

She'd fallen into his kiss that very first day.

And she hadn't stopped falling yet.

Watching him with his niece was yet another facet of the complex man. He was gentle with her, and he treated her with respect, never acting as if her questions were silly or didn't matter. Maggie could see how much he loved the girl.

She was afraid she was falling for him.

That would be incredibly stupid. He lived here, in Glorvaird. She was going back to Texas as soon as Tirith returned.

She loved the ranch. It was her home. She hated politics. Hated the power plays that happened every day among the royal family and those who revolved around them. She couldn't stay.

And there was still the not-so-small matter of Luc's relationship with her sister. He'd claimed once that they were only friends, but she'd seen pictures of Luc and Tirith in the media.

What could she believe?

"I'm sorry for my niece's nosy questions," Luc said.

Guinevere had wandered from the stables out onto the grassy embankment nearby. On the opposite side of the castle, huge cliffs guarded the private beach. But here, the grass gave way to sand that sloped gently down to the ocean. Guinevere loved the water, though he'd cautioned her not to go out in it.

He and Maggie hung back as Guinevere outpaced them.

"It's okay." Maggie's head tilted to one side, her gaze far off. He thought they'd been having a moment back in the stables. Guinevere had brought up the kiss, and Maggie had blushed so becomingly that he'd wanted to do it again.

And then something had changed. She'd pulled away, put distance between them.

"She's a doll," Maggie said softly. "I'm going to tell Tirith to invite her to the castle again. Maybe to tea. Tirith will adore her."

It was a reminder that Maggie's time in Glorvaird was short.

He swallowed. "Have you thought about staying? As yourself, of course."

She stared out at the horizon. The breeze blew wisps of hair against her cheek. "I've considered it. But not seriously. Texas is my home now."

He nodded. What more could he say? She seemed determined to leave.

She expelled a noisy sigh and then turned to him. Her arms were wrapped around her middle, her hands clasping both elbows. "How did you and Tirith meet? I've been curious."

"I tried to blackmail her."

A surprised burst of laughter escaped her. "What?"

Guinevere interrupted, waving and shouting to them from the beach.

"Don't get wet!" he shouted. He kept several large towels in his trunk, though, just for Guinevere's adventures. If she went in the water, it wouldn't be the end of the world.

When it was clear her attention was captured by something at the water's edge, he allowed his attention to return to Maggie, who watched him expectantly.

"Well?" she demanded. "I must have the story now."

He shrugged. "It isn't as dastardly as it sounds. I badly needed an introduction to your cousin Max. For reasons—well, never mind that now. I finagled an invitation to a party I'd heard she would be attending and had a grand plan to approach her. Unfortunately, there was a man hassling her. She'd shaken her bodyguard, and this guy was asking her out, saying how their mothers would think it was a perfect match." He shook his head. "He was... I don't remember. A count or something. It was clear she wasn't interested and that he was trying to push her into it."

She was gazing at him so guilelessly, listening so intently. Maybe that's why he said what he said next.

"I would love to tell you I was the gallant knight riding to rescue her, but the truth is I was looking for a way to get a favor." He wasn't a white knight, even though when Maggie looked at him like she was now, he wanted to be.

"We struck a deal that she'd introduce me to Max if I accompanied her to a school visit. Purely as friends."

Tirith was as mercenary as he was. It was why he'd abandoned his initial blackmail plan—that and the fact that the woman didn't have a single bone hidden in her closet, much less a whole skeleton full—and why they'd become true friends instead of just using each other. When he'd finally confessed to his real mission and what his father had done, she'd supported him. She'd been the one to come up with the fundraising ideas.

"She's got an incredible mind," he said. "She can enter a room full of people and see the relationships, the connections to be made as if the people were pieces on a chess board." And often, she played Queen, moving pieces around the board at will.

Maggie was intuitive and kind and open, so unlike her sister.

He'd asked whether she would stay, but he couldn't imagine her playing at politics the way Tirith did.

Maybe it was why he liked her so much. He opened his mouth to tell her so, but Guinevere had begun her trek back to them and interrupted.

Maybe it was for the best. Maggie was leaving, and if he was very lucky, he'd be working on Ernest's funding for the next year.

Chapter Seven

"Wow."

Maggie swiveled at the voice and came face-to-face with her twin for the second time in less than two weeks.

Tirith closed the door to her suite behind her. "You look incredible."

Maggie had spent a quarter hour staring at herself in the mirror. She didn't recognize the woman looking back at her. The elegant up-do they'd tamed her hair into, the darker makeup.

Mostly the dress. Floor-length, off-the-shoulder, and a pale ice blue. She looked like a princess.

She felt like a fraud.

Where was the cowgirl who lived in jeans and worn-out boots?

What was real? The cowgirl she'd left behind or the princess looking back at her?

Or, could she be both?

She didn't want to leave her life in Texas behind. She loved the horses. Loved her father.

But she hadn't known how it would feel to come home to Glorvaird. So many delightful childhood memories had returned along with her. Things she hadn't thought about in years.

Being in the public eye hadn't been as difficult as she'd feared.

And then there was Luc.

Luc, who'd charmed her and listened to her and *kissed* her.

Her whirling thoughts hadn't resolved when Tirith entered the apartment.

She wasn't sure she hid her surprise. "I thought you weren't coming in until tomorrow."

There were still shadows in Tirith's eyes, though she looked more at peace than when Maggie had left her in Texas. "I need to find a way to make reparations for what happened. The girl's father..." She pinched her lips together. "And... I wanted to be here for the gala tonight. I promised, after all."

For Luc. It couldn't be clearer, though Tirith didn't come out and say it.

Tirith was back. and that meant Maggie didn't need to attend the gala at all.

She sat on the tufted velvet sofa, her stomach roiling. She'd thought she would have one more night with Luc. But now... Now Tirith would be by his side.

A knock at the door revealed Tirith's personal assistant, who delivered two pieces of luggage and glanced between the sisters. She was trained well enough to keep her silence as she left the room.

Tirith removed something small and red from her purse and smoothed it out on the small table beneath the wall-mounted mirror. A bandana.

"How's Dad?" Maggie asked. "Did he discover the switch?"

"In the first five minutes," Tirith admitted with a little laugh. "I convinced him not to tell."

"He called Mother."

Tirith looked up sharply at this information. "Does she know?"

Maggie shook her head. Shrugged. "I don't know. She was very close-mouthed about the conversation. Only told me he'd phoned." Maggie had hoped for more time with her mother, but their schedules hadn't been able to align.

Tirith looked down at the table, smoothed her finger over the bandana. "I didn't think they talked."

Neither did Maggie, though the little girl's hope inside her had never died.

And a tiny voice inside her wondered. If she stayed in Glorvaird, would Dad come back?

Or would he remain in America? Was the damage she'd done to her parents' marriage permanent?

"It wasn't your fault," Tirith said.

"What?"

"Their separation."

Maggie had been away from her sister for so long, she'd forgotten how uncanny the twin connection could be.

"Of course it was my fault. Dad moved to the ranch for me."

Tirith leveled a look on her. "He didn't have to stay. He could've tried harder."

Maggie's chin went up. "Mother could have reached out. Gotten on a plane." She'd witnessed her father's hurt on their first missed wedding anniversary. He'd tried to hide it, but her sensitive thirteen-year-old heart had seen it anyway.

Tirith frowned. "It's too late now."

"It's never too late for love," Maggie murmured.

Tirith's sharp gaze rested on her again.

Maggie turned her attention away from Tirith and focused on the few personal things she'd brought from home. She plucked at the gown. "I suppose I should take this off." She was surprised Tirith's team of stylists hadn't already swarmed the room again. Maybe Tirith had asked them for a few minutes for the sisterly reunion.

Maggie stood.

Her stomach hurt.

"Or..."

She looked over her shoulder to Tirith, who was sending her a contemplative look.

"What if we both attend the gala tonight?"

Could they? But Maggie quickly dismissed the idea. "No one is supposed to know I'm in Glorvaird. The palace would need to make an official statement..."

Tirith shrugged. "It can be made tomorrow. It will cause a stir if we are both announced. Imagine the publicity for Luc and his brother's foundation."

For Luc.

Could Maggie really stand beside her sister? It was the one test she'd hadn't endured yet.

Tirith had been strong for so long, was still being strong, returning for Luc and the foundation when it was clear she was haunted by what had happened.

But if Maggie attended, could she still have her last night with Luc? It wouldn't be the same, not when he'd be at Tirith's side. As it had always been.

But maybe she could find a way to say goodbye.

LUC WAS STANDING in the middle of the ballroom talking with a high ranking parliament member when Princess Tirith and Princess Margaret were announced.

Around him, the assembled crowd quieted.

Both princesses descended the grand staircase that would deposit them at the open ballroom doors.

Tirith wore a gown of royal blue. Maggie's was a delicate, floor-length dress of pale blue. Tirith moved with cool, confident elegance. At her side, Maggie took each step with a quiet determination that was etched in the set of her shoulders, the most minute pinch of her lips.

Tirith was beautiful. Maybe the most beautiful woman he'd ever seen.

But Maggie slayed him. She stole his breath and every thought except a visceral *mine.*

A throat cleared beside him, and he came back to himself as the princesses entered the ballroom and the crowd came back to life, instantly swirling around him.

The man he'd been speaking to was looking at him with a sly smile that made Luc remember why he didn't allow his guard down in public.

"Does she know?"

It would be rude to excuse himself, even if all he wanted to do was push through the throng of idiots gathering around the two princesses.

He made himself smile. "Does who know what?"

"Princess Tirith. Does she know you're in love with her?"

He wanted to laugh but was afraid the desperate sound would make him sound crazy. Or give him away.

He wasn't now and never had been in love with Tirith. It would've been so much easier if he had been. They were a decent match, even if his family's coffers weren't what they once had been.

Maggie hadn't a care about politics. Maybe her innocent heart was what he admired so much.

And he knew she'd never settle for him, not when she was happy back in America.

The crowd parted, and there came Tirith, her stride purposeful as she made a beeline toward him. She had Maggie's hand in hers and was practically dragging her twin across the room.

He excused himself from the politician and met Tirith, suddenly feeling strangled by his black bowtie.

"Hello, darling." She greeted him with a kiss on the cheek. As she leaned toward him, her hand gripped his forearm. Hard.

He couldn't decipher the intense look in her eyes. Was she angry? Happy?

Every person nearby was watching them. He and Tirith were supposed to kick off the night with a dance, but Maggie's presence complicated things. He didn't want her standing at the side of the ballroom alone while he waltzed off with Tirith.

Nor was there an easy way to mention this to Tirith, not when every ear around was hanging on their every word.

But maybe Tirith had planned their entrance, because she spoke loudly enough for those around to hear. "Luc, having my sister join our little event is an honor. Would you escort her around the dance floor?"

"Of course." He'd had to speak past the relief lodged in his throat as he stepped past Tirith and extended his hand toward Maggie.

He couldn't smile at her. His feelings were already too close to the surface.

She wasn't looking directly at him, but she placed her hand in his. Her skin was like warm, like the princess herself.

The string quartet played, and music swirled around them. The crowd faded back to give them room on the ballroom floor.

And he took Maggie into his arms for the first time as herself.

He kept an appropriate amount of space between them when he wanted her closer. *Tirith is here*, he reminded himself. He would keep reminding himself. He didn't want any hint of scandal for his friend. But more importantly, he wanted to protect Maggie.

"Are you all right?" he asked. Alone on the dance floor, for now, no one was near enough to catch his words. It was a shame. If there had been a crowd, he would've had an excuse to lean in closer.

"Of course." A slight smile played about her lips. But it was the lift of her eyes to meet his gaze—the first time she'd done so since she'd entered the ballroom—that revealed the turmoil beneath her calm words.

She looked over his shoulder, but not before he'd glimpsed the vulnerability in her eyes.

He wanted to curse. No, what he really wanted to do was fold her into his arms and kiss her desperately, kiss her until every hint of that vulnerability was gone.

He didn't dare.

"Maggie," he murmured. It was the first time her name had crossed his lips.

"Don't," she whispered. She didn't look at him again, not really. Her gaze was on his ear, maybe, or his hair. Everyone watching would see her looking at him, but she wasn't.

Don't. It was the one thing she could've said to wake him up. She didn't want him to make a scene.

She cleared her throat. "Is Guinevere watching from home? Surely this will make the news."

Guinevere. Thank God one of them was keeping their head. It wasn't him.

Maggie liked Guinevere. Of course she wouldn't want to cause drama at an event that could decide the fate of Guinevere's foundation.

Was his niece the only reason she'd joined Tirith for this event? She could've slipped away into the night, no one the wiser.

It was his turn to clear his throat. "You look..." He shook his head as he swung her into a twirl. She came back into his arms. She fit there. Did she know it, too? "I can't find the right words. Everything sounds trite. Tonight, you're the most beautiful woman I've ever seen."

Roses of color bloomed high in her cheeks. "Thank you," she murmured.

"Was it a good reunion with your sister?"

Her glance flicked over his shoulder, presumably to rest on Tirith at the edge of the ballroom. There was so much emotion behind that look.

"I think she'll be okay now." When she returned her attention to him, her smile was a shade too bright. "I left her personal assistant to pack what few things I brought with me. I'll leave in the morning."

He felt as if he'd been punched in the throat. Couldn't breathe. Couldn't speak. And the song was coming to an end.

Ask her to stay. He was going to do it. He opened his mouth to blurt out his feelings, no matter the crowd that was watching them.

She spoke first. "When will you know if tonight's event was enough? Financially, I mean."

The foundation. She'd just told him she was leaving, and she was worried about the foundation. She wasn't thinking about him at all.

Could she send a clearer message? Maybe it was better that he hadn't spilled his feelings for her.

"It won't be." He'd seen the final attendance numbers already. Unless someone slipped him a large donation check before the night was over—unlikely—come tomorrow he would be scrambling for funds. "I'll figure something out," he said. "It's what I do."

The music ended, and he drew to a stop, letting his hands fall away from her.

Now. Ask her to stay. Beg. But he did none of those things.

He gave her a slight bow. "Thank you for the dance. And for... everything."

He walked away.

MAGGIE SHOULD'VE LEFT after the dance. No. She shouldn't have listened to Tirith in the first place. She shouldn't have come down at all.

Now, two hours later, she was torturing herself.

She'd tried to let herself be distracted by the myriad of people who'd introduced themselves to her.

But nothing could distract her attention from Luc and Tirith.

Her sister had been poised and collected. She'd directed numerous cheques into Luc's hands, where they disappeared quickly into an inside pocket of his jacket. She did it so effortlessly, laughing and talking with the powerful men in the room, laying a hand on their arm or drawing their wives into the conversation. Maggie would need years of lessons to learn to work a room like that. Tirith did it naturally.

And Luc was right by her side. Flagging down a waiter to refill her champagne glass when it was empty. Touching the small of her back. Even the way he angled his body toward Tirith bothered the heck out of Maggie.

She was jealous, plain and simple.

And stupid. So stupid.

He'd told her that he and Tirith were only friends. And she'd believed him. Stupid.

How could he pay such attention to Tirith, be so close to her, and not be in love with her?

Maggie had excused herself politely from the last herd of gawkers and now stood at the edge of the ballroom. She really should leave. Go back to Tirith's suite and get her bag. She could catch a few hours of sleep anywhere. Her sister's sofa was as good a place as any.

"I guess you're not staying."

She turned at the voice behind her. There was her younger sister in a simple black sheath with her hair down around her shoulders. Had she crashed the party? She hadn't been announced as an official guest.

"Bea."

Her sister reached out, and Maggie fell into the hug. Tears pricked her eyes. She dearly missed her sister.

"You could stay longer, you know. Ten days isn't nearly enough."

Maggie backed out of the hug and was blinking furiously, trying to stem her pesky tears, when Bea's words registered.

"You knew?"

Bea laughed. "You're kidding, right? You don't think I could tell you weren't miss prim and proper in the first ten seconds? It's the way you stand," she said all in a rush. "I think it must be all the riding you've done. There's something in your posture—but no one else would see it. Not unless they'd been to the ranch and knew you."

No one else but Luc.

Maggie pushed him from her thoughts. "Did Mother figure it out, then?"

Maggie had planned to speak to Mother first thing in the morning, confess to everything. Drag Tirith with her, if necessary. Smooth things over. But if Mother had figured it out, like Bea...

Bea shook her head. "She's been flustered and out of sorts ever since Dad's phone call. I don't think she noticed."

Shoot. That meant there would be waterworks and a full-fledged guilt trip to look forward to in the morning.

Maggie would welcome the distraction.

She shouldn't, but she couldn't help glancing back to where she'd seen Tirith and Luc the last time.

Tirith was gone, but Luc remained surrounded by a small knot of people. He couldn't have felt her watching, but he look up. Right at her.

Their gazes clashed and held.

And then he looked away, his mouth moving. He was in the conversation.

She'd been stupid enough to hope he'd... what? Denounce Guinevere's foundation and claim he couldn't live without her?

He wouldn't be the man she loved if he'd done that. His niece mattered to him. Helping young people mattered to him.

She'd wanted to matter, too.

As she watched, Tirith returned to the circle. Luc held out a welcoming hand to her, clasped it in his.

Maggie had to look away. Her eyes pricked with tears anew. She had to get out of there.

"I'm a little disappointed," Bea said, startling her. She'd almost forgotten her sister was there.

"Why?" If her voice was breathless with tears, hopefully Bea would be kind enough not to comment.

"The Maggie I know, the one who wrangles half-ton bulls and keeps cowboys in line, would've already walked over there and claimed him."

She looked at her sister, channeling the very best poker face she could manage. "And whom am I supposed to claim?"

Bea's nose wrinkled. "Really? That's all you've got? You're in love with him."

She'd barely admitted it to herself, but Bea had guessed.

"He's with Tirith," she murmured, looking away. It was too hard to bear Bea's scrutiny.

"No, he's not. They'd always been friends. Nothing more."

She wanted to believe her sister. But her eyes told her something entirely different.

"It's all a show," Bea said. "For everyone here. For the money."

The foundation.

She knew the foundation was important. It's why she'd come to Glorvaird.

But that didn't mean she'd ever fit here. Maybe if she'd never left the castle, maybe if she'd grown up in the bosom of politics and power, things could have been different.

But she wasn't Tirith. She wasn't a princess anymore. She was a cowgirl who valued honesty and hard work.

She couldn't reconcile the two.

That's why she didn't belong here.

She didn't want this life.

"I'm going up to my... to Tirith's rooms. I'll say good-night." She hugged Bea. There would be a tearful goodbye in the morning. For now, she needed to be alone.

Chapter Eight

Maggie didn't find the solace she'd hoped for back in Texas.

Oh, things were the same as a day, then two, then a week passed.

Her father had given her one of his bear hugs, and his worried gaze had followed her for the first few days after her return. And then it had been back to business as usual.

They'd fixed a fence line where years of runoff had eroded the ground. She and Scarlett had argued over whether to sell off part of the winter herd. She'd spent hours on horseback, half the time lost in daydreams of Luc and what could've been.

She was happy. She told herself so.

She just didn't feel it.

And now she was getting ready to walk into the boardroom for the Triple H Foundation and be thrust into the world of politics all over again.

Only this time, she had a little Luc sitting on her shoulder.

Imagining what he would say and do gave her confidence when Mrs. Evans opened up the floor to old business.

"There's the matter of the equine therapy program," Maggie said.

She was peripherally aware of the boardroom door opening behind her, of someone slipping into a chair against the wall, almost directly behind her.

She didn't look.

She couldn't allow the distraction or she would lose her nerve.

"I think we've devoted enough time to your little idea, Maggie dear," Mrs. Evans said. "And then there was the unexpected expense you brought to us last week.." The woman used the same faintly condescending, *I'm-humoring-you* tone she always used.

But this time it didn't cow Maggie, not with the memory of Luc burning a hole in her gut.

"I appreciate your help in facilitating our meetings," she said. "But I'm still the chair, am I not?"

Luc had taught her the value of silence. She let her expectant gaze drift around the table, making eye contact with each board member in turn.

Two dropped their eyes. She chose to believe it was in deference to her station. Two gave her faint smiles. And two gave her minute nods.

Mrs. Evans sat with a huff.

Had they been waiting all this time for her to find some gumption?

"My father established this foundation to benefit our local community *and* other special projects."

"Which we did with the gift last week," Mrs. Evans muttered.

Maggie shot her a quelling glance and—miracle of miracles—the woman quieted.

"The equine therapy program is needed," Maggie said. "You don't know my history. I endured something traumatic when I was twelve years old. For a long time, my horse was the only thing that gave me comfort. I couldn't talk to a therapist.

I couldn't take comfort from my father. But being with my horse gave me peace. And there are children in our county who need the same. We *will* be moving forward with the program."

No one challenged her. Not in the moments of silence she allowed. Not as she laid out the program and the next steps and demanded buy-in from each board member. Mrs. Evans only gave in grudgingly.

The Maggie from a month ago would've been appalled. She would've accused herself of throwing her weight around.

Scarlett had been right. Maggie had been too kind. So kind, she'd allowed herself to be walked all over.

There was a satisfaction in getting this done.

She should've done it a year ago.

When the meeting adjourned, Mrs. Hawes, who'd been sitting right next to her, turned in her chair.

"I'm glad you decided to do the therapy program, dear." Somehow the way she used the endearment was different from the condescending way Mrs. Evans had. "Your dad will be proud of you."

"Thank you." It was nice to be praised, but she was proud of herself.

Mrs. Hawes tilted her head to the side. "I think your young man is waiting for you."

"I don't have—" Maggie's denial cut off as she turned to look where the other woman had indicated.

Luc.

He was standing just in front of the chair he must've vacated.

Luc had been the one who'd entered the meeting and sat?

The rest of the murmured conversations behind her faded away as walked toward him. She couldn't read his expression. He almost looked... wary?

"What are you doing here?"

. . .

WHAT WAS HE DOING HERE? Did he even know?

Taking a risk. A crazy, jump-off-the-skyscraper-with-no-parachute risk.

His heart was pounding so hard that he felt it in his temples.

"Ernest's foundation received a check," he said. "For one hundred thousand dollars."

Her eyes lowered even as her lips twitched.

"From an American charity we'd never heard of before. Imagine my surprise when he told me to look up the website and I saw your picture there."

Her chin came up, and he could see the strength and determination in the set of her jaw. "As you witnessed"—she waved her hand to encompass the room and the board members who remained—"our foundation takes seriously our mission to help others."

He couldn't hold back his smile. He'd witnessed it all right. Maggie had come into her own. He'd been irrationally proud of her as she'd stood up to the board member who'd been running the meeting. Maggie had been magnificent.

He wanted to reach out for her. Wanted to fold her into his arms.

But he wasn't sure he had the right.

"Maggie, can we—?"

"You finished in here, Mags?"

A woman a few years older than Maggie had pushed open the door. She had a toddler on her hip and was noticeably pregnant. Her eyes lit on him, and instant curiosity lit her face. "Who's this?"

Maggie went to the woman, extending her arms to take the toddler.

"Maggie!" The girl patted her face.

Maggie tickled her neck, which elicited a spate of giggles.

Maggie's... friend?... was still looking at him expectantly.

"This is Luc," Maggie said when the silence lengthened.

"I'm Maggie's cousin Scarlett. You came all the way from Glorvaird? Are you coming out to see the ranch?"

He looked at Maggie. "That depends on Maggie."

She was blushing.

"Well, I'll take off and let you two... finish whatever is going on here. I just wanted to find out how the meeting went. Maggie, did you chicken out?"

"She was magnificent." Luc couldn't keep his eyes off her.

Maggie blushed more, if that were possible.

"That's wonderful!" Scarlett said. "I'm so proud of you."

Maggie shrugged off the praise.

"C'mon, booger bear. Let's go." Scarlett reached for the toddler, but Maggie held on.

"I'll carry her out to the truck."

Scarlett scowled. "I'm not an invalid. I can carry my own daughter."

The set of Maggie's chin said she was adamant. "I'm going that way anyway." She scooped up a leather satchel from her seat and headed out behind Scarlett.

Luc followed the trio out the doors.

He hadn't been able to believe his eyes when he'd driven into town in his rented sedan. He'd expected small, but the town was miniscule. Of course Maggie would've felt safe here. She must've known everyone by name.

And it was hot. It was a good thing he'd packed a bag instead of jumping on a plane willy-nilly, because he'd had to change his shirt. The soaking humidity and heat combined were like nothing he'd ever experienced back home.

Maggie buckled the toddler into a car seat in the back of a huge, four-door truck. It's wheels and undercarriage were caked with mud.

After she said good-bye to her cousin, the woman drove off with a wave.

And then he was just the two of them standing on the sidewalk in front of the squat brick building.

"You came all this way to thank me?" she asked.

"I came because I can't imagine not having you in my life."

Her eyes widened, and she stepped back.

He hadn't planned to lay it out there like that. "Maggie..." He couldn't stand it a second longer. He reached for her, rested his hands at her waist.

She didn't pull away.

"I'm sorry for that last night. At the gala. I should've found a way to extricate myself from Tirith and—"

"I didn't want that." She shook her head to emphasize the words. "I knew how important the gala was for the foundation." Her gaze lowered. "And besides, Tirith is incredible. If you felt something for her—"

"I don't."

When she raised her eyes, he saw the vulnerability in their depths. The questions that he'd put there. "I've never felt more than friendship for her. I never will. My heart belongs to you."

And he'd do whatever it took to prove it, including grovel. "I should've handled things differently. At the very least, I should've asked you to stay."

He raised one hand and touched her cheek. She closed her eyes and leaned toward his palm.

He couldn't resist any longer. He leaned down and kissed her.

It was right, that first touch of lips, without any pretense between them. Her hands rested on his shoulders.

But when he would've pulled her closer, deepened the kiss, she pressed gently on his shoulders and pushed him away.

Her expression was drawn as he looked down at her. Had he read things completely wrong?

"Luc, I have—I care about you. A great deal. But before things go any further..." She sighed. "Would you come with me? Out to the ranch?"

He'd go with her anywhere. "Of course."

. . .

MAGGIE SHOULD HAVE BEEN ELATED that Luc had come for her. She was elated—and frightened.

She figured the best way she could explain to him was to show him.

He'd joined her in the farm truck, and now they bumped over the cattle guard. She didn't drive him up to the ranch house. Dad would be up there. Instead, she drove down the rutted lane, past the barn. Out to the fields, a quarter mile in, to a hill where a good portion of the spread was laid out in front of them. She got out of the truck, and he joined her in front of the ticking engine.

For a few moments they stood there, look out over the grassland dotted with grazing cattle.

He stood slightly distant from her, his hands in his pockets. "Should I have stayed in Glorvaird?"

"No!" She turned to him, and he faced her, though there was still too much distance between them.

She took a deep breath. "This is what I wanted to show you." She swept her arm out to the side. "My family has a legacy in Glorvaird, but a part of my legacy is here, too. This land. The animals. Even the foundation and the people we help. And my dad is here."

Tirith had said differently, but Maggie knew in her heart that it was her fault her parents had split. If there was any hope of them being reunited, she'd do everything she could to make it happen. And that meant she should probably stay here, with Dad.

"I can't abandon this part of myself."

But she didn't want to live without Luc, either.

Tears threatened, and she closed her eyes against them.

She heard the sound of his shoes in the crisp grass. A moment later, she felt his presence in front of her. He clasped her elbows in his capable hands, brushing a kiss against her closed eyelids. One and then the other.

"Did you hate it so much, then? Being in Glorvaird?"

"No," she whispered, eyes still closed. That's what made

this so difficult. "It felt like being home again." Even that last tearful goodbye with Mother had been something she now held close to her heart. "But—"

"Your heart belongs here, too." He brushed his fingers against her cheek, where a tear had escaped. "Your heart can have two homes."

Could it? Was it possible she belonged both here and in Glorvaird?

Luc's voice was slightly amused when he said, "I suppose that when I said 'I can't live without you,' I should've followed that with 'if that means we're in Texas or Glorvaird or Timbuktu, I'll be happy. Because I'll be with you.'"

She opened her eyes, and he was looking at her with such a combination of vulnerability and intensity. "That is"—she heard the catch in his voice—"if you feel the same."

How could he doubt?

"These past few days," she said, "I've barely been able to function. I feel as if half of me is missing."

A slight smile turned the corners of his mouth. "It didn't seem that way at your board meeting."

"Because I was imagining you beside me. You and your politics and your charisma."

His smile was slowly blossoming into something bigger. "You find me irresistible?"

"I find it impossible not to fall in love with you."

His smile disappeared as her words sank in. Her stomach swooped the same way it had when she was tossed from a horse she was breaking.

"I can scarcely believe it," he breathed. "I don't deserve it, I'm sure of that. But I love you so dearly that I don't care whether or not I deserve your love in return."

He loved her.

The knowledge sank in deep, filling all the deep places in her that had been scarred by a decade of fighting her fears and hiding out on the ranch.

He kissed her then, tenderly. Like a man who'd just been

given everything he wanted. His gentleness gave way to passion, and she met him there in each caress, each breath.

When they finally had to draw back or risk suffocating, he held her close. She could feel his heart pounding beneath her cheek. It made her smile, burying her face in his shirt. One of his hands was tangled in the hair at the back of her head. The ponytail she'd worn all morning had tumbled down at some point, and her hair was wild around her head.

"When do you have to return to Glorvaird?" she asked softly, not sure she wanted to know the answer. Would they have a week together? A few days?

He chuckled a little, the sound rumbling beneath her cheek. "Ernest fired me."

"What?" She moved back to see his face.

"He said I'd done enough for the foundation, and he could tell I was unhappy and it was time for me to move on. I don't think he expected me to pick up and head for America." Luc shook his head, a bemused smile on his face. "I don't know anything about ranching, but maybe I can help with your foundation. I understand Americans are accustomed to having their pizza delivered by men in truck. Perhaps I could do that. Or... anything, really."

She frowned. "I'll happily let you run my father's foundation," She took a deep breath. "I think it's time for me to think about splitting my time between the ranch and Glorvaird. Being a part of the royal family again, out of hiding. I can do so much good."

Maybe if she returned to Glorvaird, Dad would too. It was a wistful hope...

He drew her close again, his chin brushing her temple. "You'll need a place to rest. Recuperate. And maybe work off some of the frustrations you'll accumulate working with hard-headed politicians. Your Triple H can be that."

Yes. It could work. For the first time, she could see a new future stretching out in front of her. A cowgirl. A royal. With Luc at her side.

<h1 style="text-align:center">Epilogue</h1>

VALENTIN STRODE DOWN THE PALACE HALLWAY toward his suite. Half his attention was on the sheaf of paper in his hand, a lengthy bill he had only muddled partway through. Every so often, he glanced up to ensure he wasn't going to mow down a member of the castle staff.

The other half of him was buzzing with tension. The same tension that had stolen his concentration in the ten days since he'd blown up at Annika.

He'd felt betrayed by her easy, flirtatious manner with his brother. Embarrassed that others had witnessed the two of them whispering, their heads bent together during his speech on the naval base.

He'd been embarrassed, but he shouldn't have taken it out on her. She'd been distant ever since he'd lost his temper and shouted at her.

He needed to see her, assure her it wasn't going to happen again. It wasn't like him. She could ask his mother, or Dad, or his personal assistant.

He could change out of the monkey suit he wore and go see her. She had an apartment in the city. He could be there in an hour.

He dropped his arm to his side, dangling the bill there as he quickened his pace. Better to fix things with Annika. Then he could devote his full attention to matters of the crown.

The door to his suite was ajar, and his heart leapt as he neared. He thought he heard Annika's voice. Had she come to him? Even better.

But his hands went cold when her voice became clearer, and he stopped just before the cracked door.

That was definitely her voice, murmuring something he couldn't quite make out.

Another voice answered. This one he recognized, too. Max.

Valentin's good intentions flew away like dandelion chaff in a stiff wind. What was Max doing in his rooms, with his fiancée?

Temper rising, he pushed open the door, only to freeze on the threshold.

Annika and Max weren't simply speaking. They were locked in an embrace, tangled together on his sofa. More than an embrace, if their mussed hair and rumpled clothing were any indication.

"What the—?"

Annika broke the kiss and gasped, pushing on Max's shoulders. Her lipstick was smeared, her lips swollen. This was no single kiss they'd shared.

But Max was in no hurry to let her go. Finally, he moved off the couch with the coiled power of a leopard in every movement.

But Max couldn't know he'd enraged a lion.

Betrayal surged, and Valentin wanted to howl. How could his brother do this to him? How could Annika?

"Get out," he snarled.

"Val—"

Valentin slashed a hand through the air, silencing Annika. "Get out. Both of you." He couldn't even look at her. "We're through."

Max wore a self-satisfied expression, and for the first time in his life, a red haze descended over Valentin's vision.

His brother wasn't moving. Wasn't leaving. And Valentin hated him.

He swung, the punch a quick jab that Max couldn't have seen coming.

It floored him.

"You back-stabbiing scumbag. I never want to see you again."

"Max!" Annika cried out and crumpled to the floor beside Valentin's brother.

At the sight, Valentin turned on his heel and stalked out. He didn't know what he'd have done if he'd stayed.

The Prince's Matchmaker

Chapter One

"Your mother is worried about you."

Valentin, crown prince of Glorvaird, looked up from the newspaper headline that had captured his attention.

His father, Cody Austin, strode into the blue breakfast room with his usual loose-limbed cowboy swagger. Valentin had attempted to imitate it once. He'd been all of ten, and his mother had politely hinted that a future king couldn't walk like that.

Mother's hints were always polite. Until they weren't.

"I'm fine," Valentin told his father as the older man settled in the chair across the small, round table covered in white linen and fine china. He folded the newspaper and laid it on the table beside his place setting.

Father leveled a look on him.

"I had my annual physical a few weeks ago," Valentin said. "I'm as healthy as a horse." He wasn't the one who spent his life drinking and carousing and doing who-knew-what. Let Mother worry about his brother. Not Valentin.

"She's worried about your emotional health." Father grimaced. "I can't believe I just said that."

Valentin could. Mother was demanding and to-the-point.

She had to be as reigning queen. But Father... Father had a sun-hardened facade that hid a soul sensitive enough that he was often the emissary Mother sent when she needed someone tactful.

Which meant the eighteen month reprieve Valentin had received was over.

The bite of eggs Benedict he'd put in his mouth turned to ash. It would be impolite to spit it out, even though it felt like he would vomit if he swallowed.

He swallowed anyway. Everyone said his heart was made of stone. Maybe the lining of his stomach was, too.

"Max phoned you, too?"

Dad's head came up, his eyes sharp. "No. He called you?"

Oh. He should've just asked Dad what was going on with Mother, not revealed something he'd rather have kept quiet.

"A few times. He left voicemails." Which Valentin had deleted without listening to. As far as he was concerned, his brother no longer existed.

But the curiosity and disappointment his father couldn't quite hide cut.

Valentin couldn't help the hit of guilt before he buried it. Max deserved what he got. Valentin never wanted to see him again, and he'd said so right to his brother's face.

But despite the fact that Max was a screw-up, Mother and Father didn't feel the same way.

"He probably blew through his allowance for the month," Valentin said grimly.

Tiny lines fanned his father's eyes. He hummed noncommittally.

It was time for a subject change. If Father called Max later to find out what bind his younger brother had gotten into, Valentin didn't want to know about it.

"If it wasn't that, what exactly has Mother worried?"

Now it was Father who laid down his fork. "We can talk about it later."

Or never. Never would be Valentin's preference.

Unfortunately, his mother was used to the entire country bowing to her wishes. And even if Father delayed, it wouldn't be long before Valentin discovered whatever this was.

"Tell me," he said.

If he wasn't mistaken, Father winced.

Valentin braced himself, imagining an invisible joist and braces shoring up the crumbling brick wall that was inside him.

"Your mother thinks it might be time to start dating again."

"What?" His voice shook slightly. His insides too, as if a light earthquake had rumbled through the foundation Valentin's being.

"It's going on two years."

Eighteen months and two days. Only that long since the day his younger brother had betrayed him. Or at least since the day Valentin had discovered the betrayal. Valentin had been completed blindsided, but it wasn't out of the realm of possibility that Max and Annika had been together behind his back for far longer.

Valentin had been devoted to Annika. Besotted with her. Blind to her faults. Or maybe that had been willful on his part.

His first duty was to his country. He'd told her that on their second date, insulated in a tiny, private booth at a coffee shop in Paris, where they'd met. He'd been in France on business, a meeting with the prime minister.

Annika had claimed to understand, to admire his dedication to his people. But all his trips overseas, the endless parliament meetings, the late nights spent reading the newest proposed bill or trade agreement instead of being out on the town...

Annika had strayed, right into his brother's arms.

And stayed there, apparently, even though Max's longest relationship before her had had a shelf life of two weeks.

Thinking about dating again, about allowing someone

into his life, made Valentin think he might yet see the return of his eggs Benedict.

Stone stomach. He attempted a smile at his father, even as his mind raced for the right answer. He folded the linen napkin in his lap, took his time placing the perfect square that emerged under his fingers onto the table beside his plate.

"I am much too busy with matters of importance to this country." That sounded too stiff, formal. Father was going to see right through him. "Dating would be too much of a distraction."

Father's pointed gaze missed nothing. "You've always felt the responsibility of the crown. But lately you've been burying yourself in your duties. Even before—you know."

Valentin's smile grew thin. "Is that Mother's opinion or yours?"

Father didn't show any sign he felt the blow, though Valentin had meant the words as a strike. His father's gaze was intent, and maybe a little sad.

"How long has it been since you took some time for yourself? Thought about something other than tariffs and treaties?"

Every night. Every night when he wondered what he might've done differently to make Annika happy. Where he'd gone wrong in his relationship with Max. How could his brother have betrayed him like he had?

But that wasn't what Father meant.

"The crown does not sleep." It was one of Mother's favorite sayings. When he'd been a young boy and asked why Mother and Father got to stay up late when he had to be tucked in early, she'd used it frequently. Later, when he'd asked why they didn't vacation abroad like some of his friends did, his Mother had answered, "The crown doesn't vacation."

"Your mother sleeps," Father said. "She relies on her staff when she needs to and she understands that if she works twenty-four hours a day, she's going to burn out. She was close to it when we met, you know. Burying all of herself in her duties because her father was dying and she didn't know how to handle it."

What was left of Valentin's smile was scraps. No doubt his bared teeth would've terrified a lesser mortal than his father. "Then it is a good thing you're in excellent health."

Father opened his mouth, no doubt to explain that hadn't been what he'd meant.

Valentin pushed back from the table, though he didn't stand. "I am not burning out. I have always loved my country, our people. I do my best to serve them diligently. Mother should recognize that." He nearly choked on his next words. "I'm only twenty-five. There is plenty of time for dating. Later. There's no royal decree that says I have to be married by thirty."

He knew, because he'd once looked. He'd been ten and Max nine when his younger brother had convinced him there was a marriage agreement that had required he marry the daughter of a visiting German dignitary, a horrid little girl who treated the servants nastily and stuck out her tongue at him whenever no adults were looking.

"You're going to have to let someone in eventually," Father said.

Valentin pictured his wall again, and his heart, which he imagined as a crumbling castle behind it. It had been bombed to the foundations. Valentin had built walls to protect it, but there was nothing there to protect anymore. He had no heart to give.

"Does she have someone in mind?" Until Annika, he'd expected to make a political match. Marry to unite two counties and all of that. He couldn't imagine trusting anyone else with the deepest parts of himself, but if it was for his country, maybe he could bear it.

But Father shook his head and wore an expression of faint... chagrin?

"What?" Valentin's tone became sharper as his temper got

shorter. He stood, straightening his shirt cuffs. He had a meeting in an hour and needed to prepare.

"She's got this idea that..." Father shook his head. He stood too, his height a reminder of how much Valentin admired the man.

"Tell me," Valentin repeated, temper dissipating like sand in a windstorm. Father didn't deserve that from him. It wasn't Father who'd betrayed him. It wasn't Father's fault his heart didn't exist.

"She heard about this high profile matchmaker lady."

"Absolutely not." The words were out before Valentin had time to think them through. It was a ludicrous idea. Out of the question.

Was that what Mother thought of his skill at attracting the opposite sex? That he needed someone to pick a match for him?

"I'll tell her myself," Valentin said grimly. "There will be no matchmaker for me."

CRYSTAL RAMOS DROVE her compact car away from the gatehouse and parked where she'd been directed, beside the royal garage. Was there a different name for it if the garage was so massive it could've fit her apartment inside at least ten times?

She'd been invited to the castle to visit Glorvaird's royal family. Well, part of it.

She was still mired in disbelief as she got out of the car. She stood on the pavers, craning her neck up to admire the castle that rose above her on two sides.

She couldn't believe she was here. Or that Queen Eloise had even heard of her.

Her! A nobody from a family of nobodies. She hadn't even finished college. And the queen had called her *directly*. Not some assistant. Not an email.

She was here to meet with the crown prince because he *needed her services.*

If she could find the prince a perfect match, she'd have her choice of future clients. She'd never have to work with sniveling, spoiled men like Ronald Frothingham again.

And maybe—this dream was so far out there that she hadn't really let it coalesce as a thought until this very moment—maybe she wouldn't have to worry about every single penny. She could pay Michael and Reid's college tuition and be able to eat more than ramen with a side of ramen. She could buy lobster.

She was shaken out of her daydream at a polite cough from nearby.

"Oh, hi!" She pushed away from the car, where she'd leaned as her happy daydreams had spun around her.

A man—not the prince—in a dove gray sweater over a starched collared shirt and pressed slacks was waiting near the corner of the garage, where a footpath led around the side.

"Sorry, I was woolgathering." Could he really blame her? She'd jumped at the chance to meet with the prince, but the only time available in his calendar had been early in the day. She'd always considered anything before seven a.m. ridiculous, but she couldn't exactly say that to her newest client, not with everything that was riding on this.

The well-dressed man was still waiting on her as she dragged her leather laptop bag out of the backseat of her car.

When she joined him, he said, "This way, miss."

She'd hoped there was a second door, maybe a servant's entrance or something, around the corner—she'd seen the main entrance at the front of the garage—but that hope was dashed as she followed the guy down the footpath around the base of the stone castle.

She'd worn a knee-length skirt and a button-up blouse with her best pair of black heels. They weren't Louboutins, or even knockoffs, but she was hoping the ensemble made her look professional and conservative. As it was, the humidity was creeping in beneath her skirt and making her underarms damp. Or maybe that was her nerves.

She tried to unobtrusively wipe her palms on her skirt.

And then the stone footpath gave way to sand as the castle wall ended and the ocean opened up in front of them, a panorama that spanned the horizon.

Her escort kept going.

"Uh, excuse me."

She stalled out on the last stone paver.

Her guide turned back and raised one imperious eyebrow.

She wondered what she'd gotten into. This was someone who worked for the prince. Did her client have that same superior attitude? Or worse?

Was he going to be another Ronald?

She made herself focus. "Let's start over, shall we? I'm Crystal."

She extended her hand and, after a prolonged moment, he shook it. "Conrad, the crown prince's personal assistant."

Ah. Gatekeeper, schedule keeper. The prince's man.

Not someone she wanted to offend.

"Conrad. It's nice to meet you. Where are we going?"

"Your meeting with his highness."

"On the beach?"

Her skepticism must've been audible because Conrad sighed with a good dose of long-suffering. She'd heard sighs like that often from her younger brothers.

"If you would...?" He gestured for her to follow him.

And even though a small part of her wondered if this was some elaborate joke Michael had cooked up—did her brother have the connections to pull this off?—she reached down and took off her shoes and followed Conrad onto the sand.

The sun was coming up over the edge of the water. The sky was all orange hues. Even the sand was gilded gold.

She blamed the romantic lighting for what happened next.

It felt like a lightning bolt. A current that zapped straight down her spine to her toes when she caught sight of the prince.

He was shirtless, his skin slicked with sweat and gleaming bronze as he jogged down the beach at the water's edge.

No, jogging wasn't the right term. There was someone a few paces behind the prince—a bodyguard?—who was puffing for air and straining for each step as he fought to keep up.

Sprinting. That was the word.

The crown prince was sprinting closer and closer, each step churning up sand behind him.

She'd known he was handsome. Yesterday, she'd pored over her computer for hours, surfing the internet and reading article after article about him. Of course there had been pictures. She was acquainted with the planes of his face, the patrician nose, the startling ice-blue of his eyes.

But this was not the polished, handsome man in a designer suit, posing for photos. Even in the occasional candid she'd seen, he was all elegant haughtiness.

This was the prince like she'd never seen him before. And she guessed not many people had.

And then he raised a hand and did a slow lope right toward them.

Lightning bolt. Prince with a hot bod. Crystal blinked as she felt a blush scalding her cheeks. She had one-point-five seconds to find her composure, but it had deserted her completely.

Think about Michael and Reid. Her brothers needed her. She needed this job.

She breathed in deeply the scent of salt water, and when she exhaled, she was back to herself.

A few yards away, the prince slowed to a walk. It didn't seem fair that he was only slightly winded. He glanced at her, his eyes wary, as he approached Conrad first.

His assistant held out a T-shirt, which the prince slipped over his head, the material quickly covering his powerful chest and the six-pack she hadn't imagined beneath his tailored suits.

Conrad handed him a small towel that he used to wipe first his face and then his hands.

And then the prince turned from Conrad to her.

"So you're the matchmaker."

"So I am." She stepped forward to meet his handshake and only belatedly remembered she had her shoes in hand. She juggled them, along with her satchel, her face heating again at her own awkwardness, before she got everything into her left hand.

She couldn't help the lift of her chin. Meeting on the beach had been his idea, not hers. "I'm Crystal Ramos. It's an honor to meet you, your highness."

He handed the towel to Conrad, who faded back, presumably heading off the beach. Which left only the two of them and the bodyguard, who stood several feet away, scanning the view back toward the castle.

The prince's grip was warm and sure. "Valentin, if you please."

If she pleased. To be on a first name basis with the prince.

But as he squeezed her hand once and then released her, she saw that the wariness in his expression hadn't disappeared. It'd been joined by curiosity, maybe. But it was still there.

It had been his mother who'd called her, not the prince himself. Of course he was wary.

He nodded back the direction she and Conrad had come from, and she fell into step beside him.

"Your highness. I mean... Valentin." That was going to take some getting used to.

His strides were so long that she had to scramble in the sand to keep up with him. She grasped for professionalism.

"Thank you for meeting with me," she said.

"I'm afraid I don't have long." And his gaze was distant. As if he'd already dismissed her. "Frankly, hiring you was my mother's idea."

She knew that, but she hadn't expected his curt dismissal.

All the dreams she'd been spinning began to shimmer like a mirage. She felt a tremble start deep inside but masked it with a polite smile.

"And you're going along with it?" *Am I wasting my time?*

They'd reached the edge of the castle wall, where the sand met the stone pavers.

He turned to her.

And she realized she was standing with her only empty hand cocked on her hip. Probably it wasn't appropriate to speak to the prince with an attitude, but she didn't like feeling misled. The queen had insinuated that the job was Crystal's.

"I'll give you four dates. With different women or the same one, I don't care. Wow me."

What arrogance!

She opened her mouth to tell him exactly where he could put his *wow me*, but what emerged was, "What are you looking for in a match?"

Chapter Two

CRYSTAL HADN'T BEEN KICKED OUT. SHE GUESSED that was something.

Her feet were hurting, and she was regretting the heels for the second time as she followed the prince and his assistant up at least two flights of stone stairs and down a series of twisting passageways.

The prince—she still couldn't think of him as Valentin—had asked her to bear with him as he spoke to Conrad. Which left her to follow and watch the rapid-fire interplay as Conrad flicked through an iPad while he spoke of engagements that the prince either accepted or rejected. There was a reminder about a new bill parliament was reviewing before Conrad handed him a single sheet of paper as they reached a doorway cut from the stone. Then the prince opened the door and held it for her as Conrad peeled off down the hallway.

"Uh, thanks." She slipped by him, getting a blast of his body heat as she passed. Inside was a sitting room that was so formal it reminded her of her grandma's parlor. There were no knickknacks or doilies here, but the air was still *don't touch*. She gave the dark, square sofa the side-eye but followed the prince through an adjoining doorway.

This room was an office. Light streamed in from a window cut into the wide stone castle exterior, illuminating floor-to-ceiling bookcases along two interior walls. They were stuffed with what looked like boring legal tomes. No novels in sight, sadly.

The prince used a remote to turn on a large flat-screen telly, and a national news channel came to life. The volume was so low it was hardly audible. He barely glanced at it before moving behind the desk, which was massive and carved out of some kind of heavy wood. It was neat, almost bare. Only a few papers were scattered across the surface along with a closed laptop. The paper Conrad had given the prince joined the others.

He didn't sit in the comfy-looking leather chair behind the desk but stood with one hand planted on the wooden surface.

"When can we schedule the first date?"

Oh yes. He was going to be as high maintenance as Ronald. At least he was handsome. And a catch, all things considered.

Think about the rewards. She could do this. For Michael and Reid.

"Do you mind if I sit?" she asked.

She didn't wait for him to answer but perched on the chair on this side of the desk. She opened her bag and vacillated between the laptop and the notepad. Notepad it was. She flipped to a clean sheet of paper.

"What are you looking for in a woman?"

His expression instantly closed off. "That's what you want to ask me? We're not doing a questionnaire from a dating site. I agreed to four dates. You provide the match."

She smiled tightly. "How am I supposed to find you a match if I don't know what kind of person you're looking for? Do you want to meet someone you can talk to about current events? Politics? What level of affection are you most comfortable with? If you like her, how often do you want to see her?"

The prince was still leaning on his desk, but his smile had turned brittle. "Miss Ramos."

"Crystal."

"Crystal. I'm sure you're aware of my history."

Of course she was. The breakup with his fiancée had been public and ugly. Although all of the media coverage had been gathered from Valentin's brother and his ex-fiancée. Valentin himself had never answered an interview question about what happened. Never spoken badly about them or how he must've been hurt by the whole thing.

Several articles had accused him of having a heart of stone. Being uncaring, because the prince had gone on as if everything was business as usual. Who knew if it was true?

She met his stare squarely. "I don't read gossip rags, but it's impossible not to know that something happened."

Now his expression turned grim. "So it is. I imagine every eligible single woman in the country knows."

She considered him. "So you've given up on finding someone."

If so, he presented a challenge that she'd never faced before. All of her previous clients had at least *believed* in love. They'd even wanted to find it. If Valentin didn't, would she be wasting her time?

So you've given up on finding someone.

Though he was supposed to be made of stone, Valentin felt like his insides were a pot, merrily simmering away on the stovetop. Every push from the pretty young matchmaker felt as if she was turning up the heat on the burner.

He'd been the one to bring up Annika and Max, and now it felt as if his lid was rattling. Ready to blow off if he didn't release some steam. His regular morning run was supposed to have done that, but it hadn't helped.

What could he say to make her understand?

I trusted them both, and look what happened.

That wouldn't be helpful. She'd probably tell him to see a therapist.

Annika was my true love.

In hindsight, he could admit that there were things about her that had driven him crazy. Surely he'd done the same to her. If she'd only talked to him, maybe they could've worked things out.

I have nothing left to give.

The truest answer of all, but one he wasn't about to share with this virtual stranger—or anybody for that matter.

He never should have brought the matchmaker up here. He'd agreed to the meeting because Mother had pushed. He'd meant to dismiss her quickly, but she'd surprised him with her sass, and something underneath her attitude made him think of kicking a puppy when he'd wanted to turn her off.

He'd said the words agreeing to four dates without thinking. He was a man of his word. He'd go through with them. But he wasn't going to find a match.

"I'm quite over what happened with my brother." His cool tone gave voice to the lie, but he couldn't look at her as he said it. He flipped open his laptop, unlocking it with a few keystrokes. It was a matter of a few seconds to pull up his diary.

"I have a state dinner a week from today. I'll bring a guest of your choice. You can make arrangements with Conrad. She'll need to be cleared by palace security."

She stared at him as if he'd lost his marbles. Maybe he had.

"You want to take a first date to a state dinner? I assume it's black tie."

He nodded.

"And you want me to choose someone for you after a fifteen minute meeting?"

"Is that a problem?" He hadn't fired her, but maybe she would quit.

He could see the wheels turning in her mind. There was a tiny part of him that wondered if she could do it, could find someone to bring his heart to life again.

Then he dismissed the thought. He would settle for companionship. That was enough. It had to be.

"If you don't mind, I have a full schedule today." He knew he was being rude, but he didn't apologize.

"Fine." There was fire in her eyes as she stood and straightened her skirt. In the blouse and business attire, he wouldn't have given her a second glance if he'd seen her at an event or in public.

But there was a spray of freckles across the bridge of her nose that he'd noticed on the beach, and now he'd couldn't stop noticing them.

She was utterly unremarkable, except for those freckles.

He decided he didn't like them.

"Thank you for your time," she said stiffly. She flounced from the room. A moment later, he realized she'd left her bag on the floor beside her chair.

He heard the outer door open and close.

No matter. He'd have Conrad return the bag to her.

His desk phone rang with the distinct tone that meant it was his private line, one that only a handful of people had access to.

He picked it up without glancing at the display.

"Valentin. Don't hang up."

Max.

Hearing his brother's voice brought back a visceral memory of those last moments. Annika's lips, swollen and bee-stung after kissing his brother. Max's flashing, unapologetic stare. The crippling pain of betrayal.

"What part of 'I never want to speak to you again' was unclear to you?"

Was that his voice? He sounded as cold as ice. He felt

anything but. His collar was too tight. He tugged, but then remembered it was a T-shirt. His run and the momentary calm he'd felt as his feet pounded the sand was long gone.

"I screwed up."

At least Max was admitting it. It was small comfort.

"I need to see you. There's something—"

Valentin let loose an expletive. "No."

"Val, I know we hurt you—"

"Don't call me again."

He hung up the phone with ruthless force. And when it rang instantly, he knew it was Max again.

He took it off the cradle and mashed the switchhook, then released it. If Max called back, he'd get a busy signal. He was already blocked from Valentin's cell phone.

He tossed the receiver onto the desk, ignoring the clatter it made.

He was threading both hands into his hair, elbows above his head, when he realized Crystal was hovering in the doorway.

He let his arms drop to his sides.

She was watching him with unconcealed curiosity. And pity.

He didn't want her pity.

"You'll forget you just witnessed that." He made it an order, channeling his mother more than he'd ever done before.

She ignored him, bending to retrieve her bag from the floor.

"I'm sorry," she said faintly, and slipped out the door.

For what? Sorry she'd taken him on as a client? Sorry she'd witnessed a private moment, witnessed his temper exploding? Or sorry for him?

Because he was a lousy excuse for a human being.

. . .

HOURS after the disastrous meeting with the matchmaker, Valentin was striding down the castle corridor when he nearly ran over his cousin Tirith.

"Sorry," he muttered.

"Me too." Her smile was genuine but muted.

"All right?" he asked. He and Tirith had grown somewhat close in the past few years. Over a year ago, she'd accidentally gotten in an auto accident that had resulted in a little girl's life-altering injuries. Before that, Tirith had been lively and free-spirited. Since then, she'd grown reserved and quiet. He quite missed her fervor for life.

"I'm fine," she said, but the shadows behind her eyes remained. "Are you all right?"

And there was a part of him that wanted to see her old smile. "Mother has hired a matchmaker for me."

"What?" She burst out the word in a single giggle before she remembered herself.

He shrugged. "She thinks it's time I started dating again."

Tirith's gaze was maybe too sharp. "What do you think?"

"I suppose I can't be alone forever." But he wasn't exactly in a hurry to meet someone. "What about you? You haven't dated since Moreno."

"I never really dated Luc."

That wasn't what it had looked like. She'd been close with the man, attending functions and inspiring media speculation as to their relationship status. But when Tirith had desperately needed to hide out for a few days, she'd asked her twin sister to switch places with her. And Moreno had promptly fallen for the Texas twin.

"I'd be more than happy to divert the matchmaker's attention to you."

Tirith laughed, as he'd hoped she would. "Not necessary. And good luck."

He'd need it if he was going to get through this unscathed.

Chapter Three

"I HAD FUN TONIGHT."

A week after his first meeting with the matchmaker, Valentin stood looking down at his date, Amy. The state dinner had been surprisingly painless. It was over now, and he'd escorted her out to the drive, where the day limo would return her home. There were still a few state officials lingering on the lawn, their cars waiting on the drive while they conversed. It was a public place for a goodbye.

He was thankful for that. It meant he didn't have to decipher her social clues. Figure out whether a kiss was appropriate or a hug would be better. Here, it was appropriate for him to tuck her into the limo and say a simple good-night.

There was a reason Annika had been his only long-term relationship.

His social skills left much to be desired. He could work a room of politicians, but reading a woman was something he'd never mastered.

"Thank you for coming," he said.

Amy smiled at him, her eyes kind and intelligent.

"I won't wait for you to call," she said with a pat to his cheek.

She got in the limo without a backward glance, and he closed the door for her, watching as she drove off.

Her intelligence had drawn him to her when they'd met in a university chemistry lab more than five years ago now. He and Amy had gone on all of two dates when they'd realized they were better off as friends.

But he had to hand it to Crystal. She'd done her homework. It was true that the media documented every time he was seen in public, but it must've taken hours of reading internet articles to find the mention of those dates from his sophomore year. Or maybe she'd just phoned his mother to ask.

It had been nice to catch up with Amy. She didn't have a royal lineage, but she was interesting and educated. She'd held her own talking tax law with the attorney sitting to her right while Valentin had been engaged with the woman's husband, a high ranking official from a neighboring country.

Amy had been demure and charming and kept conversation flowing all evening long.

If there had been any spark between them, he'd already be texting her for a second date.

Instead, he was considering whether he should text Crystal.

He hadn't been able to stop thinking about her since she'd walked out of his suite a week ago. He blamed Max for the stain on what would've been an otherwise uneventful, if uncomfortable, meeting.

But his anger at Max didn't explain why he was still thinking about *her* even now as he nodded a last good-bye to guests and strode past the pair of bodyguards standing at the entrance to the hallway that led to the royal family's private residence.

He was only paying half attention to his surroundings as he pulled his phone from his pocket and fired off a text.

Nice try. No chemistry. Who's next?

His phone beeped as he entered his rooms, pulling loose his bow tie.

I saw.

He had to bite back a smile. Events like the state dinner were televised on a remote channel that had to be special ordered from a viewer's cable provider. The local news would likely have a short clip of him shaking the ambassador's hand and little more. But if Crystal had been watching, it meant she'd worked for it.

He let the door close behind him, sealing him in privacy.

And dialed the phone.

CRYSTAL ANSWERED WITH A BLUSH.

Which was incredibly silly, given that the prince couldn't see through the device to catch her in her pajama pants and oversize T-shirt, nor could he see the evidence of the now-empty bowl of chocolate ice cream or popcorn kernels that littered the coffee table in her tiny flat.

She hadn't thought watching the state dinner on telly would have been as interesting as one of her favorite rom-coms, but she'd been riveted.

"At least you were polite," she said by way of greeting.

The prince had been the epitome of a perfect date, escorting Amy around the room, introducing her, making conversation. Crystal had been a little surprised by his good manners after he'd admitted that hiring her was his mother's idea.

But like he'd said in his text, anyone with eyes could see there was no heat between them. No spark.

"You mean like I wasn't to you last week?"

It took her a second to remember what he'd said, to figure out what he meant. Polite. He wasn't talking about their chemistry.

As he shouldn't be. It had all been one-sided. Her side.

And who wouldn't be attracted to the prince after seeing him in all his post-exercise glory?

"I didn't take it personally," she said. It hadn't been her best client meeting, but it hadn't had to be.

She'd spoken on the phone to her brother Michael earlier in the week and sworn him to secrecy before she'd revealed her job. And he'd pointed out that even if she didn't make a match for the prince, she'd have him as a client for her CV.

She'd prefer to make Valentin a success story, but she'd take what she could get. Especially since he didn't want to cooperate.

"I still feel I owe you an apology."

That was unexpected.

"I'll take it. I don't suppose you'll give me a hint as to what kind of woman you'd like to meet next?"

"I rather think I'd like to be surprised."

He might like that, but it made things more difficult for her. She mentally went through her list of single friends. Maybe Angelica would like to be set up with the prince. If he wasn't taking this seriously, she *could* do it...

"I'm supposed to visit an elementary school on Friday. Promote literacy and all that. Do you think you could send someone to come along with me?"

Three days? That was short notice.

But it wasn't as if she could refuse. "I'll do my best. Will you be doing a reading? Or just a speech?"

He cleared his throat. "Does that matter?"

She laughed a little, awkwardly. "Only to assuage my own curiosity."

She wasn't obsessed with the royals like some people she saw posting on social media, but she'd known about the prince's work to promote childhood literacy since he'd walked into the public eye as a teenager.

There was an audible pause and then, "If you'd like to come along, you'd be welcome. In the background, with Conrad."

"Of course."

Because she worked for him. Or for the queen, although the lines were awfully blurry. Employees stayed in the background, while whomever she set him up with would be front and center.

She swallowed back the irrational disappointment. "I'll check my schedule."

"Fine."

"I should go."

He said good-night and she tossed her phone. It bounced off the couch cushions and onto the floor, hitting the wood with a clatter. She didn't bother to pick it up but paced the small living room and into the kitchen, then whirled around to fetch her dirty dishes.

Valentin was being kind, not putting her in her place, even if that's what it had felt like.

He'd called her, after all, and she was attracted to him.

It didn't take a rocket scientist to figure out what was going on here.

Even as a small child, Crystal had spun daydreams. Grand ones.

Being an astronaut and going to the moon.

Dancing in a Russian ballet company.

Having a prince fall in love with her.

She needed to be very careful here. Valentin had zero interest in her. She was in his sphere for one reason only.

To find him a match.

Besides, she wasn't looking for love for herself. Her last breakup had been messy—shouting match and ugly crying messy. She'd believed Harry had been *the one,* and she'd been devastated to find out he hadn't felt the same about her.

She'd go back on the market eventually, but not yet.

Not only would she be humiliated if Valentin figured out she had a crush on him, if there was any hint of scandal, the royal family would put the kibosh on her using them on her CV.

The royal stamp of approval would give her fledgling business validation when she desperately needed it.

She couldn't mess this up.

Whatever attraction she harbored for Valentin needed to be crushed. Pronto.

VALENTIN HUNG UP THE PHONE, while using his other hand to rub his chest.

Something felt off.

Not wrong. Just different.

He couldn't place it.

He began his nightly routine. Checked his messages and emails. Nothing from his mother or Conrad that was urgent enough it couldn't wait until tomorrow. He plugged his phone into its charger in his office and retired to his rooms, where he turned on a sitcom that allowed him some time to be mindless.

But he couldn't get rid of the sensation that something had changed.

And it hadn't happened on the date, as pleasant as seeing Amy had been.

It was the phone call with Crystal that bothered him. When she'd asked if he would be reading to the kids.

She'd sounded as if... as if she admired him.

And why shouldn't she? He was doing a good thing. A lot of people admired him.

But it was different because it was Crystal.

From the very beginning, she hadn't cut him any slack. He could still picture her standing in the sand, clutching her shoes with her hand propped on her hip.

He glanced in the mirror just before he raised his toothbrush to his mouth.

He was smiling.

Because of Crystal.

He put his toothbrush back down, stared at himself in the mirror.

What had just happened?

He was thinking about a woman and smiling. Looking forward to seeing her again.

Crystal had done what he'd thought was impossible.

She'd awakened his heart. Sure, it was still barricaded behind an impenetrable wall.

But he'd thought it was DOA. Buried with a headstone.

Crystal was only doing a job for him. He wasn't interested in her. Not really.

But if he could smile about her antics, maybe he could fall in love again. Someday. With someone. Far into the future.

Chapter Four

Valentin wasn't feeling well.

Crystal could tell from his pallor and the flush in his cheeks.

But he was playacting that nothing was wrong as he read to the children, a mix of kindergarteners and first graders. He should look silly wedged into the chair meant for a small child, but he'd stretched his long legs out in front of him and crossed his ankles. The children were hanging on every word.

So was she.

So was his date.

She *had* recruited a friend to be Valentin's match for the day. Pansy was more of an acquaintance, someone Crystal had met when matching a millionaire CEO over a year ago. She'd done an initial round of interviews for each dating candidate, and she and Pansy had hit it off. Their friendship had grown to the occasional coffee date. She was an entrepreneur and one of the smartest women Crystal knew.

She'd spent the first few minutes of the classroom visit chatting with the children while Valentin spoke to the teacher. She'd been a big hit, judging by the giggles and awestruck gazes she was still getting.

While Crystal was standing at the back of the classroom, sandwiched between Conrad and a beefy bodyguard. She almost hadn't come. But then she'd wondered what Valentin would think if she didn't show up.

And the school was only a few minutes' walk from her apartment.

She was worried about Valentin. "He needs to cancel his other engagements for the day," she muttered under her breath.

"He won't," Conrad returned.

Valentin concluded his reading with a charming smile, and the children buzzed around him, their small voices clamoring for attention.

"Can you read us another one?" one little girl asked.

"My mom says she's in love wiff you!"

"I got a scrape on my knee. Wanna see it?"

Valentin smiled through it all, though his smile had grown tighter over the half hour they'd been in this classroom.

The teacher clapped her hands, and the kids quieted.

She thanked Valentin, and he and Pansy excused themselves.

The bodyguard was the first person into the hall, and Crystal hung back with Conrad as the prince and his date walked down the hallway empty of children.

Valentin and Pansy had their heads tipped close together, and Crystal forced herself to avert her eyes. Look at that artwork by creative little ones. The black and red blobs drawn in crayon were... well, she didn't know what they were supposed to be exactly, but they were something.

The bright noonday sunlight made her eyes tear as they exited the school building. Another bodyguard stood outside on the sidewalk, and Valentin's red convertible was parked at the curb. Two motorcycles for the bodyguards were parked right behind it. Valentin was supposed to drive Pansy to a coffeeshop to chat.

But as a small crowd of onlookers watched from across the street, Valentin leaned in and kissed Pansy on the cheek, and she peeled off down the sidewalk, walking briskly away with a glance over her shoulder. A lens flashed from across the street. A photographer.

Conrad hurried forward, and Crystal found herself on his heels, even though the prince wasn't her responsibility. The date was. Had he disliked Pansy so much?

But when Valentin turned to speak to Conrad, Crystal caught sight of the darker flush blazing in his cheeks and the fevered look in his eyes.

"I need a rain check," the prince said.

Before Conrad could answer, someone hailed him from the crowd across the street.

Valentin stiffened beside her. The dark-haired bodyguard moved to intercept the man—was it a man?—who was jogging toward them.

"Conrad," Valentin's voice was pained.

She realized the man approaching had something strapped to his chest. Was it a bomb? Her adrenaline surged.

The bodyguard was there, intercepting him, but if that was a bomb, weren't they in the danger zone?

"There are at least two reporters present," Conrad said. Almost like a warning.

She couldn't tear her eyes away from the bundle at the man's chest.

And then she realized it was wrapped in a fuzzy pink blanket. A baby blanket.

"It's a baby." Tears of relief pricked her eyes. "He's got a baby. Not a bomb."

She glanced at the men to find Conrad looking at her as if she'd spoken Swahili. Valentin hadn't looked away from the approaching man.

"It's okay," he called out to the bodyguard, who glanced back at him and then let the guy through.

And she realized why the man looked familiar.

It was Max. Valentin's brother.

Oh no.

She glanced at Conrad, and this time they were on the same page. They needed to get Valentin out of there.

More people had gathered, some on this side of the street. They were watching and pointing and whispering.

Valentin seemed frozen in place as Max approached. He stared at the bundle at his brother's chest.

Max had several days' scruff at his chin and looked more rumpled than she'd ever seen him in photographs.

He glanced briefly at her and Conrad but didn't waver from his course toward his brother.

"What are you doing here?" Valentin asked. She'd heard that same cold tone in his voice in his office that first morning.

"I told you, I need to talk to you."

The baby let out a wail, and Valentin jerked.

"Meet your niece. Clara."

Valentin stood still and expressionless. A muscle jumped in his cheek.

Max exhaled loudly, looking off to the side. "This isn't easy, is it?" he said. "I'm sorry."

He sounded genuine. But Crystal didn't know the man. Maybe he was a consummate liar.

Valentin didn't respond.

A shout from behind them drew Crystal's attention. The crowd was pressing closer. Perhaps they'd sniffed out a family scandal unfolding right before their eyes. The bodyguard was using himself as a buffer, arms outstretched to keep the people at bay. But one man wasn't going to stand long against that many people.

"Get him out of here." Conrad pressed something cold into her hand. Car keys. Then he joined the bodyguard to try and hold back the press of people.

She moved behind Valentin and touched his arm. He surprised her by gripping her hand. He was burning up, his skin hot to the touch.

"We need to leave," she murmured.

Max's gaze fixed on their joined hands. "Who's this?" His smile was genuine, not flirtatious.

But Valentin bared his teeth, his entire body going tense. He started to pull away as if he were preparing to throw a punch.

"Don't—" she said quietly.

And maybe it was her softly spoken word that broke him out of his distracted state. Or maybe he finally heard the crowd calling out behind them.

She tugged his hand, and he let her pull him toward the car.

"Stay away from me," he spat at his brother.

She hadn't intended to get in the car, but the flush on his face and the way his hand shook on the doorframe altered her decision. "Get in," he demanded.

She didn't want to argue, so she slid onto the smooth leather seats.

He rounded the car and climbed in, then took the keys from her when she offered them.

He could put her out of the car around the corner, when they put some distance between themselves and this craziness.

Valentin seemed to have the same idea, because he turned the corner and pulled over two blocks down.

He slid the car into a parallel spot smoothly, shoved the gearshift into park.

She was going to excuse herself, promise not to mention his brother, but he gripped the top of the steering wheel with both hands and bowed forward to press his forehead against his wrists.

"How—?" he gasped the word. She couldn't make out if he was crying or just upset.

She couldn't leave him there like that, not without Conrad or a bodyguard or someone.

She reached out to comfort him, touching his shoulder. She could feel that he was burning up even through his shirt.

"Your fever is out of control," she said. "My apartment is nearby. Why don't you come up? At least take some ibuprofen or something to bring the fever down."

He only grunted in response.

VALENTIN COULDN'T REMEMBER FEELING this miserable, ever. He'd had his share of head colds and even the flu once or twice, but none of them compared to this. Right now, his head felt like it was going to explode, and chills racked his entire body.

That was the only reason he allowed Crystal to drag him bodily across the street, through a vine-covered alleyway, and up a back staircase.

Or maybe it wasn't so much her dragging him as him leaning on her so he could remain upright.

He'd felt it coming on this morning but thought he could power through it. He'd gotten steadily worse while they were at the school and told his date—Petunia?—that he'd love to see her again another time. And then the full force of this illness had struck when he'd come face to face with Max. He'd felt like he'd been hit by a bus.

"I didn't punch him, did I?" he asked. "I was just thinking about it..."

Crystal stumbled on the top step, almost toppling them both into a door that was painted bright red.

"You didn't punch him," she confirmed with a grunt as she tried to maneuver her key into the door.

"Not this time," he muttered.

Her keys rattled against the knob, and then they were inside. It was much cooler here. Her A/C was doing a good job battling the late-spring heat.

She gave him a full-body nudge toward a sofa beneath a long window. Yes. He wanted to be lying there. And then he was, although he was a little fuzzy on how he'd gotten horizontal.

"You hit him before?" she asked. Her voice was far off and muffled by the sound of running water.

Were his eyes closed? They were. The darkness was nice. Then he couldn't see her judgment.

"I hit him. It didn't make me feel better. Just hurt my hand."

"Yeah. That's kinda how it works." She was whispering now. Something damp and cool touched his forehead. "Can you sit up? Just a little. Here."

She put a hand beneath his arm as he pushed up on a wobbly elbow. She gave him some pills and a cool drink of water and then let him lie back down.

He imagined that she brushed the hair back from his forehead.

But it was a nice thing to imagine, so he told her, "It's not supposed to hurt me."

"What hurts?" Her voice was closer than he thought it should be. Was she sitting on the floor next to him? She seemed close. He tried to open his eyes and check but they wouldn't cooperate. "Your hand?"

"No. M'heart." He was slurring a little. If he could sleep off this awful headache, he'd wake up and find it was all a dream. No Max. No baby. No pain thudding through him with each beat of his heart. "I've got a heart of stone, haven't you heard? That's what everyone says."

But if that was true, why did it hurt so badly?

"Shh. You should rest." She touched him again. A brush of her fingers against his temple. And then her voice was far away. "Conrad? He's in my apartment. Not very coherent. No, he's fine, I think. Burning up. They did what? No, no he can stay here. No one would think to look for him here. You can send a guard." She rattled off an address and then she was quiet.

He liked her. Probably too much. He didn't want to like her. Or anyone else. If he let someone else in, he might get hurt again.

But then he wouldn't have anyone to nurse him, either. No one to ply him with pain relievers and cool water. To brush his hair off his forehead.

He was arguing with himself over the finer points when the darkness finally took him.

He woke in the night, throwing off the blanket that weighted him down and pulling at his shirt that felt like it was suffocating him.

And Crystal was there again, with medicine and cool water, unbuttoning his shirt when his fingers wouldn't work. He hated to leave his undershirt on when it stuck to his body with sickly sweat, but his sense of propriety wouldn't let him strip down in her apartment. He asked her to flip on the news, but she refused.

He got all imperial on her, demanding it. But since he was as weak as a baby, there was nothing he could do when she refused to fetch the remote and turn on the telly.

She did fetch another cool, damp washcloth. This time she laid it across his face as he leaned his head back against the couch cushions.

He fell asleep like that.

Chapter Five

When he awoke the next morning, Valentin was disoriented.

It took him several seconds to remember leaning on Crystal and coming up to her apartment in a feverish haze.

Bright sunlight was streaming through the window into his face. It was making his head pound. Or maybe that was the residual effect of the illness. He could feel the weakness of his limbs, but the fever itself seemed to be gone. Thank God.

He sat up on the couch, letting his feet hit the floor. But weakness threatened to overcome him, and he put his head in both hands, elbows on his knees.

With his head down like this, he could smell just how badly he stank of sick and stale sweat. How embarrassing.

But Crystal didn't seem to be here. He glanced around the neat, eclectic space. Two overstuffed chairs brimming with colorful pillows. A half-sized bookshelf stuffed with novels, a small telly sitting on top of it. Separating the living area from the kitchen was a bar with stools. The walls were painted a soft blue. Pictures of her with two men, younger than she, hung on the walls. In one they were rock climbing, in another they were at the beach. In another they had their arms around each other, and they were laughing.

He suddenly realized he knew nothing about Crystal's personal life. Mother would've vetted her before she'd been hired, but Valentin had been so self-absorbed that he didn't even know if she had a family. Or a boyfriend.

Where was she?

She'd been nearby when he'd woken several times during the night, always replacing his cool washrags.

He winced when he remembered ordering her to turn on the television. Demanding it like a toddler. What a prize she must think he was.

By taking him home like she had, she'd gone above and beyond her duty as an employee. She'd almost acted like a... friend.

And he'd treated her shabbily.

If he were lucky, she'd be sleeping right now. If he were doubly lucky, she'd forget about his actions in the night.

And then he remembered her call to Conrad. At least, he *thought* she'd called his assistant. He could've been dreaming it. She'd asked a question that niggled the back of his brain—

Max.

Remembering his brother was like receiving a punch to the solar plexus. For a few seconds, he couldn't breathe. He felt as if he'd blacked out and was seeing stars both at the same time.

Max with a baby.

There had been photographers outside the school when he'd visited. If they'd gotten a picture of Max and Valentin, the press would be in a frenzy.

And Conrad had probably told Crystal not to let him see it.

Some sick part of his brain insisted he raise his head and look around. And there was the remote, only a scant few inches away on a low, scratched coffee table.

Where was his phone? His keys? He had options. Probably Mother and Father were trying to reach him. He could call them.

Or he could get in his car and drive as fast and as far as he could. Abdicate, even, though that would leave Max to run the country when Mother no longer could.

He'd ignored his fanciful thoughts and gotten as far as picking up the remote when Crystal walked into the room from a hallway he'd barely noticed.

She was wearing jeans and a tank top, and her feet were bare. Her hair was in a ponytail, and she didn't have a stitch of makeup on.

Those freckles.

She glanced at the remote, her gaze zeroing in on his face. "You sure you want to do that before you have coffee?"

She knew. Of course she knew.

"I—how bad is it?"

She shrugged. "I saw a couple of things pop up on my social media feeds, but I haven't turned on the news yet."

He bowed his head, though he was aware of her moving into the kitchenette area, running water, cabinets opening. And then a coffee maker quietly chugged and hissed.

He used one hand to rub his face. He felt weary, even though he'd slept.

"I've spent several weeks finessing the language in the exports bill..." He waved off his own words. She didn't care about the details of some bill parliament was trying to push through. No one else did, either. At least that's what it felt like. "And the media is probably going crazy because my brother showed up with a baby in tow."

Max was surely playing the sympathy card. Eating up the attention.

"Who knows if that was even his child," Valentin burst out. He let his hand fall away from his face, and the remote clattered to the coffee table.

And Crystal was standing right there, a glass of water in

hand. She'd abandoned the kitchen and gotten an up-close view of his temper. Again.

"I'm sorry." He stood up, ignoring the stiffness in his muscles. "You always seem to see me at my worst." Humiliation heated his neck, warmth leaching up into his face. "If you'll tell me where my car keys are, I'll get out of your hair."

He made a point of not meeting her gaze. Had it only been a couple of days before when he'd been thinking how much he liked her? And now this.

She set the water glass on a side table, and the next thing he knew, she'd reached out and touched his forearm, her fingers cool and soft.

At the touch, his frantic thoughts stopped whirling. A visceral memory fought through the haze of yesterday's chaos. Him taking her hand on the sidewalk. And knowing that because she was near, everything was going to be all right.

He looked down at the place where she touched him now, her paler skin against his tan.

And he wanted to hold her hand again. He needed it.

So he moved the few inches it took to clasp her hand in his.

For one blissful moment, everything else fell away. There was no Max, no royal duty, no scandal.

Only Crystal, only the solid weight of her hand in his, only her sweet scent in his nose.

He breathed in deeply, not realizing until she spoke that he'd let his eyes fall closed.

"What would happen if you didn't turn on the news? If you turned off your cell phone for a few hours? If you left the prince back at the castle?"

Nothing. Nothing would happen. His mother was the reigning monarch. Taking care of the country was her duty, for now and for decades to come.

Mother and Father might worry if they tried to reach him and couldn't. They'd forgive him once he turned his phone back on.

Conrad would handle anything that came up.

But—

"I'm not sure I can do it." He opened his eyes as he admitted it. He wanted to see her expressive face. "I've buried myself in my duties for so long... Apart from the prince, I'm not even sure I know who the man is."

Her eyes were soft. He wanted... he wanted things he shouldn't be thinking about.

"The man needs a shower." She said the words with an adorable wrinkle of her nose. "And then coffee. And then you can decide what to do."

CRYSTAL WAS STIRRING pancake batter in the kitchen when she heard the shower shut off. With company watching curiously from the barstools at her counter.

She needed some way to warn Valentin what was coming.

But fatigue and confusion had her by the throat. She was out of ideas. She was going to have to bluster her way through this. She made her way around the counter but was too slow to catch the prince.

Valentin stopped short out of the hallway when he spotted the two men sitting casually on stools.

She'd raided the recesses of her closet to find the track pants that had once belonged to Michael and an oversize sweatshirt that she'd stolen from Reid last winter. She'd never seen the prince dressed so casually. It was his wary expression that she wanted to ease if she could.

And then Michael spoke. "You spent the night with the crown prince?"

Reid barked, "Is that my sweatshirt?"

She pressed the ball of her hand into the center of her forehead. It didn't relieve the pressure there, but it made her feel slightly more sane.

"It wasn't like that," she hissed at Michael. "He was ill. He slept on the sofa. I slept in my bedroom." She ignored Reid's statement and turned to Valentin, who remained frozen only a step out of the hallway. "Valentin, these two cretins are my younger brothers. Michael and Reid."

Her introduction seemed to galvanize Valentin, and he crossed the room to shake their hands.

From behind the prince's back, she gave both brothers the stink eye. They knew how to behave. She'd witnessed it before.

The question was whether they would.

"How do you know my sister?" Reid asked with the same suspicion he'd used when asking about the shirt.

"I'm working for him," she said at the same time Valentin said, "We're friends."

And then Valentin was meeting her gaze, his expression frank and more open than she'd ever seen it. "Friends."

Her heart thumped, hard, as she held his stare. After last night, she knew what it cost him to say that.

I've got a heart of stone, haven't you heard?

"Friends," she whispered. She finally broke the stare and realized both her brothers were watching them with wide, curious eyes.

Reid broke the silence first. "Uhh. You're burning the eggs."

She smacked her brother on the arm. "I haven't started the eggs." She moved around them, around the edge of the bar and back into the kitchen proper. "Valentin, I'm sorry. My brothers and I have a standing Saturday morning breakfast. I tried kicking them out, but—"

"We're bigger than she is." Michael grinned.

That. And she hadn't tried very hard. She loved her brothers, and this was usually her only chance to see them during the week thanks to busy university schedules and her own crazy job.

Valentin padded into the kitchen behind her. He was barefoot. The crown prince of Glorvaird was barefoot in her kitchen.

Eggs. She tried to get herself back on track, but it was hard while he was so close. Her kitchen would never be described as "roomy," and having him in it made it feel downright cramped.

"I was promised coffee," he said.

"Yes. Coffee." The pot had finished percolating. She used her chin to point to the upper cabinet where she kept the mugs. "Milk's in the fridge."

"Shouldn't you pour it for him?" Michael asked with a cheeky grin. If she blinked, she could still see the ten-year-old boy he'd been sitting with legs swinging off the barstool.

"If you really work for him..." Reid said, suspicion still dripping from his voice.

"Not that kind of work." Valentin appeared completely unruffled, but she could sense the fine tension in the tightness around the edges of his smile. "Your sister is working on my love life."

Her brothers broke out into hoots and laughter.

She shifted from pouring pancake batter onto the griddle to cracking eggs into a bowl. She pretended each one was either Reid's or Michael's head and took particular satisfaction from cracking them open. "Watch it," she said. "Unless you want some arsenic with your scrambled eggs."

Valentin sent her a puzzled look.

"They're picturing me all dolled up and on your arm at a state function," she told him, "which they apparently find hilarious."

He frowned.

"Crystal is most comfortable in sweats and a T-shirt," Michael said. "She's not exactly in the same category as the women you're used to dating."

She was whisking the eggs with vicious wrist action when Valentin moved in next to her, nudging her with his elbow as he reached for a spatula.

He flipped the pancakes easily, not even setting his coffee mug down. He was a pro.

Meanwhile, she was overheating at his nearness.

"Maybe I'm tired of women who are all style and no substance," Valentin said.

The words surprised her so much, she looked up into Valentin's face.

One of her brothers, she couldn't tell which, snorted softly. But she couldn't tear her gaze from Valentin's as he looked down at her.

"Maybe I'm looking for someone more like your sister."

At that, her brothers fell silent.

He didn't mean it, of course. Or he did, the part about wanting someone *like* Crystal. Not Crystal specifically.

Telling herself that enabled her to finally break the stare.

She poured her eggs into the skillet, where they sizzled. "I'll remember that when I'm choosing your candidate for date number three. 'Someone like me.'"

Valentin smirked, but there was something behind his eyes that she couldn't make out.

He flipped the first four pancakes onto her brother's plates, splitting them equally.

"Good plan," she said as he poured more batter onto the griddle. "Sometimes feeding them distracts the grizzly bears from their playthings."

He laughed, then turned to ask her brothers what they were studying and how their classes were and when they'd graduate. Not soon enough.

She needed to match Valentin or she wouldn't have the money to pay their next semester's tuition.

"And what about your parents?" he asked, including her in the question as he leaned back in the corner where her counter made a V. He now had a plate full of pancakes and eggs in hand and had abandoned his coffee mug to the counter beside him. "I'm realizing I've been remiss in knowing the things a friend should know."

"Dad died right after Reid was born," she said. "And Mom passed three years ago."

"Crystal's been our mom in every way that counts," Michael offered. "Our mom worked a lot, so Crystal was always the one fixing dinners and tucking us into bed and helping us with our homework."

"Doing our homework for us," Reid said.

She rolled her eyes. That'd been one time.

"She makes a mean pot of spaghetti and meatballs." Michael let his fork clank onto his plate, a satisfied sigh escaping him as he sat back and rubbed his stomach. "We had it almost every night for supper."

"Can't get her to do our laundry, though," Reid pouted. "Not since I turned ten."

She stuck her tongue out at him. And then caught herself, stealing a glance at Valentin. He was watching her with a bemused expression.

"So she's bossed you two around your entire lives. And then she invented a career where she gets to boss other men around in the guise of finding them a woman?"

She gaped at him.

"When you put it that way..." Michael lifted a hand over his mouth as if he were considering it.

She tossed a crumpled paper towel at the prince. "What? How dare you! I feed you breakfast and this is the thanks I get?"

He didn't even have to dodge her ineffective missile. The paper towel fell harmlessly to the floor well short of him. "Bad aim," he said cheerfully, stuffing another bite of eggs in his mouth.

"Try the saltshaker," Reid offered.

"Or your pancake," said Michael.

She went back to her breakfast. "I'm not going to make a mess that I'll just have to clean up." She smiled. "I'll just choose someone really obnoxious for your next date, princey-poo."

Valentin did not look impressed.

"Let's see. There was someone from your university days.

She claimed to have been your perfect match. What was her name...? Hildy? Hilary?"

She tapped the tines of her fork against her lips.

Now Valentin was going a little green. "You wouldn't dare."

"Heidi! That was it. I happen to have her phone number in my files. I'm sure she'd love a chance to catch up."

He set his mostly empty plate on the counter. "I'll have you run out of the country," he said sternly.

"What?" Michael asked.

"She was in a couple of my early college classes and is obsessed with royalty," Valentin said. "She followed me around for weeks, constantly asking me out for coffee or drinks. There's no way—"

He broke off when her giggles escaped.

And the look he shot her was pure venom. The benign kind, a look she'd received from her brothers frequently during their childhood.

"I am relieved to know you're only cruel enough to joke about torturing me with a date with a maniac. Not actually cruel enough to submit me to it."

"I wouldn't be so sure," Reid said before he slurped his coffee. "She's got a mean streak. Once dyed all my unmentionables pink."

"That was *Michael*," she said.

Unmentionables? Valentin mouthed to her.

She shrugged, a second case of the giggles sucking her under.

SOME TIME after Crystal's brothers left, Valentin found himself lying flat on his back on the floor, staring up at her ceiling. There was a plaster patch in one corner, he thought. At some point, there'd been a leak there.

She'd shooed him out of the kitchen when he'd volunteered to help clean up. So he'd come in here and now listened to her rattling around as she washed up. He just basked in the sunshine.

"Who is Harry?" he called out to her.

He'd overheard Michael murmur to her as the two men had been leaving the apartment. *I like him much so much better than Harry.*

And for some reason, he felt a burning need to know who Harry was. A friend? An ex-husband?

He heard the tinking of dishes. She didn't answer, and he wondered if maybe she hadn't heard.

And then she did answer, hesitatingly. "Harry was my ex-boyfriend."

"Ah." What was the twisty, uncomfortable feeling in his gut? It couldn't be jealousy. He had no claim on her. They were friends.

"Are you dating anyone now?" That was a friendly thing to ask, wasn't it?

More swishing. More clinking. "No. Things didn't... end well with Harry. It's made me a little gun shy."

Join the club.

"What happened?"

She didn't answer.

"Sorry. Too personal," he called out. Though he was dying to know.

There was a clatter as if she'd dumped a bunch of silverware into her dishwasher, and then the thing started with a soft hum and glug.

"It's okay. I've pried into your personal life, haven't I?"

He caught movement from the corner of his eye, as if she was moving around the kitchen now. Wiping down the counters, maybe.

She sighed. "He wanted me to be someone I'm not. His mom didn't like my job, thought I should go to university for something else. I thought he respected what I do, but... he wanted a society wife. And I'm definitely not that."

Her brothers had joked about it during breakfast. Had

their quips hurt her feelings? Or was that just normal interplay within a functional family? He'd never questioned whether his mother loved him, but the crown demanded much of her time. There was not a lot of time for teasing or horseplay within the royal family.

So what if she didn't want to give up her job to meet the expectations of some jerk's mother? That made her independent. From what he'd gathered, she was helping fund her brothers' tuition. If she'd given up her matchmaking gig, who would've helped them?

"I'll get back out there eventually," she said. "I've just been... busy."

The truth or an excuse? He didn't know.

At least she was courageous enough to try again. Not like him. He was determined to stay out of the game. He'd agreed to give her four dates, but he didn't plan on falling in love.

No thanks.

She appeared in his field of vision, looking down at him. Time to go?

"Do you need me to leave?" he asked. "I can call Conrad." He made the offer but it was halfhearted.

"You can stay, your orneriness. How are you feeling?"

"Like I want to lie on your floor forever."

She frowned as she bent to touch his temple with the back of her wrist. "At least your fever hasn't come back."

And then she surprised him by lying down on the couch beside him, also looking up at the ceiling. He supposed there wasn't enough floorspace for them both down here.

Although it might've been cozy to try.

She was only silent for a few seconds. "I don't think you'd really be content to hide here for longer than a day. I'm quite a boring person, even with my job bossing people around."

He smiled. He'd been proud of that crack earlier, and her brothers had found it hilarious.

"I like your brothers," he said. "It's obvious they adore you."

"They adore free meals once a week." But he heard the affection in her voice.

"Do you want to know my most vivid memory of my brother? Not this last mess," he hastily clarified.

She murmured a soft assent.

"I had my fourteenth birthday party. I thought I'd grown past kiddie parties, but Max insisted we let the castle staff put on an event on the castle grounds and invite our friends from school. I was convinced no one would come. I had a hard time making friends in school." He hadn't intended to share that part. "About twenty kids came. A mix of kids from my class and Max's. We played cricket and ate cake until our stomachs ached."

"It sounds like fun," she said softly.

"It was. All the way until the party was breaking up and I discovered my brother handing hundred dollar bills to each guest. He'd paid everyone to come."

Mother had been furious. For a while, Max had insisted he'd done it as a way to help his brother. But after he was pushed, Max had admitted—

"He thought of me as dull, and he'd wanted a chance to punish me for being... I think he put it 'perfectly boring'."

Her arm slipped off the edge of the couch. He didn't think anything of it until her hand clasped his on the floor.

She didn't say anything as he let himself relive the humiliation of that day. Not only the embarrassment in front of the people he'd hoped were his friends, but how devastated he'd been to discover what Max really thought of him. He and his brother had been the best of friends as small children and throughout grade school. They'd never recovered from that one event.

"Family can be cruel." He heard her quiet words but was more focused on the sensation of her skin against his as she threaded their fingers together.

He'd called her his friend today, but that title didn't feel quite right. Not anymore.

"Don't think you can distract me," she said after a few minutes of silence had passed. "You wouldn't be happy hiding here, and we both know it."

He grunted. She might be right, but he wasn't admitting to it.

"You're a good man," she said. "A man who loves his people too much to leave them without your leadership."

He scowled. "Do you have to be so reasonable?"

Her thumb rubbed a slow line against the fleshy part of his palm. "That is not one of the usual flaws I'm accused of."

Of course he was going to turn his phone on. Return to the castle.

Couldn't he enjoy these last few moments with a beautiful woman and pretend like he hadn't any cares in the world?

He'd even face off with his brother.

"What?" she asked.

"Hmm?"

"You sighed. What were you thinking about?"

He let go of her hand, throwing his wrist over his eyes. "Why did he have to come back?"

She made to response, but he could hear her reasonable response in his head. *He said he needs help.*

"I can't trust him," he muttered. "Why should I let him back into my life just because he claims he's sorry?"

When she still didn't speak, he moved his arm so he could see her. "That wasn't a rhetorical question."

She rolled over onto her stomach and propped her chin on her hands so that she was looking at him. "Who can you trust?"

He considered that for a moment. "My father."

"Why don't you let your father talk to Max first and then trust his judgment?"

"I'd feel like my mother, using Father as a go-between."

She raised that expressive brow and he explained. "My father is more sensitive to relationship issues."

Her lips twitched in a smile. "So you're your mother's son?"

Any humor he'd felt at the mention of his father turned into a scowl. "Probably."

She reached out and patted his shoulder. "This is helpful."

He couldn't see it. "How so?"

"Oh, not to you." Her gaze had gone far-off, as if she was thinking furiously. "To me. Your perfect match is someone who can finesse difficult relationships, see the connections, ease tense situations. I'm sure I know someone like that."

He was beginning to think he did, too.

Chapter Six

JUST TURN IT OFF.

But Crystal was frozen on her sofa, her eyes glued to the cricket match on the television.

She'd meant to turn it on in the background as she folded and ironed her laundry, but her clothes were still in the hamper next to her feet on the coffee table.

Because the camera kept panning to Valentin and Pansy sitting close together in the stands, watching the match. He'd made good on his promise to connect with her again after the aborted coffee date.

And Crystal felt sick to her stomach as she watched the interplay between the two.

Leaning close enough that their shoulders touched as they spoke to each other.

Laughing together.

Unlike his date for the state dinner, it was clear to anyone with eyes that there was a connection between them.

The coverage cut to a commercial, and she blindly reached for the remote, turning off the telly completely.

But she didn't get up, didn't fold clothes.

This was good. She'd known Pansy would be a match for Valentin. Pansy was beautiful and sensitive and successful.

This was what she'd wanted. How many matchmakers could say they'd made a royal match? With a few whispers in the right ears, she'd have so much business she wouldn't be able to keep up.

So why did she feel like this was wrong?

She swiped at an errant tear. Stupid.

She stood, but only to throw a punch at the nearest throw pillow.

What had she really thought? That just because Valentin had let her offer him comfort that... what? He'd fall in love with *her*?

She might be successful at her job, but she didn't come from a royal lineage. Didn't have extensive connections in the political world.

She had two younger brothers whom she loved more than anything else in the world.

But she wasn't anybody special.

Her brothers had joked about it during that most recent breakfast together, but it was true. She wouldn't be able to hold her own in conversation about current events or the political climate. She wasn't a fashionista who could demand every eye be on her when she was in the public eye.

And most importantly, she wasn't in contention because she'd been hired by the crown. No matter how unconventional the royal family was—three princesses married to cowboys and a secret half-sister princess—royalty didn't marry the hired help.

She tried to think, but it was like trying to force her brain through frozen sludge.

The prince had asked for a meeting with her tomorrow. But if he'd hit it off with Pansy—and it seemed like he had—he wouldn't need her assistance anymore.

Maybe she could cancel.

Then she'd never have to see him again. Except in her dreams.

I HAD A GREAT TIME TONIGHT.

Valentin stared at the text message from Pansy. The day limo had pulled in to the castle garage, but he delayed as he tried to formulate a response.

He liked Pansy, but...

His phone buzzed again. *I hope it works out for you and Crystal.*

He grimaced and typed a quick, *Thanks.*

He hadn't meant for it to happen, but it seemed like every third sentence out of his mouth had been something about Crystal. He'd wondered what she'd think of a crazy fan's war paint from head to toe. He'd mentioned how funny she'd been when she was with her brothers. He'd even let it slip how much he liked her.

Fine, so he hadn't actually *said* that one, but Pansy was intuitive enough to figure it out. And she was a good sport, happy to bow out in favor of her friend.

Crystal had chosen wisely. If he wasn't already enamored with her, he'd have gotten along well with Pansy.

He followed his bodyguard through the garage and found his father waiting for him just inside.

"We need to talk," Father said, "if you've got the time."

That sounded serious, and his stomach plunged. He'd spoken to his father briefly about Max.

"Always have time for you."

They walked together to the first-floor parlor that was decorated in tones of maroon and gold.

"I suppose this is about Max." Valentin forced himself to release the tension that had taken residence in his shoulders. He propped his hands on the stone windowsill and leaned back on them.

"Tell me."

"Annika passed."

The news hit him like a physical blow. He exhaled the shock.

"How?"

"A car accident. A few days after the baby was born."

The baby. Max had a baby. Max was a single father. No doubt he wanted help. His brother hadn't been able to keep a pet fish alive for more than a few days, and now he was a *single father*? Being on his own must have been a world different from living in the palace with a staff to support him.

"Did you know? You and Mother? About the pregnancy."

Father nodded. "Your mother hired private investigators when he left. She's gotten weekly reports. And I've spoken to him on the phone a few times. I didn't think you'd want to know."

Valentin nodded. Father was right. He'd wanted ignorance.

"What does he want?" Other than a piece of Valentin's soul. Just imagining Max moving back into the palace made him want to throw something. And if he brought Annika's daughter? The daughter Valentin had imagined would be his own...?

His chest was tight as if he might be suffering a panic attack. He fought for breath.

"He wants to talk to you. To apologize."

He shook his head. "I don't think so." Tonight, he'd been lost in thoughts of Crystal. How long had it been since he'd been mired in memories of Max and Annika together? Even that morning at her apartment, being with Crystal had muted the pain.

Now the pain was back with blinding intensity.

He shook his head again. "I can't."

Father clasped his hand on Valentin's shoulder. "Easy, son. Easy."

He exhaled a shaky breath. He didn't like being this

vulnerable. Didn't want his father—or anyone—to see him like this.

But he was safe with Father. He knew that.

"I stopped loving her the moment she betrayed me. But Max—"

"He's still your brother."

How could he have done it to Valentin? How could Max hate him so much? What had Valentin ever done to him?

There weren't good answers for any of Valentin's questions. Even if he met with Max, he doubted he'd get answers that would heal the rift between them.

"You don't have to decide tonight," Father said.

Valentin took several more breaths to steady himself before he broke away.

"How was your date? Things with the matchmaker working out?"

Valentin laughed, but there was a bit of hysteria in it. "The date was passable. Crystal is..."

"More than passable, I guess?" Father asked when Valentin trailed off.

"Amazing. Intuitive. Caring. I think I'm falling for her. I thought I was..."

He pressed both palms against his eye sockets.

"How can I be falling for her if I'm still so messed up over what Max did to me?"

Father sighed. "You pulled away from everybody after what happened. You've been coming back to life these past few weeks. I'm guessing it's because of her."

Coming back to life. Like a limb that had been cut off from blood flow and lost circulation. Now life-giving blood was rushing back through each blood vessel. And it was painful. Doubly so with the wound Max had left still open and bleeding.

"I don't know what to do, Dad" he admitted. The term slipped out.

Father straightened infinitesimally. "Been a long time since you called me that. Or asked me for advice."

Had it? He'd been an arrogant fool up until things had happened with Annika and Max, and then his world had gone into a tailspin.

Dad smiled at him. "You remind me of your mother when we first met. She'd put up these walls to keep everyone out."

So had he. He'd done it gleefully, been happy to have an excuse not to put himself out there again. So he couldn't get hurt.

But he'd been withering away inside. Dying slowly without real companionship.

Until Crystal had obliterated his walls with that very first meeting.

"You want my advice?" Dad asked. "Here it is. You grab hold of that girl and don't let go."

Chapter Seven

As Crystal walked in to the palace her stomach threatened to revolt. She should've tried harder to cancel the meeting with Valentin.

When she'd texted him first thing that morning saying that something had come up, he'd responded with, *I need to see you.*

And when she'd still been chewing on how to respond to that, still telling her leaping heart to settle down, that he didn't mean it like that, he'd texted again. *Your presence is required at the agreed upon time.*

How was it possible that his pompous tone could come through in a text message? She didn't know, but hearing it had obliterated all of her softer feelings, clouded them with anger at his high-handedness.

She was clinging to that anger now, purely as a matter of survival. Following Conrad through the winding passageways meant she was getting closer and closer to the moment when Valentin would break her heart.

And then the assistant was knocking softly on a door—not Valentin's suite this time—and opening it to usher her inside.

It was a lovely, well-appointed parlor in creams and blush tones.

The romantic atmosphere of the room only served to heighten her discomfort. And then there was Valentin, rising from where he leaned against the arm of a massive brocade sofa.

He wore dark slacks and a white shirt that had been left open at the collar, as if he'd discarded his tie. His sleeves were rolled up, revealing the corded muscles of his forearms.

It was more casual than she'd seen him dressed anytime other than that morning in her apartment.

She didn't dare think about that morning right now.

"You came." He sounded... relieved? He stepped toward her, because she hadn't moved once Conrad had practically pushed her in the doorway and closed the door behind her.

"I almost didn't. I don't like being ordered around."

One corner of his mouth twitched. Not really a smile, but a hint of one.

He took another step toward her. "I've missed you these past few days."

That was... not what she expected him to say. He was supposed to tell her he'd fallen for Pansy. She was supposed to congratulate him.

But his statement had put them off the script, and she didn't know what to say in response.

There was no way she was admitting to the insane jealousy she'd experienced last night.

"The date last night went well, didn't it?" she asked stiffly.

He waved her question away. "It was fine."

Fine. It had looked more than fine in the snatches she'd seen.

"So you'll be seeing her again?" she confirmed. She needed to get out of there.

"No."

He'd come a step closer somehow and now stood at the boundary of her personal space. He filled up her vision, but she tried to look beyond him as her emotions surged in crazy directions.

She cleared her throat. "Do you want me to find someone else for the fourth date?"

The little girl inside her, the one who'd once dreamed of being a princess, was screaming *no!* even as she fought for composure. She wasn't sure she could do it, not with the feelings she harbored for Valentin. The crush that had exploded out of proportion like a stalk grown from magic beans.

Her emotions were totally out of bounds.

And then he took one more step. Into her space. Got so terribly and wonderfully close that she could smell his spicy shampoo, could see the shadow of scruff at his jaw that must have meant he hadn't shaved that morning.

He put his hands on her waist, and she froze.

"I want the fourth date, and all the dates after that, to be with you."

She'd dreamed of him saying something that crazy.

But she'd never been able to finish those daydreams. Because she was just Crystal. She'd never been able to picture the reality of how she might fit into his life.

And now that he was standing close, touching her, saying romantic words, fear rose up to choke her. She *didn't* fit in his life.

He squeezed her waist lightly. "Crystal. Tell me I'm not alone in my feelings."

It was the vulnerability behind his gruff demand that made her respond. She nodded. Then shook her head. She couldn't think.

And then he made it even more impossible when he leaned forward and bent his head.

How could she resist him?

How could she not rise up on her toes and meet his kiss?

She wanted his kiss, needed it.

Her hands came to his shoulders. To steady herself, that was all. But then she was wrapping her arms around his neck as he pulled her in closer. Her fingers weaved into the soft hair at his nape.

He groaned against her mouth, his kiss becoming deeper, more passionate. She met each one of his kisses fiercely. Because this wasn't real.

She was dreaming. That was the only explanation for what was happening. She'd fallen asleep behind the wheel and any second she was going to crash back into reality.

Valentin broke the kiss but didn't let her go as he kissed her cheek, her jaw, her temple. He was breathing hard, his chest rising and falling against hers.

This was crazy. This was—

And then reality sent her crashing back to earth.

"Val—"

The door opened.

Crystal hadn't come very far into the room, and she felt the rush of air around her.

More than that, she felt the change in Valentin. Beneath her hands, the muscles in his neck went tight.

The interruption was almost like the car crash she'd anticipated. The bone-jarring thud of running into something stationary, a hit that rattled her bones.

Max stood in the doorway wearing a look of utter surprise.

She was shaking as she tried to extricate herself from Valentin's embrace. It wasn't hard when he set her away.

What was Max doing here? She didn't think he'd been allowed in the palace since he'd broken Valentin's heart.

"I'll go," she said, but Valentin had her hand in a vice grip.

"Stay, please."

She was unmoored, out to sea without a life raft. So she let herself be carried further into the room, let Valentin pull her to the sofa, then urge her down next to him. They were sitting so close that their thighs were pressed together.

Max joined them, his gaze sharp and curious and at the same time, repentant.

What was going on?

Valentin's heart was racing. His emotions were a tangled mess. And he couldn't seem to let go of Crystal's hand as he stared at his brother across the low table.

He'd meant to talk to Crystal. Tell her everything that was in his heart and ask her not to abandon him.

But he'd kissed her instead. Because that was easier than explaining the emotions shredding him from the inside.

And now he had to deal with Max. His brother had always been perpetually late. Of course today would be the day he chose to be early. Valentin had wanted things settled with Crystal before he'd had to face his brother. She was by his side, letting him cling to her like a little kid, but nothing was resolved between them.

Max looked different. Fatigue lined his eyes, and there was a softness there that Valentin didn't recognize. Had it been there on the street last week and he'd been too angry and too ill to see it?

And then there was the fact that as Max settled in the chair across from them, he was glancing between Valentin and Crystal with undisguised curiosity. Everything between them was still new, and a fierce protective urge rose up in him. He didn't even want his brother to see the tenuous threads holding them together.

"Thanks for meeting with me," Max said when it was clear Valentin had nothing to say. He shifted in his seat, looking more uncomfortable than Valentin had ever seen him. "I... I'm sorry."

Max had said it on the street. And now for the second time. Before this, he couldn't remember ever hearing his brother say the words.

And he seemed sincere, which was even more shocking.

"I know I can't repair our relationship. I don't deserve

your forgiveness, but..." Max sighed. "I have to try. Clara deserves to know her family."

Valentin bristled. But Crystal squeezed his hand, a momentary distraction.

Max's gaze met his, but his eyes quickly darted away. "She even deserves to know her uncle, a much better man than her father."

All the breath caught in his chest. Valentin didn't know what to say, and when another of Max's glances caught what must have been the stunned expression on Valentin's face, Max laughed bitterly.

"You never knew, did you?" Max ran a hand through his hair. "I was always jealous of you. From the moment I started toddling around after you."

"You called me dull. Said I was a slave—"

"—to your duty. I remember." Max winced. "You made it seem so easy. You genuinely wanted your destiny. You and Mother were close because of it. And in Father's eyes, you could do no wrong. I wanted to be you."

Valentin shook his head. No. That was not how he remembered it.

"Is that why—?" He choked on the words.

"Is that why I romanced Annika?" Max looked down at the floor. Was this the true test, then? If he was really repentant, Valentin would find out now.

And for a long moment, it seemed his brother wouldn't answer.

Crystal nudged his knee with hers. "Are you sure you want to know?" she asked softly.

Did he want to know?

He glanced at the woman beside him, met her gaze squarely. He was a little surprised she hadn't run from the room. This wasn't her battle. Yet she'd stayed.

He wasn't just falling for her. He'd fallen. He'd dived off the deep end. He was in love with her.

Knowing why Annika had betrayed him didn't matter.

He knew, deep in his heart, that Crystal would never do such a thing.

But maybe knowing what had been the root of Max's actions would help as he tried to navigate the difficult relationship with his brother.

"Tell me," he said, looking back to Max.

Max hadn't missed the interplay between them. Thankfully, he didn't comment on it. "At first, it was pure jealousy. I thought to flirt with her and make your relationship more difficult. I didn't even know if it was possible. But the more stolen moments I spent with her..." He exhaled softly, and there were real tears standing in his eyes. "I fell in love with her. I knew it was wrong. I should've come to you. But things spiraled out of control, and then it was too late. And I let my pride and arrogance and jealousy ruin what relationship we had left."

Valentin doubted he would've understood even if Max had tried to confess to him. He had his own pride, and it would've been deeply wounded no matter what.

They sat there, Max beseeching him in silent entreaty while Valentin tried to come to terms with it all.

Would he have really been happy with Annika? He would never know. But he did know that if he'd still been with Annika, he never would've met Crystal. Everything that had happened had brought him to this moment.

Max stood with a frustrated exhale. "I won't ask for your forgiveness—"

"Well, that's just stupid," Crystal burst out.

She gasped softly and let go of Valentin to press her fingers against her lips. She looked chagrined, a faint blush staining her cheeks.

Max had stilled, a picture of wary curiosity.

"Go ahead," Valentin said. "Put us in our places."

She shook her head, still pressing her hand against her mouth. "I'm sorry. I shouldn't have..." she mumbled behind her fingers.

Max laughed. Actually laughed, a rusty chuckle. "I like her," he said to Valentin. Then, "Please, go on."

Crystal's blush was rosier now, filling her whole face, but she dropped her hand. "If it's forgiveness you want, why wouldn't you ask for it?" she said. "Pride? Or stubbornness?" She looked between them. "It seems like you've both got more than enough of both."

Valentin smiled grimly. She was not wrong.

She was focused on Max. "Maybe you'll be denied what you want. Or maybe the answer will be 'not yet.' But if you don't ask, you're only punishing yourself."

Max looked from Crystal to Valentin. All signs of humor had vanished from his expression. If anything, he looked as grim as Valentin felt. And Valentin could see the moment when he braced himself, a minute straightening of his shoulders.

"Val. I've wronged you, and I'm sorry. Can you ever forgive me?"

Valentin stood.

And Max straightened his shoulders again, as if he was bracing for a punch.

There were so many things he could hold against his brother, so many reason to hang onto his anger, his resentment, his hate. But none of those things had done Valentin a bit of good. They'd only made him angry and bitter.

Max's betrayal had wounded him. Withholding forgiveness would only would him more. He glanced at Crystal, who seemed to be holding her breath beside him. Bitterness would add jagged edges all of his relationships.

And he wanted nothing but softness between himself and Crystal.

And deep in his heart, he wanted Max back. "I forgive you. Brother."

Max exhaled a long breath.

Valentin stuck out his hand. Maybe a handshake was too

impersonal, but he couldn't offer a hug. Not yet. But maybe one day.

Max took it, his grip sure and steady. He didn't try to squeeze or play any one-upmanship games. He met Valentin's stare with a level gaze of his own. "Thank you."

And if Max's eyes were a little wet, Valentin's were slightly misty too, so he mustn't have seen it.

CRYSTAL WATCHED from her perch on the couch as Max took his leave. She felt a hundred pounds lighter on Valentin's behalf that he'd been able to forgive his brother. There would still be hurdles in their relationship. Some wounds could be forgiven but not forgotten. But today they'd forged a new start.

When Valentin turned to face her, she stood. She should've already taken her leave.

Because as she'd been sitting beside Valentin, she'd realized the reason he'd kissed her, had clung to her hand when she'd tried to excuse herself.

And she felt like she was bleeding all over the carpet. All her hopes, dashed to pieces along with her heart.

She couldn't bear to look at him, so she kept her gaze safely on the wall over his shoulder as she tried to manufacture a smile.

"I should get going."

He must've been lost in thoughts of his brother, because now she felt the sharpness of his gaze as it fixed on her. "We have things to talk about."

Her smile slipped a little. "I think we're done talking."

She stood and tried to walk past him, but she didn't make it to the door before he touched her arm.

She whirled, afraid that if she let him touch her she'd come undone. But that was a mistake, because now she was facing him.

"I want to see you again," he said. "Tonight. Or tomorrow

night, if you already have plans. Every night." His charming smile just made her angrier. She wasn't a servant to be pushed around at his whims.

"You can stop pretending now."

His smile faltered, quickly replaced by a frown.

His voice was carefully even when he spoke. "What are you talking about?"

"I get it." She hated that her voice shook. "Max saw us together outside the school. And today you wanted him to see you'd moved on. You wanted him to think we were together. To prove his betrayal hadn't hurt that much."

"It wasn't like that."

"No? You didn't let him think we were a couple?"

"So what if I did? I'd like to see where things go between us."

"I'm not some pawn on your chess board," she said. This time the shake in her voice was audible. She swallowed hard. She didn't want him to see how badly he'd hurt her. "You might have plenty of women happy to be a part of your power plays, but I'm not one of them."

She spun toward the door again, but he stopped her with a hand on her arm, turned her to face him again. "Hang on a minute."

A muscle was jumping in his cheek. He was really angry, though he was trying to control it. "Why exactly do you think I kissed you?"

"So I would look at you adoringly while you met with your brother."

"Do you adore me?"

Behind the frustration in his gaze, there was something else. Something that looked like vulnerability.

She couldn't answer him. Wouldn't. He was asking too much.

His chest rose and fell on a breath. "Is that really what you think of me? That I'm so mercenary I would kiss you, play with your emotions, to further my own ends?"

No. She didn't really think that of him. She buried her face in her hands. "I don't know."

Since she'd walked into the castle this morning, she'd been on an emotional roller coaster. Believing Valentin was falling for Pansy. Wanting him for her own. The elation of having him. And then realizing that he was using her to strengthen himself against Max.

What was real?

He touched her wrists. Gently dislodged her hands from her face. As she let her hands drop, his arms fell to his sides.

Tears were close to the surface. She could see that he was holding back his emotion as well. The stiffness of his stance, the careful blank expression on his face.

"Let me be clear," he said. "I am falling in love with you. That's the reason I kissed you. And I wanted you by my side during a difficult conversation with my brother because you bring me peace. Not because you're available or I want to show him up. Because I need you near me."

It was perfectly romantic and exactly the right thing to say.

And entirely too much. Her fragile emotions couldn't handle a declaration like that, not after everything else.

"Valentin, I can't do this right now. I'm sorry."

This time when she ran for the door, he didn't stop her.

Chapter Eight

CRYSTAL WAS STILL IN BED WHEN SHE HEARD pounding on her front door.

She answered it with bleary, tear-blurred eyes to find both of her brothers on her stoop even though it was still dark.

"What are you doing here?"

"We came to find out what's wrong," Michael said.

Reid stepped into her apartment and closed his arms around her in a hug. "You've never canceled Saturday morning breakfast before."

"We knew it must be something big." Michael followed his brother into her apartment and closed the door behind him.

How sweet. And unnecessary. She'd prefer to still be in bed, hiding under the covers with her pillow over her head.

She tried to smile. "I didn't think you'd see my text until later. I can't believe you guys are even up this early."

"Stop trying to distract us," said Michael. "What's going on?"

She brushed a stray tear from her cheek, made her way into the kitchen, and started a pot of coffee. If she was going to have to deal with these two louts in her fragile emotional state, she needed sustenance.

"What did Princey-Poo do?" Reid asked.

She laughed, but there was a definite air of hysteria to it. "No, it's me. All me."

"I knew we should've pummeled that guy." Michael punched one meaty fist into his open palm.

"He said... he said he's falling in love with me." Even as she said the words, tears streamed down her cheeks.

Her brothers stood there dumbfounded, staring at her with their mouths hanging open.

"I will never understand women," Michael muttered.

Reid ignored his brother. "Why is this a bad thing? I thought you liked the guy."

"I do!" She tore a paper towel off the roll and dabbed at her face.

Now her brothers glanced at each other. Michael shot a look at the door, like maybe he was rethinking being in her apartment at all.

Reid wiped both hands down his face. Then he put his hands on his hips. "So he's in love with you, and you like him. I don't see what the problem is."

"We'd never fit. You said it yourself. I'm not the right woman for him."

"Uhh..." Michael was looking at her as if she were crazy.

"What are you talking about?" Now Reid was starting to sound angry. "You're the best person I know."

She sniffled. For all the grief they gave her, her brothers really were good guys.

"I'm not a... a supermodel. I can barely dress myself. I don't know anything about politics. I can't date the crown prince."

"Do you really think any of that matters to him? If he's got any brains at all, he'd be snatching you up right now and never letting you go."

She hiccupped. Dabbed her face when more tears came.

"He's right," Michael said. "The guy would be a dummy not to want you." He crossed his arms. "You're always bossing us around. And most of the time"—he rubbed his side where Reid had thrown an elbow—"Okay, all the time you're right. But you're not telling yourself the truth right now."

Reid butted in. "You've got it in your head that you're not good enough for him, but you're a hundred percent wrong. Stupid Harry and his mother weren't good enough for you. You've still got their lies inside you. And you're believing them."

She listened to her brothers sing her praises for another few minutes before she kicked them out.

They were sweet. But wrong.

Weren't they?

She cleaned up the detritus of the coffee she'd shared with her brothers, her brain awhirl.

She wasn't good for Valentin. If she'd filled out a questionnaire or gone through one of her client interviews, she would never match herself with Valentin.

But did that mean they couldn't belong together?

She was trying to protect herself from the heartbreak that would inevitably come when he finally figured out she wasn't the one for him.

But what if rejecting him was wrong?

As crazy as it sounded, what if her brothers were right? What if she and Valentin belonged together?

VALENTIN PUSHED himself during his morning run.

Faster. Faster. Harder. Harder. Further. Further.

Until his muscles were aching and he was gasping for air.

He slowed. Jogged.

And then dropped to his knees the sand. The physical exertion wasn't helping the chaos in his head.

He couldn't outrun what was chasing him.

Crystal didn't love him.

Somehow it was worse than when Annika had betrayed him. Because he'd laid himself bare for Crystal. Made himself open, vulnerable. He'd shared parts of himself with her that he'd never revealed to Annika. Maybe it wasn't such a surprise that Annika had turned to his brother after all. Not when he'd kept part of himself safe, protected from her.

He hadn't protected himself from Crystal. He'd shown her all of himself. The darkest parts inside him, the broken pieces that had been left after Max and Annika had obliterated his heart. He'd offered her himself, just as he was.

And she'd walked away.

He sat on the beach, waiting for his bodyguard to catch up, and stared at the water, at the sun as it slowly rose over the horizon. First a sliver of light and then more.

He'd never claimed to be perfect. Only to love her.

And that wasn't enough.

He wasn't enough.

He felt desolate. Empty. More so even than when his life had imploded before.

He'd thought he had everything figured out. He'd foolishly thought that Crystal would be delighted by his declaration. Instead, she'd run away. He'd tried to call her twice later in the evening. She hadn't picked up.

He was nothing without her.

The thought settled. *Nothing without her.*

He played it over and over in his head.

And then he rejected it.

Crystal and Max had both said separately that he put duty above all else.

He was the monarch. The future king. He would always be that, Crystal or no Crystal. Future wife or no wife.

That truth settled deep inside him. He might be broken, might not have gotten the prize that he wanted, but he was whole enough to rule Glorvaird. To put his people's needs ahead of his own.

And for now, that would have to be enough.

. . .

An hour after her brothers left, Crystal was a little surprised the castle guards let her drive onto the grounds. No one stopped her when she parked near the garage.

The sun was barely up. This early, she'd probably find Valentin on his morning run. At least she hoped so. It would give her the privacy that she dearly wanted.

She rounded the castle, letting one hand trail behind her, fingertips touching the cool stone.

He was out there, his bodyguard slightly behind. He wasn't running. He was walking slowly up the beach toward the castle, his bodyguard trailing him.

Valentin was still a good distance away when the bodyguard said something to him. His head came up, and he looked at her.

Stupid bodyguard and his attentiveness to his surroundings.

She hung back by the corner of the castle wall.

She'd come this far, but she didn't know what she was going to say.

Valentin could've sent the bodyguard to send her away, but it was the prince himself who came to meet her. His T-shirt was soaked with sweat. How long had he been out here?

He hadn't shaved yet, and his hair was rumpled.

He'd never been more beautiful.

He stopped just out of arms' reach. "What are you doing here?"

She couldn't read his expression. He was unsmiling, his shoulders stiff.

She'd hurt him badly. What if he didn't want to give her a second chance?

Her lips wobbled. She tried to push down her emotion. She didn't want to cry all over him. But she couldn't hold it back.

So she whispered. "Valentin, I tried so hard not to fall in love with you. But I couldn't help it."

Hot tears stung her eyes, and she tried to hide her face. But his arms wrapped around her, pulled her close. "Oh, thank God."

He held her as she half-cried, half-laughed into his shoulder. He pressed a kiss into the hair above her ear.

"I'm sorry about yesterday," he said. "I shouldn't have pushed. I can try not to be so demanding, but I'm a work in progress."

She leaned back and wiped her tears. "It wasn't that."

He was watching her with such tender concern that it made it easier to say. "I'm more down-to-earth than your other matches. I'm no supermodel."

His hand came up to cup her cheek. He hadn't laughed at her fears or dismissed them outright. "I only want you. I love you."

She lowered her gaze. "And... I've worked hard to get where I am. I still have to get my brothers through university. How will it look that I've snagged the most eligible of all my clients?"

His thumb brushed her cheek. When she looked back into his dear face, one corner of his mouth was turned up. "I hadn't even thought about that. Not very considerate." His eyes went unfocused for a moment as he stared off into space. Then, "Conrad will write up a press release from my office."

She gulped. That sounded very official. "What will it say?"

"The truth is usually the easiest. That I simply couldn't resist your charms and you're off the dating market, but that you're still taking on new clients. Selectively," he murmured. "Not too many that you don't have time for me."

"Was that a complaint? Already?"

He grinned incorrigibly. "Conrad could also make a few discreet inquiries. I'm sure there must be some count or dignitary in my acquaintance who is looking for his match."

He'd do that for her?

She'd thought all her tears were spent, but new heat pricked her eyes.

When he leaned in and captured her lips, she raised one hand to clasp his wrist. She met his kiss eagerly.

She was safe here in his arms.

He broke the kiss and brushed her temple with his lips. "I'm getting you all sweaty."

"I don't mind," she replied dreamily.

"Come up and have breakfast with me?"

She agreed and he laced their fingers together as they walked.

She'd first come to the palace to make a match for her prince. She'd just never imagined it would be her.

Epilogue

Edward Bisson had chased down numerous stories in his career as a reporter. He'd exposed secrets and scandals. During the last two years, he'd been working for the American media as a foreign correspondent in the Middle East. He'd faced down bullets and once nearly been blown up by an IED.

So his current assignment should be a breeze. Go undercover as a cowboy. Work on a ranch while he tried to get close to a European princess and then expose her.

But this assignment might just be the most important he'd ever done.

Because Princess Tirith of Glorvaird had ruined his brother's life. She'd nearly killed his niece. Peyton had recovered partially, but the brain damage she'd suffered meant the bright little girl she'd once been would never be the same. The royal family might've footed all the medical bills, but his brother was a single father who now had to devote his whole life to taking care of Peyton.

And the princess had never faced one iota of punishment for what she'd done. Because the royal family had kept things so hush hush.

Even Edward hadn't known about her involvement in Peyton's accident until he'd accidentally uncovered some paperwork in his brother's messy office. There'd been a nondisclosure agreement signed by his brother. Carrick couldn't say anything to anyone—even his own brother—or the palace would pull funding for Peyton's ongoing care.

So Edward wasn't supposed to know about the accident or the cover-up. But that hadn't stopped him from snooping through the other paperwork in his brother's office. He'd managed to get some information from an aide at the hospital where Peyton had been treated.

Apparently, the princess had visited once or twice—as if that made up for what she'd done to his family.

Edward was angry. Furious that this had happened and that she hadn't paid.

Someone like her, someone who could damage a family and walk away scot-free, without a care in the world, deserved to pay. Someone like her had to have more dirt in the past. All he had to do was find it. Expose it.

Thus, the undercover assignment he'd given himself.

He sat on a dusty road outside some podunk town in Texas, gearing up for his entrance. Humble cowboy, down on his luck. Needed a job.

The princess was here for an extended visit with her father and to make some appearances for the family's charitable foundation. The public schedule on the royal family's website said she'd be here for six weeks.

This was his chance. Six weeks was plenty of time for revenge.

The True Princess

Chapter One

"I am a princess, and you will do my bidding."

Tirith, princess of Glorvaird, generally expected capitulation. If she gave an order, it was followed.

But she was out of her element. She was standing in the barn on her father's ranch and the horse standing in the open stall only stared at her, unblinking. The animal was so dark brown that it was almost completely black, all except a white blaze down its nose.

The horse was also taller than Tirith.

With hooves that could break her foot if one stepped on her. Teeth that could bite a finger off if she got too close.

If she ever managed to get the thing saddled and climbed on, she could easily fall and break her neck.

This was a disaster waiting to happen.

"This is for Maggie," she told the horse. And herself. Her twin sister was the head of the family's American-based charitable foundation and had organized a series of events over the next few weeks. A chili cook-off, a silent auction, a ball.

Oh, and a rodeo.

Who'd even heard of a charity rodeo?

Apparently, people from Texas.

In Tirith's experience, many Americans obsessed over royalty. Maggie's husband, Luc, had urged her to take advantage of her connections, and Maggie had run with the idea. Luc had been born in Glorvaird and he and Maggie split their time between the palace and the ranch. He was absolutely besotted with Maggie. And he was Tirith's former best friend.

Maggie had convinced their younger sister Beatrix and their mother to take a few weeks out of the summer schedule to fly out and make appearances. Both would compete in the chili cook-off, along with Tirith.

Their cousin, heir to the throne, Valentin, would attend the charity ball, along with his fiancée.

And Maggie was planning to ride barrels—was that even the right term?—in the rodeo. She'd asked Tirith to be a part of the opening ceremonies. She meant for Tirith to ride out into the arena, holding a flag. Probably wearing a glittering cowgirl shirt with her hair teased into a big-as-Texas style.

After what Maggie had done for her, how could Tirith say no?

She couldn't.

Which was why she'd waited until her sister and father vacated the barn. She hadn't been on horseback since she'd been bucked off as a pre-teen and had badly broken her arm. She had to figure out how to do this without making a fool of herself.

"I'm not afraid of you," she said.

But as she tugged on the rope she'd clipped to the horse's halter, the animal shook its massive head and whinnied.

Tirith startled and dropped the rope.

"I'm not sure he believes you."

The male voice from behind sent her whirling. She raised a hand to press against her pounding heart.

She didn't recognize the cowboy standing in the wide barn aisle. He had his arms crossed with one hand pressed to the underside of his opposite forearm. What a strange way to stand. He looked like any of the other ranch hands she'd seen around over the past few days since her arrival. He wore a T-shirt and grungy jeans above his scuffed cowboy boots. He had at least two days of scruff on his chin, making him look disreputable. And his cowboy hat was pulled low, blocking his eyes from her view.

"May I help you?" She said the words with the same amount of ice she reserved for nosy reporters. She didn't want or need an audience right now.

His lips twitched as if he were amused. "I should probably ask you that. You trying to saddle up?"

It couldn't have been more obvious, thanks to the saddle she'd toted from the tack room and slung over the stall wall.

"I do not require assistance," she said stiffly.

He made a skeptical humming noise that crawled right under her skin. But he said, "I could use some. Assistance. Maybe a bandage."

He raised his arms, and she saw blood dripping between his fingers.

For a millisecond, the bright red of his blood sent her spiraling back to a scene she would rather not remember. She had to blink away the memories.

And then, she jumped into action. "Go into the wash-room." She pointed to a door next to the tack room.

He bristled, but she went on.

"I'll bring the first aid kit."

His expression cleared. She didn't know what that moment had been about. Did he dislike taking orders from a woman? Or maybe she'd wounded his pride with the basic instruction.

She didn't have time to dwell on it.

Before she could step away, he drawled, "Better close the stall door, *highness*. You don't want your mighty steed wandering off."

His use of "highness" was more mocking than anything else. Not a term of respect, that was certain.

But he was right, so she quickly latched the stall door, jumping back when the horse arched its neck over.

She hurried down the hall to the small room tucked at the back of the barn. She knew her father and Maggie shared a large, open office in the farmhouse. This barn office was full of odds and ends, paperwork with columns of numbers she didn't understand. But when her father had given her a quick tour two days before, she'd noticed the red-and-white first aid kit tucked on a high shelf.

She was forced to stand on the wobbly desk chair to reach it.

When she approached the washroom, she could see the cowboy's shoulders from behind. He was standing at the sink, running water.

He was so broad he almost filled up the small space.

A prickling of nerves made her steps falter. She straightened her spine and stepped close.

She wasn't used to being in close proximity with strangers. Her life in Glorvaird was very different than the reality of this Texas ranch. Back home, she was shepherded through her day by her personal assistant. Her diary was full of appointments and meetings, appearances and events. She had her duty to the crown.

But she also had a duty to her family. And her father would want her to help one of his hired hands.

Her father had been a Navy SEAL before he'd married her mother. He was careful. Protective. She knew he would've done comprehensive background checks on anyone he allowed on the ranch.

So she did her best to put aside the nerves tumbling in her stomach.

She edged into the doorway and caught sight of the cowboy's injury in the mirror hanging above the sink. A three-inch gash on the underside of his forearm was still bleeding freely as he attempted to wash it out.

She felt her stomach lurch as the sight of that blood pinged the sensitive memory. This time, she couldn't push it away fast enough, and her face flushed hot and then cold.

The image of a little girl's crumpled body lying in the street flashed over her vision. She couldn't seem to catch her breath.

"Something the matter, highness?"

The cowboy's casual address startled her back into the present.

She met his eyes in the mirror. He'd pushed his hat back on his head, and she was caught by just how blue his eyes were. She couldn't quite read his expression. Mocking?

"You should call me Tirith," she said. "Not highness."

EDWARD FELT a beat of relief as the color returned to the princess's face. The last thing he needed was for her to faint and someone to come investigate.

As an investigative journalist, Edward had been on dangerous assignments before. But there was something deadly about the princess's father, who was former special ops.

Edward had been hired on as a temporary ranch hand for a couple of weeks to help with the charity rodeo and whatever else the boss needed. He'd been on the ranch for all of three days, and he wasn't going to compromise his cover now.

"Shouldn't you see a doctor?" she asked. "That gash looks like it might need stitches."

His gash had been carefully orchestrated to put him in this very position—close enough to speak to the princess.

"If you've got a butterfly bandage in there, I'll be fine." He nodded to the first aid kit.

She reached for the latch and bobbled the case, almost dropping it.

"Here, switch places with me," he said.

She hesitated minutely as he stepped out of the way, then brushed past him to set the first aid kit on the narrow counter.

He stepped back in front of the sink, effectively trapping her in the tiny bathroom.

Words bubbled up inside him.

What about Peyton? My brother? Don't you feel any remorse?

But he couldn't ask those questions. Not yet.

She glanced up briefly as she unlatched the case. Their gazes clashed for a beat, and something stirred uncomfortably in his gut. Probably indigestion from being so close to a lying cow.

He studied her as she rifled through the first aid kit. He'd been trying to get close to her since he'd arrived, but this was the first chance he'd had to talk to her.

He hated her for what she'd done to Peyton, what she'd cost Carrick back in Glorvaird, but that didn't stop him from noticing the fine bone structure of her face and the sweep of lashes against her cheek. Her glossy, dark ponytail had fallen over her shoulder, and he had the strange urge to tug it like he would've back in grade school.

A faint blush was rising in her cheeks, and he realized he was staring.

Surely she had to be used to that. She was in the public eye all the time.

Was he making her uncomfortable? A part of him rejoiced at that, but he had to stay focused. He needed her to learn to trust him, and he didn't have much time.

Making her uncomfortable was for later.

"How did you cut yourself?" she asked.

"Brushed up against a protruding nail. Accidentally." He tacked on the lie with no remorse. *She* was the liar. One or two white lies were well worth it if they would get her to divulge the truth.

In reality, he'd leaned into the nail on purpose. He'd been working with two other guys on building the temporary holding pens, fifty yards past the barn. He'd seen the princess slip inside the barn and needed an excuse to get close to her. He'd pretended the cut was an accident, and the ranch foreman had waved him off to find a bandage. He couldn't drag this conversation out for long, but it was a start.

She held up a large square paper-wrapped bandage. It would do.

"What exactly were you doing with that horse?" he asked. She wasn't dressed for riding, not in the expensive dove-colored slacks and silk blouse. Her leather boots were quality, but not made for the barn. The boardroom, maybe.

She ripped the package open. "That's none of your concern." Her words brooked no argument. And made him immediately want to argue.

"Whatever you say, highness."

"What's your name?" This time, her words were a demand.

He swallowed back a refusal. Forced his facial muscles to relax. "Edward."

He'd grown up in Glorvaird but he'd been on enough overseas assignments since secondary school that he'd lost most of his accent. The rest he obscured with a bit of Texas twang.

He didn't give his last name. Simpler was easier.

He'd given her father a fake name, a false identity he'd used before on undercover jobs. The name had a driver's license and social and filed taxes. It must've held up to Gideon Hale's background check, because he hadn't been fired.

He had been pleasantly surprised to be accepted so easily by the other cowboys. The bunkhouse was home to four full-time hands, and four other guys had been hired on temporarily. The guys could be ornery and play pranks, but they watched out for each other.

The Triple H Ranch would be a decent place to land, if he were a cowboy and not a reporter.

She ripped the paper off the bandage, and he lifted his arm, pretending that he couldn't easily reach. "D'you mind?"

She was frowning but didn't refuse.

Her fingers circled his wrist. He wasn't one for romance drivel, but at her touch, a physical shock traveled through his nerve endings, startling him into stillness.

He met her gaze, saw the surprise mirrored in her eyes.

She'd felt it too.

She lowered her eyes quickly, her focus on his arm as she pressed the butterfly bandage over his skin. Again, that telltale flush rose in her cheeks.

The attraction was completely unexpected.

He was a little disgusted with himself. She was an awful person. The kind of person who did something horrible and then covered it up.

But maybe he could use a mutual attraction to get close to her.

He checked the bandage. No leaks. It was tight to his skin. "I appreciate your help. But I'm pretty sure your father is going to fire me if I let that horse run you over. Do you want to tell me what you were doing?"

She kept her eyes on the first aid kit as she tucked everything back inside. "I'd like to go for a ride."

There was something else. Something she wasn't saying.

"Your dad is a horseman. And I bet you've got a big stable at your castle back home."

Her head stayed down. "Good guess."

"But... you don't like horses?"

Her lips firmed into a line. "I like them fine."

No, she didn't. The way she'd shied around the gelding was proof.

"You're scared of them."

Her head came up, and he witnessed the return of the ice princess. She glared at him. "I don't remember asking for you to psychoanalyze me."

She picked up the first aid kit, holding it against her middle, and brushed past him.

He followed at a slow walk. "Your sister's horses are pretty gentle."

Margaret Hale ran an equine therapy program, and her horses were so tame they were practically asleep.

The princess muttered something under her breath as she stalked off to what he thought was the barn office.

He waited in the aisle next to the stall where all this had started.

Moments later, she appeared again.

She didn't look happy to see him standing there.

"Don't you have to get back to work?"

He did. He didn't want Miles to come looking for him. No reason to raise suspicions.

"What if you worked up to it?" he asked. "Put the saddle on the horse today. Maybe tomorrow you ride."

She frowned.

"Why is it so important?"

Her chin jutted up. "I told my sister I'd ride in the opening ceremony for her rodeo."

"The rodeo isn't for another couple weeks. You've got time. Build up to it."

She crossed her arms over her chest, and her chin twisted to the side so he had only a view of her profile. "I'll consider it."

It was an obvious dismissal.

And he still needed to get on her good side.

"I'm happy to help. Anytime. I owe you one." He lifted his arm so the bandage was visible.

She was considering it when he glanced over his shoulder at the outside door. She was still staring at the horse with the stall door closed.

He was a little surprised she hadn't weaseled her way out of the commitment. Why hadn't she told Margaret no?

But he wasn't as surprised as he'd been to feel the instant connection when she'd touched him.

There was attraction there—on his part and hers. Now, all he needed was a way to capitalize on it.

Chapter Two

Edward held his palm against the scratch beneath the left side of his jaw. He threw open the door to the bunkhouse.

The princess jumped and whirled from the counter where she had been standing. She looked vaguely guilty, and his glance quickly encompassed the items laid out on the kitchen counter. Ground beef, a whole cabinet full of spices, a couple of cans of beans. Nothing nefarious. So why had she jumped like a startled deer?

"Don't mind me." He headed for the bathroom.

The bunkhouse was one long building. Less like a house and more like an apartment for college guys.

The kitchen ran along all of one wall, with a long counter interrupted by the stove and fridge at one end. A big window looked over the nearest field. A long dining table broke up the open room, and on the other side of it a living area was filled with a scuffed leather couch, a couple of chairs, a coffee table marked with rings, and a TV that was usually tuned to sports or news.

At one time, someone had attempted to decorate in a western style. A horseshoe was hung over the doorway. A beautiful painting of a horse galloping through a meadow hung on one wall.

But what might've once been tasteful had been disrupted by the dartboard hanging next to the painting and several ball caps had been tacked in a pattern on another wall.

The bunkhouse was most definitely the domain of several bachelors.

Past the living area was the bedroom, where half a dozen bunks and three dressers were located. And the bathroom, which was Edward's destination.

This morning was the first time he'd caught a glimpse of the princess since he'd run into her in the barn three days prior.

Miles had kept the regular ranch hands and the extra hired cowboys busy from dawn until dusk.

They'd moved cattle, pushing a big herd from one of the fields closer to the house and barn to a pasture two miles away. They'd finished constructing the holding pens and temporary chutes for the arena.

And then there were the patrols.

Edward had stumbled over that secret accidentally when he had woken coughing in the night, his allergies acting up after being outdoors in the dust. He'd gone to the kitchen to get a glass of water. That big window above the kitchen sink didn't hide a thing, and he'd easily seen two men on horseback who had passed each other in the field.

Each one had a rifle strapped to his saddle.

One walked his horse toward the barn; the other disappeared out of sight toward the fields.

In the dark, he hadn't been able to identify the men. But he recognized a security patrol when he saw one.

What he didn't know was why it was needed.

There was already a visible security team guarding the house. Unobtrusive cameras around the ranch and the gated entrance. Why did they need riders on horseback?

His gut told him there was a story here. His editor had given him the go-ahead to chase it.

He stared at his reflection in the water-spotted mirror. His fingers were still clamped over the new scratch he'd given himself, this one behind his jaw and under his ear.

He'd tanned, being out in the sun all day. The color in his face highlighted the tiny lines around his eyes. He'd hit his mid-thirties, and his body refused to do the tasks he'd done easily when he was twenty. He was exhausted from the strenuous work.

He was chafing with inactivity on the princess front. He wanted justice for Peyton, for Carrick. He'd like to return to Glorvaird and check on his niece in person.

He hadn't told his brother he was coming to the U.S. or about his self-imposed mission. He wasn't supposed to know that the princess had been negligent and caused a car accident. His niece had broken multiple bones, but the biggest injury was the TBI—traumatic brain injury. Almost six weeks ago now, he'd gone to visit his family only to find them out of the house late at night. His curiosity had been piqued, and when he'd seen Carrick's email open on his computer in his home office... he'd snooped.

And discovered the truth, including a scanned copy of the non-disclosure agreement his brother had signed.

It had stung, knowing Carrick had kept the truth from him, though he understood why Carrick had been forced to.

The crown didn't want its sterling reputation tarnished.

Edward blamed the princess for all of it, but whatever remuneration Carrick was receiving—that had to be the reason he'd signed the NDA—was on the line. No one could know that Edward had found out the truth behind the accident.

If he was going to out the royal family, he had to dig up the dirt on his own. It had taken months to set this up.

And to achieve his aim, he needed to be close to the princess.

His impatience had come to a head this morning, and he'd been lucky to see her sneaking out to the bunkhouse.

He'd manufactured another injury, and the cowboy who'd been helping him load up a farm truck with barbed wire and metal fence poles had waved him off to clean it up in the bunkhouse.

After today, he wouldn't be able to use an injury again.

There was accident-prone and there was suspicious, and he was already walking a fine line.

He turned on the faucet and pulled his fingers away from the wound, wincing as blood dripped down his neck. He hadn't meant to make the cut quite so deep.

It didn't matter. Even if he ended up scarred, getting justice for Peyton would be worth it.

He pressed some tissue from the bathroom against his new wound and found a first aid kit in the cabinet beneath the sink. He set it on the counter and then moved to stand in the doorway, facing the princess.

She stared out the kitchen window with her arms crossed, her hands holding onto her elbows. She looked a little lost. She glanced over her shoulder and caught sight of him.

"Will it offend your delicate sensibilities if I ask for your help again?" he asked.

She seemed to blink away whatever thoughts were plaguing her. "What does that mean? My 'delicate sensibilities'?"

He shrugged. "I guess it doesn't seem like you belong here. Branding steers and pulling calves." *Riding horses.*

She wore a fancy blouse again, though today she wore slim-fitting dark jeans and sneakers.

She started across the room toward him. "Do you belong here?"

"Miles is a good boss. I like working outdoors."

She brushed past him into the bathroom, and he saw her stiffen when she registered the mess. There were towels on the floor, and had she seen the whiskers on the insides of the sink? Cowboys weren't much for cleaning up after themselves.

She steeled herself, and he handed her the band-aid he'd plucked from the first aid kit. "I don't need a doctor or stitches. I just can't see at a good angle in the mirror."

She moved close and tilted her head to see his scratch. He moved the tissue away and watched her expression in the mirror. She looked serene, almost blank. He'd seen a similar expression on other faces. Celebrities. Actors. Politicians. It was an expression they wore to hide their true feelings.

She had to step closer to reach him as she dabbed at his neck with ointment. She was in his personal space now, and her scent enveloped him. It was lighter than perfume. Maybe her shampoo, or her soap. Jasmine.

She breathed in deeply, and it made him self-conscious of the fact that he'd been out in the barn before sunup. His work hauling supplies that morning had been grueling.

He shifted his feet so that he gained a half-inch of distance. "Don't breathe in too deeply. I'm a sweaty mess."

She turned away to exchange the ointment for his band-aid. In the mirror, he had a view of her profile. There was no mistaking the flush that started in her throat and rose into her cheeks.

"There." She pressed the bandage against his skin, and he felt another *zing* of attraction.

After which, she rushed out of the bathroom.

He put away the first aid kit then strode through the living area to find her at the sink, washing her hands.

He stopped near the dining table. "Was there something you needed?"

She glanced at him over her shoulder as she dried her hands, a question in her expression.

"Somehow I doubt you're in here to make the beds or bring fresh towels." He infused his voice with wry humor.

One corner of her mouth turned up. "I needed a place to cook."

He raised his brows. "Isn't there a kitchen in that big farmhouse?" No doubt it was miles better than the fifteen-year-old appliances and Formica counters in here.

She moved restlessly to where she'd laid out her ingredients.

"You cookin' up a secret?" he asked quietly.

She shook her head, not looking at him. "It's not a secret. But I'd rather my family not watch over my shoulder."

There was something in the way she said the words. Some hurt. Something about her family. His journalistic instincts were buzzing.

"I'm a confirmed bachelor. You want some help? I owe you, after all." He gestured to the bandage when she glanced over at him.

"You cook?"

"Sure." That was an exaggeration. He could make scrambled eggs. And Peyton's favorite: grilled cheese.

He worked a lot. Had never had time to learn to make himself meals. But if it meant getting close to the princess, he could be a chef. "I can follow a recipe," he added easily as he rounded the dining table.

"Won't Miles be expecting you?"

He shrugged. "I can spare fifteen minutes. I'll work overtime later tonight if I need to."

She seemed to accept that. She nudged a piece of paper across the counter to him. A computer-printed recipe. *Texas chili*.

He glanced curiously at her. "I heard about the chili cook off. Don't tell me you're entering."

She fiddled with the spices, lining them up like toy soldiers. "My whole family is participating." There it was again, that uncertainty in her voice. "I don't want to make a fool of myself."

That was exactly the kind of sentiment he'd expected from her. She wanted to save face. Uphold her public image.

"You could always drop out." He had to work to keep the hardness out of his voice.

She shook her head. "My sister's foundation does a lot of good. I want to help." She blinked rapidly and turned her face to the window. She cared that much?

Or she was a good actress.

Except he was the only one here. And she probably didn't care what he thought about her.

So what?

He had written enough exposés to know that everybody was made up of shades of gray. Even the most notorious criminals usually cared about and wanted to take care of their families.

It didn't matter that the princess had a single kind-hearted bone in her body.

She'd been careless and covered it up while his family suffered.

But the knowledge that she wasn't all bad made his stomach twist in a knot.

———

Tirith watched Edward hesitate. He'd clearly been on his way to the door, but now he hovered just between the kitchen and the dining table.

There was a part of her that wanted to urge him on.

The man had nearly caught her sniffing him. She'd been standing close to put that silly band-aid on his neck, and she'd been tantalized by the scent of his skin, a mix of Texas grass, saddle leather, and something that was uniquely Edward.

Thank goodness he'd said something about being sweaty and edged away. He'd saved her further embarrassment. She could only pray he hadn't noticed.

It had obviously been far too long since she'd dated. She had her reasons. Edward was the first man in a very long time she'd been attracted to.

"I'm happy to help you get started," he offered now. "And you've got a crew full of cowboys that'll stampede in here at lunchtime, scrounging for food. They can test it for you. Give you an honest opinion."

She wanted to refuse. Save herself further humiliation. She knew he had to feel the attraction between them too. It had crackled through the air both times they'd been in the same room together.

What was his motive? Had he made the offer out of the goodness of his heart?

She didn't know.

But she was desperate.

And there was a part of her that wanted to stay as far away from the ranch house as possible.

Her mother had arrived that morning, with Bea in tow and an entourage of guards. She'd been cool and distant when she'd greeted Tirith.

It wasn't a complete surprise. Mother had treated Tirith differently ever since Tirith had proposed a new royal initiative. Tirith had battled anxiety for years and wanted to help erase the stigma of mental illness.

Mother had some old-fashioned ideas.

Lately, whatever warmth Tirith remembered from her childhood was gone. Mother hadn't smiled at her in weeks. Not a real smile, anyway.

So Tirith had escaped the ranch house with the excuse of cooking up a practice round of chili. She'd dithered too long in the bunkhouse, long enough for the cowboy to come in and find her staring into space. She wasn't used to asking for help. In the palace, there was always someone to see to her needs. Sometimes even before she realized what she needed.

Now she smiled a trembling smile at him. "I suppose you could help me get started."

He saw through her attempt at making it seem as if she was the one doing him a favor. Something sparked in his eyes, but he didn't comment.

She was completely inept in the kitchen, and she caught the smile he tried to hide when she didn't know how to use the crank can opener he found in one of the kitchen drawers.

He might be a cook, but he certainly wasn't familiar with this kitchen. While she browned the meat, he opened and closed all six of the drawers, familiarizing himself with their contents.

She knew her father and Maggie hired a cook part time to help feed the ranch hands so that Scarlett didn't have to do all of it. The hired cook, Daisy, used the ranch kitchen. Which meant this kitchen was furnished with only the bare minimum.

Edward muttered about the lack of appropriate utensils, his shoulder brushing hers as he moved around her to fish in one of the drawers again.

He moved with an easy grace that she envied. It had taken her years to learn to relax in her own skin, and she only managed it when she was alone. It was safer that way.

"You're smoking," he cautioned.

She jumped, blinking out of her wandering thoughts. The ground beef in the pan was starting to smoke. What should she do?

"You need to stir." Standing at her back, he reached around her and grabbed the floppy rubber spatula from the counter.

He was too close. Her heart beat in her ears. But he had her boxed in as he stirred the meat in the pan. It stopped smoking and went back to sizzling.

He stepped away and turned on the faucet.

"What's it like, living in Glorvaird?" His question was asked casually. He wasn't looking at her as he rinsed out the can of tomato sauce they'd added to a large pot on the second burner.

But she was still flushed from his close proximity.

And aware that every word she said could end up in a tabloid.

She stuck to her usual public answer. "The countryside at home is like nothing you've ever seen. The seaside cliffs and how the city rises above the water. But what I love most about home are the mountains."

She didn't usually add that last part.

She hadn't thought so as a child. The mountains were inland, remote, too far from the city with its bustling tourism. They were too isolated. It felt as if she could get lost and never be found.

But after the accident, during her recovery, she'd gone away and found herself in the mountains.

"It must be nice, not having to cook for yourself. Always having someone there to look after you."

His words hummed with disgust that he couldn't quite mask.

She heard that tone from people who didn't know her. People who didn't understand that the royal family worked hard for their country. Before the accident, there had been days when she'd been so busy she'd barely had time to eat.

It stung to hear Edward's censure. The fact that it stung was ridiculous.

They didn't know each other.

It was only the connection that flared to life when they were together that made it feel as if they did.

"Ground beef is browned," he said. "You want to add it to the chili pot?"

The skillet was unwieldy, and some of the meat dropped onto the stovetop as she attempted to pour it into the stock pot.

Edward went for the paper towel roll by the sink. "Did you ask your dad to help you ride that horse?"

She shook her head. Her father was an expert horseman. She wasn't ready to admit to him that she hadn't been on horseback in over a decade. "It's impolite to remind a lady about her imperfections."

He snorted slightly. And then, his voice overly casual, he

said, "Your dad's probably been too busy to help, anyway. What with the extra patrols he's got running at night."

She looked up from stirring the pot. "What patrols?"

The morning sun streamed in the window, highlighting the dark stubble at his jaw. "Not sure I'm supposed to know about them—me bein' the new guy and all. But a couple of nights ago, I saw the changing of the guard."

What was he talking about?

He must've recognized her cluelessness. "One guy rode toward the barn. One rode out into the night. Both of 'em had rifles tied to their saddles."

She picked up the skillet and moved to the sink, forcing him to step aside. She ran water into the pan, considering what to say.

Edward spoke before she did. "I might only be a temporary worker, but I'd like to know I'm not going to get shot while I'm riding fences."

A shiver went through her at the thought. "You aren't."

The raise of his brows showed his skepticism.

There were always threats against the crown. Most were anonymous emails or letters. They were all investigated. Most turned out to be nothing.

Occasionally, there was a threat that the royal security team took seriously. Her father had mentioned that there would be heightened security over the next weeks, but she'd thought it was because of Valentin's presence.

But her cousin wasn't set to arrive until just before the ball.

Why would Father have extra patrols now?

"Are you in danger?" His pointed question brought her out of her thoughts. It was past the bounds of curiosity and bordering on nosy.

And she didn't have an answer for him.

"If you have concerns, I'm sure my father or Miles can answer them. You should bring your questions up with them."

His expression closed off. "I might do that."

A soft pop and hiss sounded. He turned to the stock pot and used a long-handled spoon to give it a stir. "This looks decent. We didn't botch it too badly. You want to taste it?"

"I thought it had to simmer for three hours?"

He dipped the spoon into the pot. "You got that right. Cooking it for that long will enhance the flavors, infuse them into the meat. But you can still give it a test and get an idea of what the final product will taste like."

She wasn't expecting him to step toward her and extend the spoon. It felt a little too intimate, but after he had helped her, how could she refuse?

She opened her mouth. Behind the spoon, his gaze was warm. Almost as smoky as the chili smelled. He gently tipped a small bite into her mouth.

Flavor exploded over her tongue, but not in a good way.

Hot!

She swallowed after barely chewing and lunged for the faucet, quickly turning it on and cupping her hand beneath the stream of water. She drank directly from her hands, mouth burning too badly to be embarrassed.

"Too spicy?"

She couldn't answer him. Her eyes were tearing, and she blinked rapidly, watching as he reached for the drawer and pulled out another spoon. He took a bite for himself. Smacked his lips.

"It's got a kick, all right."

She was still gulping water when he chuckled. "Let me get you some milk. It'll soothe the burn better than water."

She let the rest of the water run off her hands and reached for the towel to dry off as he filled a glass.

She took the milk from him and gulped it down.

"Slow down," he said. He wasn't laughing out loud, but she saw the way his eyes were dancing. "You sure you measured the spices right?"

She nodded. She tried wiggling her tongue inside her

mouth. Maybe she hadn't burned every square inch of her taste buds.

"I bet the other cowboys will like it."

She finally got her mouth working. "We can't serve that." So her words sounded more like a gasp than anything else.

"It's Texas chili. Texans don't mind the heat."

She considered dumping the whole thing in the garbage. But she hated to waste it. "Do you really think they'd eat it?"

He smiled. A real smile that made her belly flip. "I'll report back when they come in for lunch."

She wrinkled her nose skeptically, but he didn't seem to see it as he dug a ballpoint pen out of the junk drawer at the end of the counter. He took her hand in his and wrote something on her palm.

His number.

"Text me, and I'll have your number. Then I can let you know about the chili. And you can call me when you're ready to go for that ride."

Her stomach did a second slow flip.

He was flirting with her. Like she was a normal woman, not a princess.

It wasn't real.

But she carried the warm feeling with her all day.

Chapter Three

Tirith would not cry.

She simply refused.

At least not until later tonight, in the privacy of her room.

Although even that wasn't private anymore, not while she and Bea were sharing the small space.

Today was chili cook-off day.

And Tirith didn't have a partner.

The mayor of nearby Taylor Hills was a family friend, and Maggie had cajoled him into taking part in the event. But he'd notified them only an hour before that he had a stomach bug and wouldn't make it.

Tirith didn't look at the spectators milling around the perimeter of the spacious room. The 4-H building was more like an empty warehouse, with a concrete floor and cinder block walls. But it suited Maggie's purposes, and everyone in the community knew where it was.

Bleachers that looked like they belonged in a high school gym had been set up at one end of the room. They were mostly empty, as it was early yet. Maggie's team had cordoned off the center of the area, and a security team was spread throughout, attempting to blend in to the crowd. Some of her dad's cowboys were milling around too. She'd had a brief glimpse of Edward earlier.

While the chili was cooking, Maggie and her dad would hold a short press conference and answer questions about the foundation. When the chili was ready, the crowd would have a chance to taste all of the selections.

There were twelve cooking stations set up around the inside of the roped-off area. Each one had a small countertop with two hot plates that would serve as burners. A cutting board, knives, and assorted utensils made up the rest of the gear each pair of amateur chefs would be allowed to use. There was a central area where all the ingredients were kept. The teams wouldn't be allowed to choose ingredients until the cook-off started.

How was she supposed to do this on her own?

Tirith glanced down at the two pieces of paper on her station—an ingredients list and a rough recipe. She was aware of her father and Bea at the station to her left. Her mother and Maggie were on their other side. Maggie had set it up so the royal family was competing against family friends and prominent local celebrities—like the veterinarian who, based on the way he'd greeted every person by name, knew *everyone* in town, and the high school principal, who'd been surrounded by people since he'd walked in.

A cameraman ducked beneath the barrier, and Tirith chose to squat behind her counter, pretending to search for something on the shelf below. Not her smartest move, since there were only three steel mixing bowls and a cutting board down here.

Maggie had hired a group of kids from the local community college to video today's event and run live segments on the Foundation's social media pages throughout the day. There were four or five of them running around, and since they were approved by Maggie and the security team, Tirith wouldn't be able to avoid them forever.

She usually didn't mind cameras. But today she felt unsettled.

That morning, Maggie had found her sipping a cup of tea in the kitchen. She'd come to break the news that Tirith no longer had a partner for the event.

Mother had been on her heels.

Tirith hadn't blinked when Maggie had asked whether she was good to complete the event on her own.

But Mother's words had been a cut. *"Perhaps you should stay behind the scenes, dear."*

And Tirith had heard what she didn't say aloud. That Tirith couldn't be trusted. Mother looked at her differently now. She thought Tirith might make a scene and ruin Maggie's event.

Mother couldn't have known that her lack of faith in her daughter was sending Tirith perilously close to a panic attack that very moment.

Breathe.

She counted out several slow breaths, her head still bowed, crouched behind her work counter. She focused on listening to what was happening around her. Father was nearby, his voice a calm counterpoint to Bea's bubbly excitement. They were arguing about peppers.

There was a young child somewhere in the crowd, chattering about ice cream flavors. Someone was humming. Outside, the breeze was blowing. It was a sound that belonged to her childhood, the constant Texas wind. Like a little girl, she was still holding onto a childish hope that her mother and father would reconcile someday.

Her stomach felt jittery, but she forced her wobbly legs to hold her as she straightened.

Maggie had posted a large digital countdown timer on one wall. There were five minutes before the official start to the cook-off.

If she was going to do this by herself, she needed a game plan. At least she wasn't flying blind. Edward had helped her practice in the bunkhouse only a few days before, so she knew there were several steps to the process that needed to happen simultaneously. She would just have to juggle.

It was as if thinking about him had conjured his presence.

Edward was at the edge of the roped-off crowd, speaking to one of the security guards.

And then he ducked underneath the barrier and strode toward her.

"Where's your partner?" He stopped on the opposite side of her counter.

"Sick. I'm on my own." She sounded airy and unaffected. But to her horror, her lips trembled.

And he saw.

For a moment, the connection between them—or attraction or whatever it was, a feeling she hadn't been able to name —leapt to life.

He rounded the counter. "You got an extra apron? I won't hold it against you that you never texted me to find out how the hands liked your chili."

It took her a beat too long to realize he meant *he* was going to cook with her.

"You can't just..."

But he was *just*. He'd already removed the blue apron that matched the one she already wore from the hook on the side of the counter and was slipping it over his head.

"I'm employed by the Triple H. That's gotta count for something."

He waved at someone behind her, and she turned her head to see her father watching them. Bea said something to him, and he returned his focus to their workspace.

"Same recipe as before?" Edward's question brought her attention back to her new partner.

"Absolutely not. I still can't taste anything on the right side of my mouth."

He grinned, and her stomach took a tumble. "It turned out all right. The cowboys emptied the pot."

She didn't know why he'd chosen to come to her rescue, to be her partner, but there were thirty seconds left on that countdown clock and she wasn't going to send him away now.

"The old timers in the crowd would give you their vote for that fire alarm chili."

"I would prefer not to involve the fire department," she said primly.

He laughed, a low sound that made her heart pitter-patter. He almost looked... surprised.

Was it so shocking that she could make him laugh?

He glanced away.

Five seconds left.

She picked up the ingredients list from the counter and quickly ripped it in half. She offered him one of the pieces. "We'll have two minutes to grab all of the ingredients."

His fingers closed over hers briefly as he took the list. "You want me to misplace ingredients while I'm at it? Make it diffi-cult for the other teams?"

She hadn't thought to be that devious. "This is a charity event. We'd better play it safe. No cheating."

"I thought you'd say that."

But when he smiled at her, it didn't feel safe at all.

———

THE ROYAL SECURITY force was out *en masse* today. There was definitely something going on.

Which is why Edward had done the stupid thing and joined up with Tirith for the cook-off.

He wanted to find out what all the security was about.

It didn't have anything to do with the pinch in his gut when he'd noticed her hiding behind her counter. Or that her hands had been shaking when she'd swept a stray strand of hair from her face.

He didn't feel sorry for her.

She didn't deserve compassion.

He'd seen a chance and taken it. He wanted the story.

And if this unwanted attraction they shared would get him closer to her, he needed to use it.

They worked together to do the quickest "grocery shop" in history.

"You want to chop?" he asked back at their station.

"Yes. And you'll brown the beef?"

They set to work. He had the ground beef sizzling in a skillet while she chopped a green bell pepper.

He moved to sort through the dry spices she'd tossed in a brown sack. "Lot of security here today. Because of your mom?" He held his breath, waiting for her answer. Had that been too obvious?

Over her shoulder, he caught Gideon Hale shooting him a look from the next station over. It'd been a risk, approaching Tirith in such a public setting. Edward was putting himself under the rancher's scrutiny. He needed his identity to hold up for a little while longer.

Tirith was opening her mouth to answer when a college-aged kid approached, holding some kind of apparatus with a high-tech video camera on top. A second kid was with him and asked Tirith a question about her sister's charity.

Tirith gave an answer that seemed authentic, a smile that was genuine, as she spoke about the children Maggie's foundation was helping and why the work was so important. She was charming and perfectly at ease.

It couldn't be real, could it?

But the kid behind the camera was eating it up. He looked a little star-struck. Or maybe just enthralled by the princess and her beauty.

When Tirith turned that smile on Edward, part of him started to get lost in her magnetism too.

Except he knew better.

He pressed his lips together in an expression that meant to show her he saw through her.

She switched to chopping a jalapeño while the kid asked Edward what he was doing behind the stove.

"I'm usually riding fence lines for the Triple H, but today I found out the princess needed an extra hand, so I volunteered."

The kid didn't seem interested since Edward wasn't anyone famous, and that was fine with him. The less attention shined on him, the better.

Tirith used the cutting board to tip her peppers to the sizzling meat in the skillet. She wiped her hands on her apron.

He was glancing at her from the corner of his eye when he saw her swipe that same strand of hair out of her eyes.

She gasped. Had she seen something? Where exactly was the danger?

But when he looked at her, her eyes were tearing, and the tip of her nose was red.

"What's—?" And then it hit him. "You had oil from that jalapeño on your fingers."

His hand was at her elbow before he'd given it a thought. There had to be a medic here—

She was tugging against his hold. "We can't leave the station. The meat will burn."

She couldn't be worried about the stupid chili at this point. Her eyes were streaming tears. She waved her free hand as if she wanted to touch her face but knew better.

"I barely touched my face." There was a hint of whimper in her voice. "How can it hurt so much?"

"You need to flush your eyes with water."

He looked around. There was an arrow pointing to the restrooms at the back of the building, away from the crowd.

His gazed clashed with Gideon's. Concern was etched on the man's face.

He refocused on Tirith when she spoke. "You stay here and watch the chili."

By now her eyes were completely closed, still tearing.

And then he caught sight of the kid approaching again,

camera pointed toward Tirith. He'd somehow caught wind that something was going on.

Edward scowled at him. "Turn the camera off. You can come back to us later." He didn't realize he'd pulled her to his chest until he was looking down into her face. He didn't wait for the kid to follow his instructions but moved the half-done ground beef off of the burner, setting it on the cutting board, where he hoped it wouldn't melt through to the counter below.

"Just point me toward the women's restroom." Was she still arguing with him?

"C'mon." He kept her elbow in his hand and ushered her toward the back of the building. "I took the food off the burner. We'll come right back." Unless she was in bad shape, in which case, someone could drive her to the nearest hospital.

She let him lead her away, one hand shielding her eyes. "I can't believe I made such an amateur mistake." She sighed. "Everyone saw, didn't they?"

"Dunno." He'd been more concerned with her than everyone else.

No one answered his knock on the women's bathroom door, and he pushed inside. He used the lever above the door to prop it open and then led her inside.

"Soap and wash your hands first," he said. "Or you'll spread the oil."

Except, how was she supposed to see the soap dispenser? He turned on the faucet first, then pumped several squirts of soap into his own hands.

It felt entirely too intimate as he lathered her hands over the sink. His fingers moved between hers, smoothed over her palms.

Her eyes were still closed, her face tilted toward him.

As if she trusted him.

His gut clenched into an uncomfortable boulder. He

forced himself to guide her hands under the stream of water and let her go. "Okay?"

She made an indecipherable murmur and bent to splash her face.

At the last second, he saved her long ponytail from falling into the sink.

There was no sign of the composed princess as she sought only relief. She even let some of the water run into her mouth.

He grabbed some paper towels and waited.

"Just give me a second," she gasped. "I think I'm all right."

"Good. I think your father might come after me if we're gone too long."

She made a sound that might be a laugh. Grabbed the edge of the sink and straightened. He pressed the paper towels into her hand.

"He's a little overprotective." She blinked and opened her eyes for the first time since they'd left their cooking station. They were red-rimmed. Her makeup had been washed off.

There was something different about the small smile she gave him. Something warm and open.

And it made that rock in his gut burn hotter.

Which was why he said, "Overprotective enough to hire all those extra bodyguards?"

She hadn't answered him back at the station because they'd been interrupted.

Now, his question seemed to put her defenses back up.

Good. That was what he needed. He couldn't think, couldn't remember the real reason he was here, when she looked at him as she had before, with tenderness and trust.

A man in a dark suit appeared in the doorway. Tirith must've seen him in the mirror.

"We're coming," she murmured. Then to Edward, "We've got to get the chili in the pot."

She didn't want to talk about the security. Which only made his curiosity burn hotter.

She leaned closer to the mirror and wrinkled her nose at her bedraggled appearance. He half expected her to call for a makeup person or even refuse to go back out there without a full face of makeup on. But she only straightened her shoulders and made for the door.

He followed, determined to press her about the bodyguards. He was a half-step behind her at the doorway, but as he crossed the threshold, there was a loud explosion. The sound echoed off the high metal ceiling. It had come from inside the building?

He reacted with pure instinct, honed from months of overseas assignments in a war zone.

He grabbed Tirith's waist and pulled her back into the bathroom, around the doorframe so she was behind the cinder block wall. He pressed close, put himself between her and the danger.

What was it? An IED? A grenade?

There was shouting, and he peered around the doorframe to see the security guys in dark suits mobilizing through the crowd. The guy who'd come after them in the bathroom was doubling back.

Edward looked down into Tirith's face. Her eyes were wide and frightened. Her breaths were shallow.

He wanted to comfort her.

He wanted to *kiss* her.

The outlandish thought was replaced quickly as the guard approached. He was listening to some message coming through his earpiece, his weapon out and pointed at the ground.

"We're clear," he said to them—no, to Tirith. "One of the cooks blew the lid off of a pot."

A cooking disaster. That was all it was.

But the princess was shaking. Or maybe he was. She took a moment to smooth out her apron before nodding to the guard, who escorted them back to their station.

If the explosion was nothing, why did Gideon Hale have

Princess Alessandra away from her station? They were talking in low voices—arguing?—behind a wall of three guards.

Others were sweeping through the crowd.

Finally, Tirith's mother and father returned to their stations, though the rancher's expression was like granite.

Tirith noticed Edward noticing all of this. And maybe something had changed between them when he'd pushed her behind him in the bathroom. She leaned in and whispered, "There's been a threat against my mother. An email, I think. She doesn't think it is anything to worry over."

But obviously Gideon Hale didn't agree. The man's gaze flicked through the crowd, not stopping anywhere for long.

"He almost lost her once," Tirith said, voice low. "When they first met." There was nostalgia in her tone, and behind it, sorrow.

That wasn't the information Edward needed, even if it was juicy.

But the camera soon returned to their station, and Edward didn't have a chance to push for more. Not yet.

Chapter Four

TWO DAYS AFTER THE CHILI COOKOFF, A SLENDER figure detached itself from the growing shadows outside the barn as Edward approached on foot.

Tirith.

The sun was setting behind the structure, and he had to squint before he could make her out. Definitely her, and he couldn't explain the beat of relief that coursed through him.

He didn't have to seek her out. Mission on.

That was all it was.

That and the fact that he was exhausted.

He'd been assigned a job repairing fence lines in the far pasture today. He'd suspected he'd been sent so far from the house and barn because Gideon Hale had seen him in close proximity to the princess during the chili cook-off.

Call it a hunch.

His horse had come up lame late in the day. When he'd called in on his two-way radio, he'd been told there wasn't a truck or trailer to send after him. He'd been forced to walk with his horse, and during the long walk under the hot evening sun, he'd wondered how Hale had engineered this punishment.

If he'd known he'd come face to face with the princess at the close of this unending day, it might've made everything worth it.

She had a slightly-too-big cowboy hat smashed low on her head and wore a T-shirt and jeans and boots that might belong to Margaret, because they were faded and broken-in.

He'd never seen Tirith so casual.

The yard was quiet. There were lights on in the farmhouse and bunkhouse, but everyone seemed to be inside. The setting sun was changing the light around them, lengthening the shadows.

"I need to ask you a favor," she asked at his approach. Her head was tilted so that silly hat hid her eyes from him.

He still had the reins in hand. He was exhausted and dirty and desperate for a shower and his bunk.

But this was Tirith. Waiting for him.

He stopped within reaching distance of her, the horse behind him. "What do you need?"

He heard the soft catch in her breath before she cleared her throat. "I was wondering if you'd saddle one of Maggie's horses for me. I'd like to take a quick turn around the corral."

She would, huh?

He let her request hang in the air between them for a long moment. She still hadn't looked up.

"It's almost dark," he said.

They both knew there was a big spotlight for the corral near the barn. It wasn't currently on, but that was an easy fix.

"Why not ask your dad?" he said when she remained quiet.

She shrugged.

What was going on?

He reached out and used his finger to tip her hat up. Her eyes flicked to him, and with her face fully revealed, he saw that she was close to tears. Her eyes were glassy and the tip of her nose was pink.

She was upset.

And she didn't want her dad. She'd come looking for Edward.

That had to mean he was getting closer to what he'd come here for. His gut knotted.

"I've got to take care of this guy first. Then I'll take care of you."

He saw emotion pass over her expression. Usually, she was better at hiding it. Was that gratitude? Or something else?

She trailed him and the horse into the barn, keeping her distance from the animal. He unsaddled the horse and gave it a rubdown and some grain. He'd already told Miles about the lameness. He'd remind the foreman in the morning, make sure the horse got checked over.

He detoured to the tack room and pulled the saddle for the horse the princess had wanted saddled a week ago. He carried it on his shoulder and joined her.

Tirith had hung her hat over one of the posts. When she caught sight of him, her gaze flicked to where his shoulder muscles stretched to carry the saddle.

Either she was getting worse at hiding her emotions from him, or she was letting him in.

He slung the saddle over the stall railing and moved to open the gate. When he reached up for the horse's halter, he did a surreptitious sniff of his armpit. He'd been doing heavy work out in the hot sun. He wasn't fresh, and he wished for a moment that he'd had a chance to shower in the bunkhouse.

Not that that was necessary. Just because she'd sought him out didn't mean she wanted him close.

She'd asked him to saddle the horse for her. *She* was the one who would be riding around the corral. He'd watch and make sure she didn't take a spill.

This was a perfect opportunity to press her about the accident. Or her mother. When he'd shot off a rapid-fire email to his editor, his boss had wanted any kind of information on the royals that Edward could get.

The exploding pot at the cook-off had been pure accident.

But the guards—and Gideon Hale—had been on high alert during the rest of the event. Gideon and Miles had called a meeting in the bunkhouse later that night. They'd kept it vague but let the cowboys know there was a threat against Tirith's mother—and the princesses by extension.

Edward had feigned sleep in his bunk until all the other hands were snoring. He'd snuck outside to sit on the back stoop with the small laptop he kept hidden in his rucksack and spent hours when he could've been sleeping digging into what the threat might be.

Turned out there was more than one person who disliked the royal family enough to make threats against them.

He needed to narrow his search. And maybe tonight he could get Tirith to give him a clue what direction he should go.

His mind whirled as he walked the horse out of the stall and slowly saddled it up. He slipped the bit into the animal's mouth and buckled the bridle.

"Thank you," Tirith murmured from behind him. "I know you've worked hard today and must be ready to get some rest."

He finished with the bridle and held the reins loosely as he turned toward her.

"I've always got time for you, highness."

He saw the hint of vulnerability in her gaze before she dropped her eyes.

Had she always been so slight? Tonight she seemed to almost fold in on herself, her hands clasped on her elbows, her arms across her midsection.

For the first time, he felt a pang of guilt at his deception.

Think of Peyton.

He imagined his niece lying bandaged in a hospital bed.

But even as his imagination overlay the image of this moment, his insides twisted. This wasn't as easy as he'd thought, in his righteous anger, it would be.

He cleared his throat and extended the reins to her. "Here you go."

She took the few steps that separated them and reached out. The hand that closed over the reins was trembling.

She stared at the animal past Edward's shoulder.

She hadn't overcome her fear of the horse at all. She was determined to bulldoze through it.

When she stepped forward and would've brushed past him, Edward reached out and stopped her. "Wait."

She was close now, close enough that he could've put his arm around her waist. Almost as close as they'd been right after the sound he'd thought was an explosion.

He gently pried the reins from her fingers and closed the tiny distance between them, stepping so he was beside her. He nudged her one step closer to the horse, took her wrist in his hand, and raised it. He pressed his right palm against the back of her left hand so that her hand was sandwiched between his and the horse's shoulder.

At this angle, they had some protection if the horse turned its head with malicious intent—not that he was expecting that to happen. Not with this docile animal.

She was holding her breath.

He let go of her hand momentarily only to replace it with his opposite hand. He stepped so he was behind her and reached for her other hand. He placed this one against the horse's neck, just beneath its mane.

He was effectively trapping her against the horse, but if she needed to move, he would let his arms fall away.

This wasn't about blocking her. He was trying something.

They stood there breathing in time with each other, with both hands pressed against the horse. The horse's skin shivered, and Tirith shivered too. He could feel her warmth, even though their bodies weren't touching. Their only point of contact was through their hands.

He angled his face toward her. He desperately wanted to

close the inch between them, press his scruffy jaw to her cheek. But he didn't.

"He's just flesh and blood," he whispered. "Just like you and me."

The truth of his words knocked into him.

Tirith might be royalty, but she wasn't so different from him. He'd seen her terror at the chili cook off. If there'd been a real emergency, she could've been injured.

She had fears. Hurts. Desires. Hopes.

What was he doing? He didn't want to see her as a real person. Only a figurehead, someone who didn't care about others, who covered up their mistakes.

He felt the tension leave her, bit by bit, even as his own tension ratcheted up.

He never should've tried to get so close to her.

He was close enough to see the curve of her cheek, the tip of her nose. She blinked, and he saw her lashes move.

She turned her face toward him, tipping her head back so that she just touched his shoulder.

"Would you ride with me?" she whispered.

———

TIRITH WALKED beside Edward as he led the horse out of the barn.

He hesitated for one moment near the industrial switch that would light up the corral. And then he kept going without flipping it.

Outside, the sun was at the horizon. A few minutes of sunset remained, and the Texas twilight could last for some time. There would be at least thirty minutes of riding time.

Edward bypassed the corral entirely, then finally paused and turned to her with raised eyebrows.

She nodded to his unanswered question. She was doing this.

But it was a relief not to have to do it alone.

She took a deep breath just before he boosted her into the saddle. The leather creaked underneath her, and her stomach dipped.

He watched her, one hand at her knee and the other still holding the reins. She firmed her chin and nodded. All the while, she was shaking inside.

He stepped into the stirrup and slid into the saddle behind her, his chest brushing her back as he settled into the seat.

He offered her the reins he held in his left hand, but she shook her head.

"One thing at a time."

Her voice was a little breathless. Maybe she could blame it on the horse, but really it was Edward's nearness that made her pulse thrum in her earlobes and her skin feel tight over her bones.

He kept the reins and settled his opposite hand at her waist. She couldn't tell whether he was trying to hold her away from him, keep some distance between them… or keep her close. He'd gone quiet back in the barn. Something kept her from asking why.

His legs flexed, and the horse began to move beneath them, taking a few slow steps.

"You gotta breathe," he said, close in her ear.

She was trying.

He made some kind of grunt and then said, "Maybe one of these days you'll catch me fresh outta the shower instead of after working for hours in the hot sun. Stinkin' of manure."

He was worried about that? Something warm lit inside her, something she didn't want to examine too closely. "You don't stink." She wrinkled her nose, rethinking the words. "It's simply… the smell of a successful day at work. Something to be proud of."

He laughed, the sound a short burst of amusement. "They teach you that in princess school? How to schmooze everybody you meet, no matter how lowly?"

"What's princess school?" She couldn't help smiling. But then she schooled her voice to be more serious. "I'm not trying to schmooze you, Edward. Or charm you."

He didn't respond to that, and she choked back the words that wanted to escape. *I like you. There's something about you that draws me.*

The horse trudged along, slowly leaving the barnyard behind. Edward made some kind of clucking sound, and the horse picked up speed, though not much.

Edward rode with a quiet confidence, completely in control. She breathed in deeply, the scents of horse and Texas wildflowers a reminder of her childhood. But those memories weren't all pleasant. It was the man at her back who somehow calmed her.

"You gonna tell me why you're so scared of horses?" he asked.

She didn't like talking about it. Didn't like thinking about it.

"You sorta owe me." His words sounded both teasing and as if he'd ground them out through clenched teeth.

She sighed. "I was thrown from a horse just before my thirteenth birthday."

Before that, she'd been as horse-crazy as Maggie. They'd been raised on the back of a horse, with Father so often riding behind, just like Edward was now.

"I was on the palace grounds in Glorvaird, and the groom who was watching over me thought perhaps the horse had been stung by a bee." She'd been a capable rider. Overconfident, maybe. Sure of her own invincibility.

"And your father didn't insist you get back on the horse?"

"My father was here, on the Triple H." With Maggie. It'd been months after the two of them had been kidnapped and held for ransom. Tirith had been trying to swim through the currents of terror to find some semblance of normalcy. Maggie hadn't been able to swim at all, and Father had brought her to the ranch, the one place she felt safe.

She never spoke of the kidnapping. It had been kept from the press. Mother never spoke of it. It was as if it had been erased. Only not in her memory.

The pause had stretched too long.

"I broke my arm rather badly. Surgery, hospital, the works. It was months before my doctors approved being back on horseback."

And when she'd tried, terror had encompassed her. She'd rushed away from the horse and vomited.

"Your father didn't figure it out?" he asked.

"No. He rarely visited Glorvaird after—it happened." And when he had, they'd only had stiff, awkward visits in the palace.

She couldn't think about that without thinking about her mother, and she didn't want to think about Mother right now.

She forced a smile into her voice. "You're a good rider. Were you raised on a ranch?"

She realized she didn't know anything about Edward. She'd been selfish to this point, thinking only about the charity events and her family's expectations.

"My brother and I had lessons when we were kids." There was something in his voice, some vagueness.

"And you ended up a cowboy."

He made a non-committal grunt.

"Are you close?" she asked.

"Our parents died when we were teens. It's been the two of us ever since. At least, until he married. I have a ten-year-old niece."

He'd tensed up, but she didn't know why.

He rushed on. "My brother's wife left when my niece was small. It's been the two of them for years. I don't get to see them as often as I'd like."

It was a niggling itch that he didn't use names. But maybe he just wanted to ensure she understood who he was talking about.

"I don't see Maggie as often as I'd like," she offered. "She and Luc split their time between Glorvaird and the Triple H. Not that I'm blaming her or anything," she hurried to say. "They're newlyweds."

"What?" he asked.

"Hmm?"

"There's something you're not saying. Weren't you—" He cut himself off. "Do you dislike your brother-in-law?"

He'd started to say one thing and then changed to something else. Why?

"Luc and I get along. We were friends before he met Maggie."

"Ah. So you've lost your sister and your friend all at once."

"I haven't lost anyone."

She hadn't. Not really. But somehow Edward had picked up on what she hadn't said.

Now his arm came around her waist. Her pulse pounded, but he only pressed the reins into her hand before she had time to protest. "Time for you to try."

The horse was still rambling along, and though adrenaline pumped through her, she was doing it.

Dusk was falling now. The moon wasn't out, and pinpricks of white stars against the velvet blue sky above decorated the night.

She knew they shouldn't stay out for long. Father had shared about the threat that had come in an e-mail and then a package delivered to the palace. She didn't want to worry her father.

But she didn't turn the horse back toward the barn. Not yet.

Riding was more familiar than she'd expected. The movement of the horse beneath her. The slight adjustments she needed with the reins. All of it came back to her in a long-dormant muscle memory.

And then she allowed herself to lean back against Edward until her head rested against the shoulder. He froze.

And then eased, adjusting slightly so that she was nestled against him.

"I needed this," she said softly. "To spend a few minutes with someone who has no agenda for me."

She felt a new tension take over his body. Had she revealed too much of herself in that simple statement?

"We should get back," he said quietly, the words a rumble against her back.

She turned her face toward him, seeking answers to his tension.

In the near-darkness she couldn't see his eyes clearly, but she could make out the planes of his jaw and the sharpness of his cheekbones.

He breathed in, every muscle she could feel against her wound tight. On a sharp exhale, he reached up to cup her cheek.

She leaned forward, and there was only a breath between their lips. A breath passed from him to her.

He held back, maybe studying her features. Why did he hesitate?

And then he made a sound low in his throat, almost a groan. It sounded of defeat.

He crossed scarce space between them and kissed her.

The ever-present connection between them sprang to life, and she felt with a deep certainty in her belly that this was right. Her heart thrummed against her breastbone like a hummingbird's wings.

The kiss began gentle and searching, but her passion seemed to ignite his, and soon she was breathing hard.

He broke the kiss, quickly turning his face away. His hand moved from her face to scrape over his lips and jaw.

"We probably shouldn't have done that," he said. He still didn't look at her.

The bottom of her stomach dropped out.

He regretted it?

Her face flamed as she guided the horse back toward the barn. There was no hesitation as she used her legs to tell the horse to speed up. Amazingly, the animal listened.

And then she was pulling up in the barnyard.

Edward dismounted first and reached for her, but she clung to the saddle horn and stepped down herself.

She couldn't look at him and stared at the saddle instead, "I'm sorry for forcing myself on you."

"Tirith."

She couldn't bear to hear what he might say, so she rushed away in the darkness toward the house.

We shouldn't have done that.

His words circled through her head on repeat.

Was he right?

She planned to return to Glorvaird after the ball. Edward was a temporary employee. She didn't even know his plans.

They came from different worlds.

But she'd started to hope that the attraction that sparked between them was real.

Apparently, she was the only one who didn't regret that incredible kiss.

Chapter Five

EDWARD SPOTTED THE PRINCESS AS HE CROSSED from the barn to the bunkhouse. Twenty-four hours had passed since he'd seen her last. He barely glanced toward the ranch house in the gathering dusk but caught sight of her standing beneath a stately maple nearby.

His feet changed direction to go to her before he was even conscious of doing it.

Maybe it wasn't her.

He could only see her from a distance. Her lips were moving as if she was talking. To the tree? Maybe the girl staring up into the tree branches overhead was Margaret. Or Bea. Or even Tirith's mother.

But his heart knew. It pushed blood singing through his veins as his feet carried him toward her.

He'd come to a decision after that disastrous kiss and her softly spoken words, *someone who has no agenda for me.*

He couldn't keep lying to her. Not now that he'd seen the real Tirith. He still didn't know why she'd agreed to the cover up after the accident, but the kindhearted princess he'd come to know would never have hurt Peyton if she could help it.

His emotions had gotten involved. His boss would tell

him they were clouding his judgment, but Edward rather thought he was seeing more clearly than ever before.

He still couldn't believe she'd kissed him.

He couldn't stop thinking about it. Couldn't forget the tiny catch in her breath just before he'd claimed her mouth. The way she'd smiled against his lips, the softness of her skin...

She wasn't the monster he'd come here to expose.

He'd lied to her from the very beginning. He couldn't change what had already happened.

Carrick didn't even know that Edward had come here. Edward had had a knee-jerk reaction when he'd seen that nondisclosure. But exposing what had happened would mean exposing Peyton to media attention too.

His boss was expecting a story. He'd given himself a self-imposed deadline. Twenty-four more hours to find out who was behind the threats against Alessandra. That would have to be enough for the paper.

He probably shouldn't go to Tirith, though he was incredibly curious about why she was talking to a tree.

He definitely should keep his distance. He wanted too badly to hold her in his arms again.

He was in trouble.

But no matter how his thoughts tumbled, his steps didn't waver.

What was she saying? He wasn't close enough to hear. Her face was uplifted to the branches above her head. She didn't seem to register his approach. Where was her bodyguard? There, standing near the corner of the house with hands loose at his sides.

The man in reflective sunglasses didn't seem to care about Edward's approach.

Edward was about to call out to her when she reached her arms above her head and jumped. He watched her disappear into the green canopy.

"Tirith?" He jogged the last few steps to stand where she'd just been. He craned his neck.

She was there, crouched on a thick branch; she held onto another near her shoulders with a white-knuckled grip. She wore a similar outfit to the one she'd worn the last time he'd seen her, though she'd exchanged the cowboy boots for sneakers.

She glanced down at him, clearly terrified. And then perturbed, her lips pinching into a white line. "What do you want, Edward?"

He let his gaze take her in.

She wasn't that high. Only six inches above his head. He could reach up and touch her ankle if he dared.

He didn't.

"One wonders why you jumped into the tree if you're scared of heights."

"One should know it's none of his business," she muttered, glancing up into the canopy above.

Ah. She was angry with him. As she should be.

"Do you want to come back down?" he asked conversationally.

"No, thank you." The words spoken through gritted teeth told him in no uncertain terms that he wasn't wanted there.

"Why not?"

She was looking upward again, and Edward didn't think she was that determined to avoid looking at him. He let his own gaze wander up through the tangle of leaves until he caught sight of the skinny orange cat that usually slunk around inside the barn. It was sitting on a branch at least ten feet above Tirith's head, near the maple's trunk.

Its tail was curled around its paws, and it stared unblinking at Tirith.

"I think he's stuck."

His heart did a funny shiver in his chest as he realized the princess had followed the cat into the tree.

"I didn't realize you were a firefighter," he said evenly.

This time the look she shot him was more exasperated

than fearful. "It's a myth that fireman use their ladder trucks to rescue cats in trees. It's not a good use of their resources."

He laughed. He couldn't help it. It was a little ridiculous. That cat was at least ten feet above her, and she hadn't moved an inch since his approach.

Even under her exasperated stare, the connection he felt when he got close to her flared to life. If she'd been on the ground, he might have taken her waist in his hands, pulled her close.

She felt it too, he was sure of it, because her gaze shuttered and she glanced away.

He cleared his throat. "That cat isn't stuck."

She stared up at the animal. "How do you know?"

"Cats climb things. We had a tabby when I was a kid. She would climb straight up the side of our chimney and sit on our roof. I've seen that cat in the hayloft." Which meant it must've figured out a way to climb the wooden ladder in the barn. There was no other way up.

But instead of dropping down, Tirith gripped the upper branch more tightly and tried to straighten her legs. The branch beneath her was wide, but it still wobbled.

She gasped and crouched back down.

He'd had a sudden terrifying vision of her falling just out of his reach. "Tirith. Come down." Was his voice shaky?

"My sister loves this ranch," she said through her teeth. "and every single animal on it. Even an annoying barn cat. I can't just leave him. I'm not frightened."

Why would she lie? He could see the terror in the way she clutched the branch, the white lines around her mouth, the flutter of her eyelashes.

There was something deeper going on here. Her determination almost reeked of desperation.

"The cat climbed into the tree," he said gently. "It can climb back down. We can stand here until it does. Even if it takes all night."

We. He'd used the pronoun to get her attention.

It worked.

She glanced down at him, and he saw the hurt she'd been trying to hide. It was there in the depths of her eyes. So was everything she wasn't saying.

What if it was another mistake?

Was he going to push her away again?

Why was he doing this?

He'd been the one to pronounce their kiss a mistake—after he'd engineered opportunities to pull her close.

We probably shouldn't have done that.

He'd handled things badly from the very beginning.

"I'm sorry about last night," he said. "Things got complicated, and I panicked."

"Complicated how?"

He took too long to answer. She looked off into the distance, her eyes narrowing.

The cat watched them with gleaming eyes. Edward was a little afraid it was going to pounce down on top of him.

"Complicated because... I like you."

She looked back at him, vulnerability and hope shining in her eyes. It was the vulnerability there that unmanned him.

He reached up and gently clasped her ankle in one hand. "Will you please come down?"

She finally glanced past him to the ground. Took a shaky breath. "I don't know how."

She'd pulled herself into the tree—a feat of strength—but was afraid to drop down?

She closed her eyes and shook her head slightly, clinging to that branch. He was a bit jealous of a tree; he'd like her to cling to him. "Last time I fell, I broke my arm."

"Then I won't let you fall."

Her eyes opened and connected with his. He saw the struggle she was going through. He'd hurt her once. Could she trust him?

He ignored the guilty pang inside.

She shifted slightly, and he knew her legs had to be tired of holding that crouching position.

"Sit on the branch like it's a swing. You can drop down, and I'll catch you. I promise."

————

"DROP DOWN and I'll catch you."

It sounded easy when Edward said it.

But Tirith couldn't seem to let go of the branch her arms were wrapped around.

Edward's hand was warm on her ankle. She tried to tell herself she wasn't that far from the ground. If she could land on her feet, even if Edward didn't catch her, she would probably be all right.

But there was no guarantee.

Why had she chased the stupid cat up into the stupid tree?

"I know you're thinking about when you got thrown and broke your arm. You must've been lonely and bored during those months of recovery. You probably missed your dad like crazy."

How had he guessed?

Edward's eyes were warm and compassionate.

It was a reminder of what she'd wished for so long ago. For her father to be there with her. For him to look at her like that. Wrap her in his arms and tell her everything was going to be all right.

But Maggie had needed him, too, and Tirith had never told him how much she needed him on the rare phone calls she'd shared with her dad.

"I'm right here," Edward said. Edward, who wasn't going to let her fall. He'd promised. He watched her with a steadiness that comforted her.

She wanted to believe him.

He must have seen acquiescence in her expression,

because he let go of her ankle. "Sit down on the branch instead of crouching. You can drop right down."

Moving felt too scary. When she'd tried to stand, the branch beneath her had swayed She'd thought she was slipping off.

Edward didn't falter. "Sitting or standing, I'm going to catch you."

She exhaled a breath that was more tremble than air. She wrapped her arm fully around the branch that was at chest level and slowly maneuvered until she was seated on the wide branch where she'd been squatting.

Edward reached up to squeeze her calf. "There we go. Now for the easy part. Let go of the branch and drop down into my arms."

She scrunched up her nose. "I have to let go?"

"'Fraid so."

She glanced back at the ornery cat who'd fooled her and gotten her into this problem. "Did you know, this branch is more comfortable than I thought. Ralph and I can live up here. You can bring me food and water."

His eyebrows rose. "Ralph?"

"He looks like a Ralph, doesn't he?" She nudged her head toward the cat.

His eyes were warm and if she focused only on them, she could ignore the dizziness that wanted to distract her. He looked tired. Worn out.

He tugged on the tip of her sneaker. "Come on, highness. Let go." There was warm affection in his voice instead of the sarcasm she'd heard that first day.

He took a half-step back so he wasn't directly underneath her. He held out his hands.

She let go of the branch above her and pushed herself slightly forward. She slipped off her seat on the lower branch.

She saw surprise in his eyes, but he caught her against him as she fell, her belly against his chest. His arms came around her waist, and then he set her on her feet. He steadied her with his hands at her waist.

"That was fast. After all your dawdling, I was expecting you to count to three. Or three hundred." One corner of his mouth tipped up, but his eyes were serious.

She tipped her chin. "Princesses don't dawdle. A princess is always perfectly on time."

"Ah. My mistake."

His teasing words were a reminder of the way they'd ended things last night. Awkwardness descended. He let go of her waist and stepped back.

She lowered her gaze and murmured, "Thank you for the rescue."

She expected him to make some excuse and return to the bunkhouse, but his hand clasped hers.

"Do princesses sit on the grass without a picnic blanket?" He didn't wait for an answer, just tugged her toward the base of the tree. She sat, and he lowered beside her, shoulder-to-shoulder.

He tilted his head up to see the furry animal in the branches above. "How'd you end up out here anyway?"

She didn't know if he was talking to the cat or to her. "I'm supposed to be cataloguing the last-minute entries for Maggie's silent auction. I just... needed a break."

Mother had come to check on her one too many times. It was stifling, being in the same room with her, with so many things unsaid. And heaven forbid Father be inside the house at the same time Mother was.

Tirith leaned her head back against the trunk. She closed her eyes. "You were right," she said quietly. "I did miss my father after I broke my arm." *I still miss him.* She swallowed back the unhelpful words. "I never asked him to come see me, though. So it's partly my fault."

It took a moment before Edward responded, his voice low. "Why not?"

"Because Maggie needed him."

Just the fact that he'd stayed, that he was keeping his promise to wait for the silly cat with her, made something open up deep inside her.

"Just before our twelfth birthday, Maggie and I were kidnapped from under our bodyguard's protection." She'd never told anybody that before.

Edward went tense beside her and his hand seemed to tighten involuntarily on hers.

"It didn't last long," she said quickly. "And we weren't harmed. Just frightened. After... Maggie couldn't handle being in Glorvaird. Making appearances. Being in crowds. Father brought her back here, to the Triple H, where she felt safe."

"What about you?" There was a harshness in his voice. "Where did you feel safe?"

"On my horse," she whispered. The silver gelding had been so fast... fast enough to race away if someone came too close.

"Only that turned out to be dangerous, too," he murmured.

He saw through her too easily.

She tilted her head upward. Checked on the cat. Still there.

Edward angled toward her. He brushed a strand of hair from where it was caught in her eyelashes. He was close, his gaze both tender and probing.

"Hey," he whispered.

She smiled. There was something about his presence that made those painful memories fade.

His fingers slid across her cheek, his touch soft and seeking. His fingers slid into her hair, tipping her head back slightly.

"What are you doing?" she breathed against his lips.

"Complicating things." And then his lips closed over hers, and she didn't have time to wonder what he meant.

He kept the kiss gentle and light, filled with such tenderness that it warmed her from the inside out, filling up all the cracks from her broken childhood.

When he turned his head and eased back from the kiss, her stomach twisted. But he only settled her closer against him, his arm around her shoulders.

He glanced up into the tree. Apparently the cat was still there.

"And your mother?"

It took a moment for her to register his question, remember what they were talking about.

"Did she help you through those months?"

Usually, thinking about her mother brought on so many difficult feelings. But with her head leaning against Edward's shoulder, she only felt a ghost of the usual swirl of emotions.

"Mother was in the middle of a long and difficult trade negotiation with one of our neighboring countries. She was often at home, but she was so busy..."

He pressed a kiss to her temple. "And?"

"And I didn't want to be a bother. I told myself I was fine."

Only she wasn't. She hadn't been fine in a long time.

"I started having panic attacks when I was fifteen. I didn't know what was happening at first. And then... I hid it. Anxiety isn't a very royal emotion. The attacks got worse. And then, two years ago, I—"

She blinked away memories of the flashing emergency lights, of Peyton's crumpled body.

She'd caused that.

This was the moment. Talking about her fragile mental state made her terribly uncomfortable, and she felt the discomfort seeping in now.

She edged away from Edward, but he caught her hand and twined their fingers together. "Tirith. Whatever you tell me won't go any farther."

She turned her face away, hiding from him. Shame suffused her. "I've only spoken about it to my therapist."

She was still working through the muddle that was her life. A part of her wanted to get up. Put some physical distance between Edward and this difficult conversation. He must've felt the slight way she turned from him. Barely a movement at all.

"If you can't tell me, then just... stay."

Did he care? Because she was starting to fall for him. And if she stayed, her heart would only get more tangled up.

She settled back against him, ignoring the way her derrière was going numb sitting on the hard ground.

She'd managed to tell Edward about her panic attacks, her anxiety, and he wanted to stay close to her.

Maybe it was dangerous to allow her heart to get involved with him. They were certainly different. She didn't know where he would go after his time on the Triple H was done.

But when she was with him, she felt... at peace. As if she could, one day, like herself again.

Chapter Six

Edward ran the words through again and again as he sidled up to the horse secured in its trailer and untied its lead.

He had to tell Tirith the truth. Why he'd come. That he'd had a change of heart.

That he'd lied to her.

His plans to dig into the threat against Alessandra and leave had changed after Tirith's heartfelt confessions under the maple tree. He didn't want any negative attention pointed toward her or her family.

She wasn't a monster. She was a woman trying to deal with the trauma in her own past.

His cell phone buzzed in his pocket. He glanced at it and refused the call. He couldn't talk to Holly right now. His boss would be furious that Edward had spent weeks on this story and would have nothing to show for it.

He had morals. Professional ethics.

And what Tirith was going through was nobody's business but hers.

But sometime over the past few days, he'd begun to want

to be a part of her life. To be the one she shared her hurts with.

He didn't know if that would be possible once he told her the truth of his identity.

But he had to try.

He used the horse's halter to lead it down the ramp before he tied it off on the side of the trailer.

There was noise and activity all around. The parking area where all the horse trailers were congregated was packed with trucks and horses and competitors preparing for the rodeo. Barrel racers and ropers were settling their horses. He'd seen one teen girl giving her horse's tail a fancy braid.

He had to admit he'd been a little starstruck by some of the famous rodeo names the royal family had managed to wrangle into this event.

Edward hefted the fancy saddle and began to secure it, aware of the heavy boot steps approaching from around the truck.

Gideon Hale's strident voice rang out, calling out the false name Edward had given. "Bouchard."

Edward had had a recurring nightmare about the ex-operator discovering his identity and making him disappear forever. The man was probably just checking up on his daughter's horse.

Edward worked to keep his voice even and unaffected. "Mr. Hale. What can I do for you?"

"You can leave my daughter alone."

Edward glanced only briefly at Hale, long enough to see the black vest over his dress jeans and fancy felt hat. Was he entering an event? Edward kept working on the currycomb, running his free hand over the horse's shoulder and side. "I'm not sure what you're talking about."

Gideon stepped closer, forcing Edward to drop the currycomb and focus on him. "Don't play games with me."

Not good. "What game?"

Hale's stare was hard. "Do you want to tell me who you really are?"

Everything inside Edward went still. Had Hale found him out? What did he know? Edward hadn't been grabbed and escorted bodily off the premises. Maybe Hale was simply bluffing?

The horse stamped one of its front hooves, obviously picking up on the tension Edward was attempting to hide. Hale knew horses. Edward was going to have to do a better job if he didn't want to be found out right this second.

Edward showed his teeth. Not quite a smile. "I'm Edward." He left off his last name. No use lying now, not when he didn't know how deep Hale had dug.

"That's the name you gave us, but the more I look into you, the more your background seems a little too put-together to be real."

Edward's pulse was still pounding, but his thoughts were clear. Hale was guessing, fishing for information.

Edward had been on the *asking questions* side of the interrogator's table enough times that he knew the best thing he could do was stay calm. Miles had tasked him with readying Tirith's horse. So he kept on securing her saddle, tightening the girth, buckling the stirrup into place.

"Why're you so interested in me?"

Hale didn't hesitate. "Because you seem to be interested in my daughter."

Where had the man's protective nature been when Tirith had been a hurting teen? When she'd needed her father's comfort and he'd been absent? Edward wanted to push for answers to those questions, though he knew he didn't have the right.

Edward had barely finishing securing the saddle when Hale grabbed his shoulder and spun him around so they were face-to-face. Edward worked to hold on to his temper even as Gideon stared at him with hard, glittering eyes.

The horse's tail swished. Its ears twitched on high alert.

"There are some really nasty people who've threatened my family. If one of them decided to try and get close, masquerading as a ranch hand would be a good way to do it."

"I don't want to hurt your family."

The words tasted like ash in his mouth. Edward had come here intending to do just that. He'd planned for Tirith to be humiliated, her family exposed when he'd uncovered what she'd done to Peyton. He'd arrived on the Triple H full of self-righteousness.

And then he had gotten to know Tirith.

He had let himself get confused. Peyton and Carrick deserved justice. But if what Tirith said was true, if her inattention had been due to a panic attack, as he suspected, and not negligence, that changed everything. And she'd tried to make things right by paying Peyton's medical bills, if he'd understood what the NDA and Carrick's emails meant.

Hale somehow saw Edward's whirling thoughts. Or maybe he just sensed blood in the water. "If you aren't one of the Bello family's minions, then what are you? A reporter?"

The accusation hit too close to home. Edward worked to keep his expression neutral. "Why? Do you have skeletons in your closet? You got some reason for staying separated from your wife all these years?"

He knew the words were a mistake as soon as they left his lips.

Hale grabbed the collar of his shirt, and Edward braced for a punch.

It didn't come.

"I want you out of here," Hale said, voice dangerously low. "Off the Triple H tonight. You can check in with Miles at the ranch house and pick up your pay."

Edward started to protest, but before he could get a word out, Tirith rounded the back of the trailer.

Hale let go of Edward so fast that he almost stumbled.

Confusion passed over Tirith's expressive face. "What's going on?"

"Nothing," Hale answered firmly. He shot a look at Edward, who considered blurting out, *Your father just fired me!* But that would sound like sour grapes. And then he registered her outfit.

She wore a vest of the colors of the Glorvaird flag over a bright white shirt with sequins down the outside of each sleeve. Her hair had been fussed and sprayed into a traditional Texas style that made him smile. Her face was too made up, probably so her features would be visible under the harsh lights of the stadium. She wore fancy jeans with blue sequins down the side of them too and red cowboy boots.

He'd never seen a more beautiful rodeo cowgirl.

And he couldn't ruin her moment. Not when she was nervous about getting on the back of the horse.

"Daddy, what—?"

"We're fine." Edward brushed past Hale. When the man would've stopped him, he raised his chin and glared.

"You look beautiful, highness." He brushed a kiss against her cheek. "I'll see you later."

Let Hale think he was complying.

Things weren't finished between him and Tirith. He needed to talk to her. Find a way to tell her the truth. Find a way to be in her life.

But this was her moment. And he wouldn't take it from her.

———

She couldn't do this.

Tirith stood next to Ace's head, holding the horse's reins with shaking hands. After Edward had disappeared, Father had helped her check the horse's cinch and bridle and left her with Maggie at the bustling area outside the arena gate.

Maggie was already seated on her horse several yards away, chatting with a girl who held a Texas state flag. Maggie's

United States flag was secured in its special leather rig attached to the saddle.

Tirith eyed the Glorvaird flag attached to her own saddle. It didn't seem to bother the horse. All she had to do was hold it steady with one hand. Hold the reins in the other.

It would be just like riding around the corral at home.

Except it wasn't the same at all.

Flood lights illuminated the stadium. The stands were packed. Maggie should be proud of herself. This was a great turnout.

Tirith didn't know where Father had disappeared to. Maybe checking on Mother and Bea, who were watching from the viewing box installed on the far end of the arena, near where the announcer was stationed. There'd been words exchanged between them earlier. Father still didn't want Mother to be out in such a public setting.

Mother hadn't raised her voice, had used only stilted and polite words, but she'd scoffed at Father's worry and told him in no uncertain terms that she would attend Maggie's rodeo.

Tirith had been on the other side of Mother's cold dismissal just that morning when she'd brought up her proposal again.

Anxiety rose inside her, choking off her breath.

Mother thought Tirith was going to muck things up. Maybe she was right.

"You okay there? Need help mounting up?"

She shook her head as she waved off the friendly cowboy who'd approached. What she needed was a time machine so she could go back and tell Maggie she wasn't doing this.

It didn't matter that she'd ridden the horse around the corral all on her own yesterday. There hadn't been a thousand pairs of eyes watching her yesterday.

She caught Maggie's worried gaze and tried to smile. She turned away quickly, afraid her expression had looked more like a grimace.

All of a sudden, the chatter around her seemed to quiet. Was she having an all-out panic attack?

No.

Everyone had mounted up.

It was time to go in there.

Tirith attempted to swallow her fear. She slipped her foot in the stirrup and pulled herself into the saddle. The leather creaked beneath her weight. Her horse blew and shook its head as it felt the tension she was holding in her back. It took one step to the right.

She wasn't going to be able to keep the horse under control. What had she been thinking? She was going to get thrown.

From her perch on the horse's back, she had a better view of the crowd.

She squinted against the bright stadium lights. Earlier when she'd seen Edward near the horse trailer, he'd been wearing a blue-and-white checked shirt with silver snaps. Under the black cowboy hat, his jaw showed two days' worth of stubble.

A man sitting in the third row of the stadium seats could've passed for his doppelgänger.

As she watched, his stare zeroed in on her. It *was* Edward!

He nodded at her, his mouth hinting at the curve of a smile.

I'll catch you.

Edward believed in her. He'd listened to her, encouraged her.

Even if her nerves got her tossed from the horse, he'd be there to scoop her up.

She forced herself to relax the hand that held the horse's reins. She exhaled a long breath and some of her jangling nerves.

The wide gates into the arena were opened by two long-legged cowboys, and she heard a deep voice over the loudspeaker, though she couldn't make out the words. And then Maggie was beside her.

"You ready?" Maggie asked.

Tirith reached out her left hand and steadied the flag pole attached to her saddle. She glanced past her sister to catch Edward's eye once more. "Let's go."

She lost sight of Edward, concentrating on getting the horse into the brightly lit arena the way she and Maggie had practiced earlier in the day on foot. Tirith stayed on the inside, with Maggie at her right, a half step ahead.

She was doing it.

Her chin lifted in triumph as she rode past the glass-enclosed box where her mother must be sitting. *Look at me. I'm all right.*

She was going to push her proposal past Mother. Earn the approval of her aunt, the ruling monarch. Maybe even later tonight.

There was one terrifying moment when Maggie kicked her horse into a trot. They hadn't practiced that, but her sister sent her a look with her eyebrows lifted. A dare. Tirith was rusty in the saddle, but she wasn't going to let her sister best her.

She posted up and asked her horse for a trot. Her form must look terrible compared to Maggie's, but the faster pace allowed the flags to unfurl behind them in all their glory.

And then it was over.

Tirith's cheeks were aching from smiling so widely as she followed Maggie out of the arena. The other riders who had paraded in the arena behind them crowded around, and she felt a moment of nervousness as her horse shifted beneath her. Maggie tipped her head, and Tirith followed her out of the chaos into a holding area closer to where all the horse trailers were parked.

Both sisters dismounted, and Maggie reached for Tirith's reins. Tirith might have overcome her fear, but she was content to let her sister take the horse. Maggie nodded to someone behind Tirith. She turned to see that Edward was there, striding toward her.

She was so intensely happy that she threw herself at him, not caring who watched. He caught her with his hands at her waist while her arms went around his neck.

She was exultant. A laugh rang out of her throat.

She had done it.

She gazed up into his face and knew that everything she was feeling must be written on her face, but for once she didn't care. She saw recognition in his eyes and the warm affection that followed. He tipped his head toward her. She lifted her chin for his kiss.

But her father's strident voice broke through the haze of her joy. "Tirith."

And then, "I told you to stay away from my daughter."

Edward's hands fell away from her waist. She was forced to step back as Father invaded Edward's personal space.

She hadn't understood the scene near her horse trailer earlier, but she'd had only minutes before her ride into the arena. She hadn't had time for questions. She didn't understand the tension between the two men now.

"What is going on?" she demanded.

Father's gaze turned to her, and her stomach dropped at the fierceness in his expression. "Your *friend* here is a journalist." His disgusted tone said exactly what he thought of Edward's friendship.

The bottom of her stomach dropped out. A journalist? It couldn't be true.

Father turned back to Edward. "One of my contacts sent over your file ten minutes ago."

There was guilt written clearly on Edward's face even as his eyes pleaded with her.

"Edward?" Her voice sounded far away to her own ears.

"Let me explain."

But Father was pushing him away from her. "I told you to

stay away from my daughter. You've got two minutes to vacate this property."

A bulky bodyguard was closing in behind Father.

She was frozen in place, both hot and cold at the same time.

Maggie was there, her hand at Tirith's elbow.

Maggie.

Tirith had told Edward about Maggie. About the kidnapping. About her resentment, her sorrow. The panic attacks.

Coldness slipped over her body like an icy blanket. There were people all around, voices and curious stares. This felt surreal, as if she was watching from outside her body.

Edward had lied to her.

His eyes were almost wild as he stared at her.

"Tirith, it's not what you think. Just give me five minutes."

She couldn't give him that. She couldn't bear to see him any longer.

She closed her eyes and let Maggie lead her away.

Edward called out after her. She heard a scuffle as he must've tried to follow. She couldn't look back.

What had she done?

She started to say something, apologize to Maggie, but the sound that emerged was more moan that words.

Maggie shushed her. "We'll figure everything out. Just not right this moment."

This was Maggie's moment. Maggie's fundraiser.

And Tirith had caused enough chaos for one evening.

She opened her eyes. Squeezed her sister's arm. "You've got to get ready for your ride." The barrel racing portion of the evening would begin soon, and Maggie was the crowd favorite.

Maggie watched her with concern, compassion clear in the depths of her eyes. Maybe she hadn't understood. She hadn't been standing near when Father had revealed Edward's occupation.

Or maybe she understood too well. They'd always had an uncanny knack at reading each other's feelings.

"I'm fine," Tirith insisted. She wasn't. She might not ever be again. "I'll join Mother in the box." It was the last place she wanted to be but probably the safest place on the property.

No doubt Mother would have something to say about what Tirith had done. She'd let a journalist get close to her, uncover family secrets. It wasn't the scandal Mother had been worried about, but it was another strike against Tirith.

Maybe Mother was right. Maybe she wasn't the right person to head up a new royal initiative.

She was a disaster.

Chapter Seven

EDWARD DIDN'T KNOW WHAT HE'D EXPECTED, BUT it wasn't to see Peyton sitting cross-legged on the floor across from a young woman in scrubs. His niece was giggling at something the woman had said.

She looked so... normal.

Edward hung back in the hallway, his brother's living room open before him as he watched his niece. He'd used his key—Carrick might take it away after Edward had a frank conversation with him tonight—to gain access to his brother's Glorvaird apartment. His flight had landed late enough in the evening that he'd thought Peyton would be in bed.

Apparently, he was wrong.

She was taller than he remembered. It had been months since he'd been home.

Too long.

Peyton was growing up, and he was missing it. She still looked as sweet as ever, with the spray of freckles across her face and her lashes making dark fans against her cheeks when she looked down.

She was still Peyton.

His heart swelled with love for his niece. He backed up a

step, not wanting to interrupt. When he glanced down the hallway, Carrick was watching him from his office doorway.

Carrick's expression was closed-off, his gaze cool. He nodded farther down the hallway, and Edward moved silently into the kitchen. His brother followed.

"You mind if I make some coffee?" Edward asked, voice low, not wanting to disrupt Peyton and her helper.

"Fine." Carrick's shortness was probably merited. Edward had shown up out of the blue.

He needed to find the right words to apologize, but he was exhausted and heartsick.

He hadn't had a chance to speak to Tirith. Last night, he'd been escorted not just off the Triple H, but all the way to the airport. His burly, armed escort had followed him until he'd boarded the plane. Destination: London. Apparently, Gideon Hale's contact had discovered everything about Edward, including his home address. Edward had caught a flight from there directly to Glorvaird.

During his layover, he'd tried to call Tirith, but she'd blocked his number. His texts had never been delivered.

He hadn't slept.

He couldn't stop thinking about the shock and betrayal he'd seen on her expression before she'd carefully blanked her features.

He'd tried to get to her, but her father had blocked his way and then physically restrained him. Edward had gotten a punch in the stomach and his arm twisted behind his back before she'd been out of sight and he'd gone limp. Given up.

He'd hurt her with his lies. His quest for revenge.

During the airplane ride, he'd tried to imagine a way that he could see her.

This couldn't be the end for them.

She'd return to Glorvaird after the charity ball. Maybe he could make an official request to see her through the palace. Unless she refused him.

His exhausted brain hadn't been able to come up with any good ideas.

Because he knew he didn't deserve a second chance. Or her forgiveness. He wouldn't blame her if she never wanted to see him again.

Right now he needed to focus on Carrick and Peyton.

The single-cup coffee maker had stopped its drip, and he took the mug and faced his brother.

"What are you doing here?" Carrick looked tired. Lines fanned his eyes, and his shirt was rumpled. Edward felt a beat of guilt. He should've come sooner, been here to help his brother.

"I... did something stupid."

Carrick crossed his arms over his chest and waited for Edward to go on.

"I came home to see you guys. About two months ago."

He'd surprised Carrick with that information. Probably because he hadn't actually seen either of them. "I got in really late. I knew you were at the hospital, so I stopped in to sleep for a few hours." He'd planned to join them at the hospital first thing in the morning. "I had a thought for an article I didn't want to forget and went into your office to find a pen. Your computer was booted up. Your email was open."

Carrick's eyes flashed fire. "You snooped through my emails?"

Edward met his angry stare head-on, coffee forgotten. "I saw the royal seal and I..." *Couldn't help myself.* He didn't say that. He could've. He'd just chosen to override his good sense. "I invaded your privacy."

Carrick turned to face the cabinetry. He gripped the counter and dropped his head. "I signed an NDA. You broke into my computer, got into my private emails, but I guess it's still my fault. I should've had it password protected."

"That's not all of it."

Carrick's head came up, and Edward flinched at the fury in his expression. "Please tell me you did *not* write something

—" He cut himself off, shaking his head. "Of course you wrote something."

Edward's throat was dry, but he forced the words out. "I went to America. To confront the royal family. I made a mistake. They know I'm a journalist and it won't take much for them to link me to you." Saying the words brought back the memory, not of those terrible final moments together, but of Tirith's quiet trust when she'd shared with him about the kidnapping, about a young girl who'd missed her dad. She'd shared her deepest wound with him.

Carrick slammed one hand on the counter, apparently no longer trying to be quiet. "How could you? Do you know how exorbitant Peyton's hospital bills are? Every bill for her care has been paid for"—he lowered his voice, apparently remembering they weren't alone in the apartment—"by the royal family. But only if I honor the NDA." He let loose a stream of curse words that Edward had never heard his usually-reserved brother say. "Where am I going to get the funds to pay it all back?"

Carrick's anger had morphed into desperation.

Edward's chest felt tight. He'd done this. Pushed Carrick to the point of tears with worry over his little girl. "I'm sorry." The words were so inadequate. "I'll pay whatever it takes." He had a small nest egg saved up, and his apartment in London. He could sell that, though his equity wouldn't be enough to pay *exorbitant* hospital bills.

"I don't want your money." Carrick's voice had gone cold. He stared at the wall, not even looking at Edward. "And Peyton and I don't need someone like you in our lives."

The words cut like a knife. Edward had come here to make things right, but he'd only hurt Carrick. Hurt Peyton. His eyes burned. "I'm sorry."

Carrick shook his head, still unable to look at Edward. "You've always been more dedicated to your job than our relationship. I don't know why I'm surprised that you'd do this."

Edward flinched as if he had been struck. "That's not true." His words were an instinctive denial.

"You missed my high school graduation because you were too busy playing journalist." Carrick didn't even have to think about the accusation. The words were quick cuts, as if he'd played the duel of this part of the conversation over and over.

The old grief expanded in Edward's chest, joining the other constant pain. "That's not why."

Was Carrick even listening?

Edward rushed on, afraid his brother was about to throw him out of the apartment. "After Dad died, I could barely keep your tuition current." Carrick had needed consistency. At least that's what Edward had believed. He'd thought the Glorvaird boarding school would provide it. And Edward had been sent on assignment all the time. He was gone more than he was home. "I wrote sixteen hours a day." He'd freelanced on top of his journalist work, writing for any publication that would pay him. "You couldn't go on to university without your transcript, and I knew they wouldn't release it if your tuition was unpaid."

Carrick peered at Edward now, his eyes flashing disbelief.

"It killed me not to be there. I made the best choice I could." His boss at the time had been particularly hard-nosed. Edward had been on assignment. If he'd left to attend Carrick's graduation, he would've been fired. And then he wouldn't have been able to pay the tuition.

"Why didn't you say anything?"

"Say anything like what? We were both in survival mode."

Carrick's voice was choked with emotion. "If you had just told me that you wanted to be there. Just a phone call to let me know that you cared, I wouldn't have felt so alone."

Carrick had felt this way for years? This was what had driven the wedge between them?

Edward didn't know how to cross the gulf between them. But he had to try. "I wanted to be there. For all of it."

Carrick stared at him with a grim frown. Maybe Edward's emotional declaration was too little, too late.

And then Carrick's expression crumpled. "I needed you. I need you. But not as some avenging angel. Peyton and I need you in our lives every day."

Edward's throat was hot and tight. Was Carrick giving him a second chance?

———

TIRITH KNEW SHE SHOULDN'T, but she hit the spacebar on her computer, and the footage played again.

She recognized the interior of the 4-H building, the setup for the chili cook-off. But this clip wasn't edited like the pieces that had been added to Maggie's charity website.

Maggie had sent it to her directly. It was a rough cut of the excruciating moments when she'd touched her face after chopping that darned jalapeño pepper.

She zeroed in on Edward. He scowled directly into the computer screen. *"Turn the camera off. You can come back to us later."*

And then he pulled her to his chest. She remembered that moment. Remembered the way her eyes stung and watered so badly, remembered the feeling of safety when he'd tucked her into him.

Right now she couldn't stop staring at his face, recorded for eternity. The way he looked at her puffy, tearing face...

That wasn't the sly look of a man who was using her for his own gain.

He looked at her like... like she was something precious. As if he was surprised to find a treasure in his hands.

She blinked and glanced up from the screen, not really taking in the sleek hotel suite's sitting room around her. She closed the laptop, wishing she could close off her roiling emotions just as easily. She needed to clear her head. She was expecting company. Why had Maggie sent this clip to her?

Late into the night after the rodeo, there'd been a family meeting—with the PR team from the palace joining via video —and Tirith had been forced to confess to all of it. Her growing friendship with Edward. The things she'd confided to him.

She'd kept her true feelings to herself, not willing to divulge to her judgmental mother just how deeply she'd fallen for Edward's con. But later that night, Maggie had come to her room, and Tirith hadn't been able to keep the truth inside any longer. She'd told Maggie everything. How Edward had charmed her. How he'd listened. How her feelings for him had grown.

Maggie had told her that she hadn't done anything wrong by opening her heart. It was Edward who had lied to her.

The knowledge he'd gained was a PR nightmare.

But two days after the rodeo, not a hint of it had hit the media. Was Edward simply biding his time?

Her heart wanted to believe that because no story had appeared in the news, it meant Edward hadn't betrayed her.

Maggie's video clip was making the confusion worse.

Tirith couldn't afford to hope. Whatever relationship she'd believed was unfolding with Edward was fiction. She'd needed to show her mother that she was capable of running this new initiative.

And then the fiasco with Edward had happened.

She'd only begun to believe in herself again.

And this thing with Edward—as awful as it was— couldn't take that away.

A soft knock on the door brought her out of her thoughts. Her cousin Valentin stuck his head inside. "Can I come in?"

"Of course." She stood to receive the hug he offered.

She and Val had become close after Maggie and Dad had left Glorvaird. They'd commiserated over living under their mothers' thumbs in the palace.

She was ashamed that she'd let their friendship fade after

the accident. She hadn't wanted to share her struggle with him.

It was time she took back her life.

"Thank you for meeting with me," she murmured as they sat on adjacent sofas. He didn't settle into the furniture but sat forward with his elbows loosely on his knees, giving her his full attention.

"Crystal will be sorry she missed the chance to see you."

His fiancée, Crystal, was a delight. They would have to catch up later.

"I know you don't have long to chat," she started.

She was surprised when he reached out and put his hand over hers. "I have as long as you need. What's up?"

Tears smarted. What had she done to be so blessed by the family she had?

"I want to start a new royal initiative. A charity, maybe."

She saw his slight hesitation and guessed at the cause. "I've spoken to my mother, but she's worried about the image of the royal family." Mother's thoughts on this subject were outdated and wrong. Still, Tirith needed to finesse this conversation.

Valentin nodded for her to go on.

"Have you ever been close to someone who suffers from anxiety or depression?" Her chest tightened at the question. She wasn't used to speaking so openly about this. But she'd learn to grow comfortable.

Valentin considered her. "I don't know. Have I?"

Her cousin was perceptive. His steady, compassionate manner made it easier for her to find the words to tell him about what she'd been through. About the things she'd learned about herself, how she'd grown, where she still needed support.

He listened to all of it, including her ideas on how the royal family should be speaking out against the stigma of mental illness. She told him her preliminary plans and where she wanted to go with the charity.

By the time she was finished, Val had cast off his suit jacket and loosened his tie. He sat back in the sofa with one leg crossed over his knee. One hand rested across the back of the furniture while the other hand tapped against its arm. He was deep in thought, considering every angle.

"This is important work," he said.

The last little bit of tension she'd held as she'd explained herself was whisked away. Her cousin, her dear friend, understood. Even when Mother couldn't.

"I'll speak to my mother," he said, "but her agreement isn't necessary for you to start your work. If you'll write up a proposal, I can present it during the next council meeting."

Her eyes blurred with tears as she moved across the space to hug her cousin.

He patted her back and then let her ease back into her seat.

Valentin's acceptance would help her get one step closer to the goal she'd set for herself. She was both elated and filled with nervous anticipation. Now, she must get to work.

After the charity ball in two days.

And maybe throwing herself into this work would help her forget about Edward.

Chapter Eight

THIS WAS IT.

Tirith stood at the top of a wide staircase, the expansive ballroom laid out before her. Men in tuxedos, women in dresses of every color. The guests mingled and chatted.

And watched as the members of the royal family were announced. Including Tirith.

She had imagined this moment numerous times over the past few weeks. In some of her most far-fetched dreams, she had pictured herself standing at the top of this elegant staircase on Edward's arm.

But she was here alone.

And she was going to have to learn to be content with that.

She had her family.

She and Maggie had dressed together, both of them giggling the way they had when they'd been young girls.

Val had promised Tirith a dance after he took a turn around the parquet floor with his fiancée. He'd already spoken with his mother about Tirith's new charity. Tirith would hit the ground running when she returned to Glorvaird.

She and her father had finally cleared the air about those lost years after the kidnapping. Dad had apologized for not being there when she'd needed him. Admitting her feelings hadn't been that bad. They were already finding a way back to the closeness they'd once shared.

This solitude wouldn't last forever.

Her elegant designer gown swirled around her when she took her place at the top of the stairs after she'd been announced. Her gaze caught on the two massive chandeliers overhanging the ballroom. They were huge works of art, curls of metal and crystal.

There was applause from the assembled guests and, for one breathless moment, she thought she saw Edward's dark-haired figure among the crowd.

She was being ridiculous.

Edward wasn't a knight in shining armor. She didn't *need* a knight in shining armor.

She had herself.

She smiled as cameras flashed, the approved media wearing noticeable name tags on lanyards around their necks.

She barely felt the stab of hurt at the thought of another member of the press.

She moved downstairs and was mingling with the crowd when she caught sight of Maggie several yards away. Her sister's eyes were huge, and not with excitement. Why did she look anxious? She made a motion with her hand that Tirith couldn't decipher. A tall man interrupted Tirith's view of her sister, and the press of people obscured her.

Tirith made her excuses, intending to go find Maggie, when the crowd parted.

All of a sudden, she came face to face with Edward.

He was wearing a tailored tuxedo with a black bowtie, and he was so intensely handsome with his chiseled jaw shaved clean and those piercing eyes that she stumbled. She stared openly at him, unable to comprehend what was happening.

Other people swirled around then, moving around in the ballroom. But she was frozen.

"Hello, Tirith."

How did he have the brain function needed to speak? Her heart was pounding. She didn't think she could form words.

"Can we talk?" His expression read grim.

"I have nothing to say to you."

She spoke the words she was expected to say—she wouldn't share anything with him, not when he had the power to hurt her family—but it cost her. Oh, how it cost her.

And he saw it too. She saw the echo of her hurt in the twist of his lips.

She couldn't do this. Couldn't face him in this public space and keep her composure.

She spun on her heel, frantically searching the periphery of the room for an escape.

But he caught her elbow in his hand. "Tirith, please. Just for a moment."

She wouldn't cry out, wouldn't give him the satisfaction of causing a scene. She glanced over her shoulder at him. Where was his press badge? Had he been able to waltz right in the front door?

She didn't have a chance to pull her elbow from his grasp.

There was a loud *pop*. Then another.

Several voices in the crowd cried out.

A distinct ripping sound overhead had both Tirith and Edward instinctively looking up.

One of the massive glass-and-metal chandeliers was swaying.

Before she knew what was happening, Edward pushed her out of the way. She tripped on the wide skirt of her dress and fell flat to the ground. She lost her breath.

Edward covered her body with his.

There was an explosion of sound, metal against metal. Glass shattered.

When she peered under her arm, she saw that the chandelier had crashed to the ground.

Someone was shrieking, but the sound seemed muted.

Edward's warm hand clasped her bare upper arm. He helped her scramble to her feet. "Are you all right?"

Her heartbeat was pounding in her temples. She couldn't quite take stock of her body.

"Tirith."

He moved back slightly just as there was another *pop*. She flinched.

Was that a gunshot?

One of Father's guards ushered her toward the wall. "We've got to move."

She grabbed for Edward. He pressed closely against her back even as the guard kept her right behind him, so she was sandwiched between their two bodies.

Who would shoot into a crowded ballroom?

It seemed to take forever, but only a few seconds had passed by the time the guard ushered her and Edward into a utilitarian hallway.

They kept moving. Where was Maggie? Bea, Val, Mother, Father?

She couldn't breathe.

Why hadn't the guard separated her from Edward? She thought of those terrible gunshots and reached behind her blindly. Edward seemed to understand she needed reassurance because his hand closed over hers. His other arm came around to brace her shoulder.

The guard unlocked and threw open a door, his gun aimed in front of him as he peered inside. He motioned for her and Edward to enter. He stood inside the door, peering out. He seemed to be listening to his earpiece.

He glanced back at Tirith, who waited with bated breath.

"There's conflicting information coming across. It seems everyone is secure. But your father is requesting backup. Stay here until someone brings the car around."

Before she could ask why Father needed backup, the guard was gone. He'd said everyone was secure. That meant safe, didn't it?

She struggled to remember the layout of the facility. Her father's team had gone over everything in a security briefing this morning, but she hadn't paid enough attention. Like Mother, she hadn't believed the threat was real.

She'd gotten turned around in the chaos of the ballroom, but it was obvious this was a storage area. The room was full of stacks of extra chairs. Round tables were leaning against the walls on both sides with a narrow walkway left between. At the end, she saw part of a doorway, the lighted exit sign above it.

And she and Edward were alone under the stark fluorescent lights.

"Are you all right?" He dropped her hand and stepped back, his eyes scanning over her.

"I don't know."

She started shivering. When had it become so icy cold in the building? Only moments before, she'd been overheated in the ballroom.

He noticed, of course. Edward noticed everything.

He brushed his thumb over her cheek. "You've got a small scratch here. Probably from the flying glass."

But it would've been much worse if he hadn't shoved her out of the way. She might've been crushed by the chandelier.

He'd blocked her body from the flying glass and metal. The elbow of his tuxedo jacket was ripped, and his hair had a sparkle like he'd picked up glass shards.

He shrugged out of his jacket and threw it out around her shoulders. She let the warmth close over her, breathed in deeply of his familiar scent. She put her trembling hands through the sleeves.

He seemed satisfied that she would be all right for the moment. He paced toward the exit door and then back, glancing all around as if he might find a secret passageway. He stopped several feet away. "What is this room?"

"What are you doing here?" she blurted. "And where is your press badge?"

He had the audacity to smile at her. "I'm not here as a member of the press."

"How did you get in? My father—"

"Your father is pretty scary. But I explained to him exactly why I needed to see you, and he relented. He gave me one chance."

She found that hard to believe. How in the world had Edward convinced Father to put his name on the guest list?

He answered the question she hadn't asked.

"I told him the truth. I'm in love with you."

———

EDWARD WASN'T ready to register the shock on Tirith's face. He hadn't meant to blurt out his feelings quite like that, but nothing about this night had gone right.

"I quit my job." Saying the words still felt a little surreal. In the very best of ways. In the beginning, he hadn't minded when his editor, Holly, had kept him busy, hopping from assignment to assignment. But the CEO wanted higher revenues, Holly had started pushing harder on Edward. This wasn't the first time he'd been encouraged to leave his ethics behind. On other assignment, he'd found ways around compromising his morals. Or hadn't minded so much if digging up a story required getting his metaphorical hands dirty.

Until Tirith.

Knowing Tirith had shined a light on the ugly parts of his job. The parts he couldn't live with any more.

He'd injured his elbow taking Tirith to the ground when the gunshots started. He worried he'd hit her too hard, that maybe she'd been hurt, but she seemed to be unharmed except for the scratch on her face. Maybe that outrageously huge ballgown had some kind of body armor sewn into it.

"You can't quit your job."

It was the last thing he had expected her to say. Maybe *I never wanna see you again* or *leave me alone.*

"The stories you write matter." She blushed, the roses of color striking against her pale skin.

Warmth spread through his chest. Hope surged. "You've read my work?"

Her blush darkened, but she didn't deny it. Her chin jutted out at the stubborn angle he loved so much. "You tell the truth without putting a spin on it. We need more voices like that in the media."

What he really wanted to do was stride over to her and take her in his arms. Reassure himself that she was really all right. Kiss all the fear out of her—out of both of them.

Instead, he went to the door where the security guard had exited and pressed his ear to the portal. He didn't like being trapped in this airless room. Not knowing where the danger was coming from. Not knowing how best to keep Tirith safe. When would the guard be back?

"I can find another job," he said, looking back at her. "My editor and I stopped seeing eye to eye."

He saw the unspoken question in her eyes. He hated to disappoint her, but he wouldn't lie to her again.

"I came here of my own volition. I'm sure your dad has uncovered everything by now. Carrick is my brother. Peyton is my niece."

No surprise crossed her expression, but he saw the hurt. He hated that he was the one who put it there. Even if she never forgave him, she deserved the truth. "You and I met under false pretenses. I engineered our first two meetings. I was trying to get close to you to uncover the facts about the accident. I was sure you'd done something illegal or immoral, and then paid my brother off to make sure it stayed covered up. I was full of self-righteousness. I was wrong. I'm sorry. You'll never know how sorry."

She stood with her hands clasped over her elbows. Holding herself together. "Why haven't you published anything I told you? You're one of the very few people who know about what happened to Maggie and me."

His heart hurt. "Nobody should profit off of what happened to you years ago. That's your story to tell, or keep to yourself."

There was still too much distance between them. Earlier he'd spent fifteen terrifying minutes with her father, confessing his feelings and begging for a chance to apologize and make things right.

He had been gifted these few moments. He wasn't going to waste them by giving up. "I went to see Carrick and Peyton after your father kicked me off the ranch. My brother and I had grown apart, and a lot of that was my fault. We were able to clear the air between us."

Her expression softened.

"We haven't been close for a long time. I tried to take care of him by providing for his physical needs. I hadn't realized... He told me that what he needed from me was... just me." He still got a little choked up over the words. It seemed impossible to believe. He was just Edward. A bit of a workaholic. Nothing to write home about. Not like Tirith and her warm spirit, her kind heart that shined through every action she took. He cleared his throat. "After Carrick set me straight, I realized that maybe what you need from me is the same. Maybe I'm way off base. Maybe you'll never forgive me—and you have a right to feel like that. But I came here tonight to tell you that I love you. I think I started falling for you from the very first time you spoke to me. You surprised me at every turn. I am truly, madly in love with you."

There was a long moment of silence while his heartbeat pounded in his ears. His skin felt hot and prickly, as if he might slip right out of it. Why wasn't she saying anything? Had he gotten it all wrong?

Did she feel nothing for him?

And then he saw that her eyes were welling with tears. She took a step toward him. "Can you come over here?" He'd never heard her speak in such a tremulous, uncertain voice.

"Is that an order, highness?" His heart leaped and he strode toward her. She met him in the middle of the room and came easily into his arms when he reached for her. His own eyes were a little misty as he cupped her cheek in his palm.

"Did you really ask my dad to get you into the ball?"

That was what she wanted to know? "It was terrifying, but I knew that if I wanted to get farther than a few inches in the doorway, I was going to have to win him over."

"I watched footage of you. Of us together."

She had?

"From the day of the chili cook-off. I couldn't stop watching because of how you looked at me."

"I couldn't deny it, even then." He brushed a kiss on her cheek.

"Edward, I fell in love with you too."

His heart beat powerfully in his chest.

"I love you," she whispered.

And he finally let himself do what he had wanted to do since the moment he'd seen her in that crazy dress at the top of the stairs. He bent his head and kissed her.

It was there in the press of her lips against his, the way she touched the back of his neck. He felt how powerfully she loved him. His heart recognized the connection they'd shared from the beginning.

Tirith was a true princess. Goodness radiated from her heart and flowed into everything she did. He didn't deserve her, but he was never going to let her go. He was home now. He'd found what he'd been seeking for so long.

Tirith was it for him.

She broke the kiss, and he realized someone was knocking on the door. He turned their bodies so he was blocking her from whatever danger was coming.

It was Luc, her sister's husband, who stuck his head in the door. "Everyone all right in here?"

"Where's Maggie?" Tirith demanded.

"We're safe," Edward added.

"Maggie's okay. Shaken up."

Tirith relaxed in Edward's arms.

The man went on. "Your mother was injured. I don't know how badly. I can't get any information out of the guards other than that your father took her away."

Edward looked to Tirith, saw the worry and fear in her eyes. He clasped her hand and she clung to him.

Whatever the future held, they would face it together.

His Forever Princess

Chapter One

Once a Navy SEAL, always a SEAL.

But Gideon Hale wasn't a young and foolhardy warrior anymore.

It was early summer, but an inch of snow had covered the road through the Rocky Mountains of Colorado—a road that was more of a track than anything else.

The remote cabin stood empty and had been for months, judging by the dust covering every surface.

It didn't matter if there was an inch of dust accumulated on the countertops. That it was cold outside and getting colder. There was no room for him to be complacent, not when the princess had nearly been killed.

His wife.

His wife had nearly been killed.

He held a 9mm at the ready as he moved on stealthy feet across the cabin. It belonged to an old friend and there wasn't much to it. Not many places to hide. Maybe the curtained-off lower shelf beneath the minuscule kitchen counters. Gideon swept it aside with his foot. Empty.

He heard a soft sigh behind him as he bypassed the bed

and headed for the only other door in the place. A bathroom? He nudged open the door, 9mm pointed ahead of him. Careful.

Alessandra's next sigh carried a hint of impatience. Or maybe exasperation.

He didn't stop. Couldn't. His need to keep her safe was primal.

It was also the only thing holding back the fury pounding through his veins.

He swept aside the shower curtain. For one microsecond, the motion cast a shadow on the wall. He almost pulled the trigger.

But good sense prevailed.

He turned back to the room. "Clear."

Alessandra, in her charcoal sweater over dark-colored jeans, ignored him. He'd insisted she wear a hat to cover her golden hair, but she'd taken it off sometime in the last hours driving the empty mountain roads. Now she stared out the bank of floor-to-ceiling windows.

Neither one of them had slept in almost forty-eight hours, but he wouldn't have guessed it by looking at her. She looked as regal as ever. Perfect posture, every strand of hair in place, a hint of disdain in the slight frown she wore. Disdain for their accommodations? Or because she was stuck here with him?

He didn't let the thought land. Couldn't afford the distraction.

Yet he couldn't stop his memory from shifting to provide him a glimpse of Alessandra when he'd first met her. She'd been on the run then, too. Not dressed for the weather, pale and terrified. And beautiful.

He blinked away the memory that felt like a punch.

He secured his gun into the holster at his hip and crossed to the windows, where he began lowering the blinds.

Alessandra shifted. He didn't hold out hope that she would argue with him. It had been the silent treatment ever since they'd left the Triple H's ranch house. She'd argued then, on a video call with her sister, the Queen, and a security team from the palace in Glorvaird.

Gideon and Alessandra's sister Eloise rarely got along, but this time Eloise had agreed with his plan. Which meant Gideon had overridden Alessandra's protests about this plan. Twice.

She'd iced him out since.

When he reached above his head to pull the cord for the upper blind, the bullet-wound in his side screamed against the movement.

He ignored the pain.

These windows were a direct invitation for a sniper to take an easy shot.

"You can wash up, if you'd like," he told her.

He didn't look over to see whether or not Alessandra moved. They'd only stopped when the SUV had needed gas. And each time Gideon had followed her to the bathroom. It hadn't been a trip fit for a princess. But he didn't care. This was the only way to keep her safe.

Especially since she'd left him in the dark about the threats against her.

He was so angry his hands shook. They hadn't been on the same continent since Maggie's wedding. Before that, it had been at least five years.

She didn't need him. She'd made that perfectly clear years ago. But that didn't stop him from video conferencing with her security team once a week. He always knew where she'd be. What legislation or trade agreement she was working on. The threats against her.

Until this recent threat.

She'd ordered her security team to hide the truth from Gideon, to make the threat seem less severe. She'd almost died because of it. And put their daughters in the crossfire.

Gideon had made sure all three of his daughters, along with Maggie's husband and Tirith's beau, had been sent to secure locations as a precaution. He felt reasonably secure that his daughters would be safe. After all, the letters and emails had threatened Alessandra directly. Not his family.

Now it was up to him to keep Alessandra alive.

"I'm going to walk the perimeter. Then I'll bring in your bags."

He didn't expect a response, and none came.

Exhaustion buffeted him as he stepped outside into the darkness. The sky was littered with stars. No moon out tonight.

He leaned one arm against the side of the house, sagged against the wall, letting it take his weight. His side ached. He wanted to sleep.

Focus.

He had to keep going. This had been *his* plan. Isolate Alessandra until his team, not hers, had neutralized the threat.

It had been a long time since he'd been a Navy SEAL, but he still had connections with that world. He only hoped they would be enough.

He walked the perimeter of the cabin, eyes alert for any sign that someone had been here recently. Everything was dark and quiet.

At the SUV, he pulled out Alessandra's duffel bag and one of the brown grocery bags. His side protested.

He needed to check the wound. He'd only had time for the doctor to put in a few stitches and toss some antibiotics in his duffel. It had been twelve hours since then.

Inside, Alessandra wasn't immediately visible, and his pulse skyrocketed.

There.

Maybe the bathroom door didn't latch or something because it stood open a couple of inches. He caught sight of her blonde tresses, saw her face pressed into her hands, shoulders trembling.

His first instinct was to go to her. It was a visceral tug, the desire to pull her into his arms, reassure her, comfort her.

Except he wasn't the right guy for the job. Not anymore.

He dropped the bag of groceries on the counter with a thud. "Everything is clear outside."

He crossed to the bed and put her designer leather bag on the end of it. He'd need to scrounge up sheets and a blanket. A chest under the window seemed the likely place for them.

He was bone tired and didn't want to add one more thing to his to-do list, but there was nothing for it. Alessandra didn't need to sleep on a bare mattress.

He was propping the the lid of the chest open when he felt a trickle of warm liquid trail down his side, underneath his T-shirt and the flannel shirt he'd thrown over it.

He bit back a curse word. He needed to be at full speed, full strength. His wound would slow him down if he didn't take care of it.

When Alessandra left the bathroom, he set the sheets and blanket on the end of the bed and went into the bathroom himself.

Pain flared as he took off his shirt.

This was bad.

———

ALESSANDRA COULDN'T SEEM to get warm.

Gideon had noticed on the drive up. He'd turned on the heater and the heated seats.

Gideon noticed everything.

She hated that about him.

She didn't want to be here. To be sequestered with her husband. For him to find out the secret she'd been keeping all these years.

She'd argued for a different solution, but after the attack at Maggie's charity ball, Gideon and Eloise's security team had overruled her.

"It's only a few days." She barely breathed the words, but it was so quiet here—completely silent, unlike the constant bustle in the Glorvaird palace or the steady stream of cowhands at the Triple H—that her whisper sounded as loud as a shout.

"You say something?" Gideon spoke through the cracked bathroom door—the thing had a faulty latch.

She took her cell phone out of her pocket. She hadn't turned it on since yesterday, at Gideon's demand. If she powered it up now, she could guess that there would be no bars. No service.

"Is there wifi?"

She knew the answer before he said it. A remote place like this, more than an hour from the nearest town.

"No." His voice commanding, even with the partly closed door between them. "Keep your cell phone off."

She knew why. Location services could be hacked. But it still rankled to hear him order her around.

"I have the meeting with Ambassador Cain in a week," she said. "There are documents I need to read through. Send changes back through my assistant, Clara."

"You can mark up the paper copy your aide sent." He was maddeningly calm.

There was a rustle of clothing. And that was it. Just mark up the paper copy.

Her temper sparked. "I can't be out of communication for an undetermined period of time. There are people I need to talk to."

He didn't answer. She looked toward the bathroom, imagining banging on the door until he responded to her—

Then she realized he was shirtless.

It was so unexpected that she lost her composure for the briefest moment.

And he was staring at her, dark eyes unreadable.

"Who?" he asked. His voice held a dangerous undertone.

Who, what?

Afraid he would see her icy mask slipping, she shook her head and turned away.

But that didn't stop her brain from fixating on the memory image of him. Gideon wasn't the kind of rancher who sat behind a desk and ordered his cowboys around. He never had been.

And his years of work showed, even on a fifty-something year old body.

She hadn't aged as well as he had. She'd gone soft in some places, especially after Bea's birth twenty-four years ago.

Gideon didn't have an ounce of softness on him.

She closed her eyes, willing away the image of his broad shoulders and the ropes of muscles down his abdomen.

It didn't help.

What had they been talking about? Communications. Or the lack thereof.

"I need to be able to communicate with Eloise. And Clara. And there are others." She opened her eyes to a wavy reflection of him in the outdated stainless steel fridge.

He remained in the doorway, one arm propped on his hip.

Not on his hip, she realized.

Her surprise had her reacting before she'd thought it through. She whirled and took two steps toward him before her thoughts caught up. She stopped short.

"You're hurt."

Blood, stark red, was soaking through the wad of tissues he held against his left side.

She caught the flash of surprise in his eyes before his expression went carefully blank.

"I got nicked. I'm fine."

She'd seen his nicks before. Once at the ranch, he'd nearly sliced his finger off while filing a horse's hoof. He'd declared it so minor he didn't need to see a doctor.

She'd overruled him.

But back then, everything had been different. That was

before their marriage had transformed into this cold, barren wasteland full of pressure mines.

They stared at each other, all of it hanging almost palpably in the air between them. The words they'd spoken and the ones they hadn't. The missed anniversaries. Their daughters growing up without him. Both of them missing Maggie so deeply for so long.

He looked away first, a muscle jumping in his cheek.

He didn't like this either, she realized. He didn't want to be here with her.

Why had he insisted so furiously, then?

His sense of duty.

Of course.

Like recognized like. She understood duty. She was good at it.

It was everything else that she could never seem to manage.

"The mirror is too high." It seemed as if he was speaking through gritted teeth. "I can't get a good look at it." He twisted and she saw dark stitches against his skin. "Would you... please... take a look for me?"

She had to clear her throat to push words past the lump that wanted to choke her. "Yes. Of course."

Her feet took her to him before she could truly steel herself. The bathroom was minuscule, so she stayed in the doorway and bent to examine his wound.

"Was it...?" She couldn't say the words.

"A bullet. Just grazed me. Doctor checked it out and it passed right through. I'm fine."

He sounded so matter-of-fact, but all she could do was remember how they'd stood together at Maggie's charity ball. One moment, he'd been at a polite distance. Not so far that anyone would know they were estranged. He had once found it difficult to be more a few inches from her. He'd often stayed glued to her side, his hand at her back.

There'd been a crack that split the air, and she'd found

herself unceremoniously pushed to the ground. Gideon had covered her body with his.

Was that the moment he'd taken this bullet? One meant for her?

"I just need to know if the stitches held." His voice had gentled.

Had he guessed that her thoughts would spiral in terrible circles?

She breathed in deeply and was shocked by the familiar scent of his skin. He'd used that same soap since she'd met him. She just hadn't been close enough to smell it in ages.

Suddenly uncomfortable, she straightened. "The stitches look all right. But I'm not a doctor."

He nodded, meeting her eyes in the small rectangular mirror that was shoulder-height for his tall frame. "Can you stick a bandage on for me?"

She glanced past him to the sink, where he'd carefully laid out a white gauze square. It had tape on all four sides. All she needed to do was press it over his wound.

She reached past him to pick up the gauze. Her hand brushed his bare arm and the shock of the inadvertent touch sent her eyes flying to his in the mirror.

His gaze was hooded, telling her nothing.

Maybe she was the only one unmanned by the graze of skin against skin.

She grabbed the bandage and carefully lined it up before she pressed it against his skin. This time she was better prepared for the sparks that coursed through her.

"Good enough?" she forced a cool tone into her voice and when he nodded—she couldn't quite meet his eyes now—she turned to retreat.

There was nowhere to run, so she began making up the bed.

It had been a long time since she'd touched a man. That's what she told herself as she kept her eyes on her task. That was the reason for her overblown reaction. She missed touching, being touched.

It didn't mean anything.

And she needed to get ahold of herself if she was going to keep him from discovering her secret.

Chapter Two

Alessandra opened her eyes. She didn't know how much time had passed or whether she'd dozed off or not.

She rolled over.

The sheets on the bed at this remote cabin weren't the same quality she was used to. The feel of them against her legs was just a shade off uncomfortable.

Or maybe it was the company making her so restless.

There was Gideon, standing where she'd last seen him. He had one shoulder propped against the wall and stared out a sliver of exposed window.

She sighed softly. And she knew he heard, because his eyes flickered briefly.

"It's the middle of the night," she whispered. "You need to sleep."

"I'm fine."

His stitches had just barely opened. He hadn't lost much blood, but a gunshot wound was a gunshot wound. And they'd driven sixteen hours straight to get here.

She had a sudden urge to growl, like some kind of wild animal. Or chuck a pillow at him.

The man was so stubborn. So stubborn.

Well, so was she. Years ago, she had single-handedly convinced the royal council to uphold one of Eloise's only edicts.

She sat up in bed, the sheets folding around her bent knees. Her hair was loose and fell over one shoulder.

"You're not a machine," she argued softly. "You need rest just the same as I do."

Saying the words aloud was a good reminder for her, too. She'd lived in survival mode for so long. Sometimes it was easier to think of Gideon as a machine. A thing with no feelings.

Because if he was a machine, he couldn't mean to hurt her.

Alessandra hated that what had once been a warm relationship, one she'd been sure she couldn't live without, had faded into the same kind of sham marriage as her parents had.

Now he grunted, shifting a little on his feet. Was he in pain?

"I didn't pack a sleeping bag," he said.

Confusion pinched her brow.

Maybe he had 20/20 peripheral vision, because he continued as if she'd spoken her confusion. "There's only one bed."

Oh.

Did it bother him to think about lying in the same bed with her? Heat crept into her cheeks. She turned her face to the side.

"We shared a bed for years," she said. Was that her voice? Husky and soft? "It doesn't bother me."

He was silent and motionless for a moment that stretched long. The longer it stretched, the more she wondered if he was finally going to say all the things that were broken between them.

But then he was a blur in the darkness, taking the two steps from the window to the bed. He sat down gingerly on the edge. He must be in more pain than she'd guessed.

He moved his legs. She heard his shoes thunk onto the floor.

She stretched out again, lying on her back, scooting away to give him room. It wasn't enough. His shoulder still brushed hers, and she felt the awareness of his touch skitter down her spine.

He was lying on top of the covers. Still fully dressed.

But at least he'd relented. Maybe he would even get some sleep.

She stared at the ceiling, feeling more wide awake now than when they'd arrived.

The hours together had opened her eyes, made her remember that Gideon was tough, a product of his upbringing and his time as a SEAL and the nature of his profession.

He was a man, but he was human. He bled. He hurt.

And he kept that part of himself from her.

Who had started the rift, years ago? The memories were fuzzy now, nebulous. They could blow away if she breathed too heavily.

Thirty years ago, she'd pledged her life to Gideon. She'd trusted him. She'd loved him—and she still did. That was the secret she held so close. Because it was one-sided. And it made her weak.

"Where did we go wrong?" Had she meant to say the words? She'd held them close to her heart for such a long time. Afraid of the answer. Afraid that if she asked, every-thing would become final. There would be no coming back.

He made a noise halfway between a grunt and a sigh. "I thought you wanted to sleep."

She did. But now that she'd dared to speak the words, she also wanted to know. The question was out there, waiting to be answered.

But he remained silent, and she'd used up all her reserves of bravery for the moment.

Gideon could be reasonable, she reminded herself. She'd

fought against this plan, the isolation. But fighting against him hadn't gotten her anywhere. If he was her only chance of ensuring the trade agreement reached Ambassador Cain, she'd make nice.

"This agreement is vitally important," she said softly.

"I know." There was some resignation behind his words, something she didn't understand.

"I have to be back in Glorvaird by next Friday."

It gave her a little more than a week to somehow get her changes on the document to Clara. And the flight would take a whole day.

"Your safety is my priority," he said.

She turned her head slightly toward him. He moved, and they were looking at each other from only inches away. For one breathless moment, she thought about crossing the small space. She missed his kisses. Desperately.

"If you have to miss the press conference with the ambassador, is there someone who can speak in your place?" he asked.

She didn't want to think about that, but sighed and tipped her chin toward the ceiling, breaking eye contact. "I suppose Ronald Arnault is the one who knows most about it."

Gideon was lying still, but somehow when she spoke Ronald's name, he froze. Was he even breathing?

"We'll talk about it tomorrow." He spoke the words with finality and rolled over onto his side, facing away from her.

What had just happened? For a fraction of a moment, she'd thought that maybe he would soften toward her. Maybe they would have a chance to clear the air.

But her timing was off, as usual. He must be exhausted. He was injured.

And she was suddenly buried under the weight of all of it. Trying to keep up her facade. She had never used to hide her true self from Gideon. But there was such a chasm between them.

She would prove she could hold her own during this perilous time. She wasn't helpless like she had been when they first met.

And she had a duty. A job to complete for the crown. She wouldn't shirk her responsibility.

Gideon was reasonable. She held on to the reminder tightly. They could work together.

———

Where did we go wrong?

Alessandra's words echoed through Gideon's mind even after she'd fallen asleep.

Her head had turned toward him on the pillow and her even breaths sent warm air across the bare skin of his neck.

All of this was wrong.

He knew that's not what she'd been asking, but he couldn't help thinking it.

It should never have come to gunshots in a crowded ballroom.

If he'd lived in the Glorvaird palace with his wife, he would have known the seriousness of this threat. She wouldn't have been able to hide it from him.

It was thoughts of the other things she wouldn't be able to keep hidden that had kept him from her side all these years.

Ronald Arnault.

Gideon had known the other man would be trouble the moment they'd met in one of the many palace meeting rooms. He should've listened to his gut. He should've been there when his wife needed him.

Not that she would've asked. Ten years after their marriage, the Triple H had experienced a span of difficult years. A country-wide drought, a larger-than-usual loss of cattle to sickness, and Carrie's husband, Trey, had gone through treatments for cancer.

Gideon had come back to Texas, even knowing that

Alessandra was tied to Glorvaird, to her duties to the crown. And that's when everything had gone wrong.

How he hated that word. Duty.

If it weren't for his duty to the family ranch and legacy...

If Alessandra had a few less responsibilities...

What had once been a happy, if busy, marriage hadn't survived their individual lives tearing them apart.

And Arnault had been there to pull the pin on the grenade that blew everything up.

He'd never told her he knew. Was too humiliated. Gideon should've been enough for his wife.

Where did we go wrong?

Gideon shouldn't have come out here with her, alone.

He'd kept his hurt to himself for a decade now, along with the knowledge that she'd been having an affair. That Arnault was the one making her laugh and buying her flowers.

Just thinking about it made him want to howl. He clenched his teeth against the desire to make any noise.

Alessandra was his.

That kind of caveman mentality wasn't something Alessandra would appreciate. He'd always kept that side of himself hidden—the greedy, selfish side that wanted her all to himself.

After all these years, he was sure she didn't want to see it now.

He should call in reinforcements. Or take Alessandra to the nearest airport and put her on a plane straight back to Glorvaird and the palace that was built like a fortress.

But this whole thing had been his plan. Keep Alessandra hidden away until time to meet with the Ambassador. Give the FBI team back in Texas long enough to track down the assassins that had attacked during the ball.

His plan to hide Alessandra away was the opposite of her usual modus operandi. Her every move was published by the crown, she took every photo opp. Eloise had relied on her to be the face of the royal family for decades. Everyone in the kingdom, and even on an international level, loved Alessandra.

Gideon loved her, too.

He'd never stopped.

And maybe that was clouding his judgment now. Lord knows, he'd failed Maggie when she'd been twelve and needed him most.

No.

He couldn't think like that.

He turned his head slightly. The moon had come up in the hours since he'd walked the perimeter and light filtered through the blinds he'd closed. It was enough to see her expression relaxed in sleep.

She looked ten years younger.

He'd known her in her twenties, and she was even more beautiful now than she'd been then.

Her lashes formed dark fans against her cheeks. Her mouth was slightly open, and he forced his eyes away from her kissable lips.

He never got to see her like this. Relaxed. At peace.

When they were in a room together, she was always hiding behind a polite, distant mask.

He did it, too.

With every secret they held between them, taking off those masks was too painful.

Stop staring. He pointed his chin up to the ceiling again.

She doesn't want you.

He wasn't going to change the plan now. Not when they'd found safety in this remote cabin. He'd made sure they weren't followed. He'd turned off both cell phones and secured them in a Faraday bag in the back of the SUV after she'd patched him up.

Alessandra was safe.

It was his peace of mind that was in jeopardy.

How long could he stay in this tiny cabin, locked away

with the woman he loved—who didn't love him back anymore—and keep his distance?

He'd thought being separated from Alessandra was the hardest thing he'd been through.

This was worse.

Now she was close enough to touch, but she still wasn't for him.

He had to get through this. Keep her alive. Keep his emotions to himself.

Deliver her back home.

Do the job.

Chapter Three

Gideon woke disoriented.

His pillow smelled like Alessandra and in the hazy, half-awake place, he only knew that he ached for her. He reached out and his hand encountered only cool, empty blankets.

Instantly, he came awake. Everything snapped into place in his brain.

His wife.

The danger.

The cabin.

He sat up, rubbing one hand down his face. He ached, but it was the physical pain in his side, not the fanciful imagining his sleep-addled brain wanted him to believe.

Something was sizzling quietly, and he shook his head, still trying to clear his thoughts.

Alessandra stood at the stove, a rubber spatula in hand. She was watching him over her shoulder. He read the concern in her face.

"Are you all right?"

He cleared his own expression, just in case any lingering pain might be visible. "I'm fine."

He was always fine. The bitter thought was quickly shoved away.

He stood up and pretended he wasn't staggering those few steps past the cast iron, pot-bellied fireplace to the bathroom. He'd grown older when he wasn't paying attention. He couldn't go days without sleep. Not anymore. His body was fit for his age, but he wasn't kidding himself that he could go up against a twenty-five-year-old without risking injury.

His most important weapon now was his brain. And he intended to use it.

He splashed his face with icy water and rubbed his skin briskly with the rough hand towel. His side pulled, but he ignored it. He'd pop an ibuprofen along with the antibiotic the doctor had prescribed. He could handle this.

When he re-entered the main room and caught sight of Alessandra scraping scrambled eggs onto two plates, he almost turned around to duck back into the tiny bathroom.

Seeing his royal wife doing such a domestic chore brought him right back to those early days, when she'd found herself sequestered on the Triple H with a bunkhouse full of rowdy cowboys. She was as bad with inaction as Gideon. She'd cleaned the ranch house top to bottom. Cooked for them. Made the house a home.

The ranch house still bore some of her touches, but nothing was the same without her there.

He pushed those thoughts away as he joined her at the counter, reaching for the chipped coffee mug she pushed toward him.

"Thank you," he gruffed. She'd always called his rough morning voice his bear growl.

Would the hits keep coming this morning?

"You're welcome." She was watching him, her gaze curious. Checking to see if he was really all right?

He raised his mug. She did the same, taking a delicate sip.

His brows crunched together, and he lowered his cup before he'd taken a drink. That wasn't tea in her mug.

"Since when do you drink coffee?"

She lowered her cup, her eyes following the motion as she set the mug on the counter. "I acquired the taste about five years ago. And there's no kettle."

He hadn't thought to pack one. They'd been in such a rush. He knew he'd put her tea bags in one of the grocery sacks, but he hadn't given a thought as to whether or not there'd be a way to heat up the water.

"Sorry," he muttered. He hid his frown behind a sip of coffee. It was something else he didn't know about his wife. They were practically strangers now, weren't they? Even with three grown daughters between them.

The coffee turned bitter in his throat.

He scarfed down the eggs and toast she'd made, earning himself a sideways look that viscerally reminded him of their first meeting.

Then he took his meds. Started pulling on his boots.

"Are you going for firewood?" she asked. "It feels colder in here today."

He glanced around at the threadbare furnishings. There was no more wood in the iron holder near the stove. "Older cabins like this aren't always insulated that well. I'll grab some wood after I do some reconnaissance."

A haughty, bossy expression came over her. "What does that mean?"

He opened the door to find a light snow falling.

"I'm going to take a look around. Maybe hike down toward the road and make sure nobody's been in the woods since last night."

Her frown turned fierce. "It's snowing."

I know. He didn't say the words.

"And you're injured."

He grabbed the black vest from the small pile of belongings. "I'm fine. I'm hale enough to keep you safe. Let me do my job."

Her mouth trembled before she firmed her lips, a hardness overtaking her expression. Somehow he'd said the wrong thing.

He shrugged into the vest, ignoring the pull in his side. "I might be gone an hour. There's a second pistol locked in the case. There."

He pointed to a high shelf on the wall where he'd stashed his backup weapon. He'd given Alessandra shooting lessons himself, but that'd been years ago. He didn't know whether she'd kept up the practice. He didn't ask.

"I'll bring in some firewood when I come back."

He'd seen a pile stacked neatly between two trees, last night when he'd walked the perimeter of the cabin. It was set off from the cabin, at the edge of the woods.

He ducked outside without waiting for her to speak.

Last night, he'd been sure he could handle this. But being faced with a wife who had cooked breakfast, taken care of him? Not to mention how incredibly beautiful she was with her hair loose and a too-big sweatshirt.

For a long time, he'd been the only one who'd seen the softer, private side of the princess. The woman she could be at home, not the public face she showed when necessary.

He grumbled under his breath as he hiked away from the cabin. He needed to find his equilibrium.

He didn't walk a straight path through the pine forest that surrounded the cabin. For one thing, the mountainside grew steeper and steeper, and he had to take a roundabout path to keep from sliding down on his tookus. He also wanted the chance to catch any footprints or broken twigs, and he didn't know which direction an enemy might've come from.

It took longer than he'd thought to reach the winding mountain road they'd driven up yesterday. The air seemed to grow colder as he followed the road in both directions, from far enough away that he remained mostly hidden in the trees.

He didn't see any signs that anyone had been there.

That was good.

What wasn't good? His extremities numb from cold. It was well into spring back home in Texas. He hadn't packed winter gloves or thick wool socks. He hadn't been prepared for a spring mountain snowstorm.

His fault.

His side burned with every step now. Had he overdone it?

He stopped to lean against a long-dead tree. Its lower branches were gone, and some animal had stripped the bark from the trunk. At least it still held his weight as he tried to catch his breath.

He couldn't see the cabin through the snow, falling more thickly now. He'd thought he'd be back by now. Had he gotten turned around?

Was Alessandra still cold in the cabin? Had she packed better than he had? Did she have warm clothes to bundle up in?

His brain was getting sluggish. That was the real danger.

He forced himself to keep moving. If he died out here, who would keep Alessandra alive?

SOMETHING BIG HIT the side of the cabin.

Alessandra jumped, several pages of papers she'd spread across the counter floating to the floor.

What was that?

Heart racing, she stood on trembling legs.

More than an hour had passed since Gideon had gone out. Closer to two.

Then a sound like scratching against the outside of the wall. On the north side. Where there were no windows. The door was on the west wall.

Was it an animal? A bear, able to smell the food she'd cooked earlier? She'd read news stories of bear attacks.

She glanced at the metallic case on the high shelf Gideon had motioned to earlier.

She had some training, but she was nervous to even hold a gun.

What should she—?

A moan, louder than the wind that had been rattling the windowpanes.

She strained her ears to hear over the pulse pounding through her head. More rustling.

"Allie."

That was Gideon. She was sure of it. Sure enough to go to the door and pull it open, though she kept her body hidden behind the wooden panel.

"Gideon?" she called.

If it wasn't her husband, he was going to be angry with her.

"Allie. Help."

That was his voice, for sure.

She'd slipped into her shoes earlier, more because her feet were cold than any notion of going outside. She didn't bother with a coat now, just rushed out into the biting wind. Big, fluffy snowflakes landed on her hair and the exposed skin of her neck and hands.

He was leaning heavily on the house as he rounded the corner, moving slowly toward her.

"Gideon!" She went to him without a second thought, her arm going around his waist to support him.

His vest was covered in a thin layer of snow, his hand a block of ice when he grabbed onto her shoulder to steady himself.

"Why aren't you wearing gloves?" It was a silly thing to ask, but it was the first thing her mind latched onto.

"D-didn't h-have any," he mumbled through chattering teeth.

"Come on," she urged. "We have to get you inside."

It was only a few steps, but with his weight heavy against her and his feet dragging, the door seemed so far away.

One step. Two.

He stumbled. Even with her feet braced apart, they both almost went down.

She cried out. He gasped. Was he in pain? Was it his injury?

"You make me so angry," she cried out as she made a huge lunge toward the door.

He caught himself on the door frame, keeping them both from falling. Somehow, they shouldered him inside.

She was panting now, sweating a little beneath her layers from the exertion.

"You aren't thirty anymore," she said quietly, angrily. Tears were gathering in her throat and that made her angry too. "You can't just hare off into the woods. What if you'd frozen to death out there?"

His eyes were half-closed, his teeth chattering. He didn't answer.

He could be suffering from hypothermia. Her brain started to whirl in useless circles. She didn't know what to do. She couldn't get on her phone to find answers.

Get him warm.

That's all she could think.

New anger rose, anger that she hadn't gone out to find the woodpile herself. The small heater wasn't keeping up with the temperature outside, though it was warmer in here than out in the elements.

She needed to get him dry. Then she could build a fire in the pot-bellied stove in one corner of the cabin.

He hadn't moved since they'd come inside, only remained leaning against the wall. Was he even coherent?

"Come on," she demanded. "You need dry clothes." She reached up to unzip the vest and push it off his shoulders.

He gave a mumbled protest when she dragged his shirt over his head, grunted in pain when she made him raise his left arm. His bandage was still in place. She'd need to check it, but not now.

She went for the blanket from the bed as he struggled out of his pants.

"Get in the bed." She threw the blanket over his shoulders, but he seemed disoriented and didn't move.

She thought of giving him a little shove, but worried about his wound.

When she tugged him by the hand, he followed her the few steps to the bed, more docile than she'd ever known him to be. When she tried to step away so he could lie down, he wouldn't let go of her. He kept hold of her hand, pulling her close until she was tangled up in the blanket with him.

"Gideon!"

Maybe he fell or maybe it was intentional, but he took her onto the bed with him. He was behind her, snuggling like two spoons. He nuzzled his face into her hair.

"You're warm," he mumbled.

This wasn't a real embrace. He was only trying to get warm. And they'd both be embarrassed when he came to his senses and realized how he was holding her.

But she didn't tell him to let go. Didn't roll away.

One of his hands gripped the blanket, just in front of her midsection. She covered his icy hand with both of hers, settling there. Trying to share her warmth with him.

He didn't move, didn't speak for long minutes. He shifted slightly, and only then did she realize she'd relaxed against him.

"I'm sorry," he whispered into her hair. His teeth were still chattering, his words slightly slurred.

"You should be," she whispered back. "I didn't think you were coming back."

Just the thought of it now set a spiral of anxiety loose in her stomach.

"I lost your trust." His words slurred. "I saw it happening, and I couldn't stop it."

She tried to turn her head to see him, but his arm was heavy, trapping her where she was. Was he talking about today? It sounded as if he was having a whole other conversation.

"Gideon—"

"I tried to find Maggie, but I couldn't."

A shudder shook him.

Maggie? Find Maggie? Was he talking about the kidnapping?

Those had been dark days. Alessandra had been so worried about the twins, and she'd taken out her fear and anger on Gideon, even though he didn't deserve it.

"Maggie is fine," she whispered. "She's at the safe house with Luc. Tirith and Bea are safe too."

He rolled his head, the movement anxious. "I should've found her. I should've been the one."

Did he really believe that? The palace had invoked emergency help from every agency available to them. The police, the palace guard, international law enforcement, private investigators.

A local Glorvaird policeman had found Maggie at last.

"You did everything you could," she whispered.

It was my fault.

Those words she kept inside. Maggie and Tirith had been at an event Alessandra had planned. The palace security team had made mistakes, yes, but it was Alessandra's event. She didn't dare ask forgiveness from Gideon, not when she couldn't forgive herself.

A soft snore startled her. How long had she been lost in the past?

Was it dangerous for him to sleep?

She slowly ran her hand up his arm. His skin seemed to be warming. Would he be all right?

Even in his sleep, his arms tightened around her.

"Don't see Arnault again," he demanded in a sleepy voice. "I hate him."

"Gideon—"

Another snore. Was he talking in his sleep?

Why would he say such a thing? Ronald was a close member of her team. He was instrumental in the work Alessandra did for the crown. He'd become a friend over the past decade.

Maybe Gideon was dreaming about something else.

Though she was still worried about him, she slipped from his embrace, throwing a glance over her shoulder to ensure he was still sleeping.

She put on an extra sweatshirt and went out into the snow. She had to find that firewood.

Chapter Four

Gideon came to when the door quietly closed. Unlike earlier—or was it yesterday?—there was no disorientation.

The bathroom door was open, the light off.

Where was Alessandra? Had she gone outside?

He sat up in the bed, and as the blanket fell away, he realized he was mostly undressed. He remembered being out in the snowstorm, losing track of time and direction, but his memories of reaching the cabin were fuzzy and full of holes.

He'd been glad to see Alessandra. So glad. He'd wanted to grab her and kiss her.

He'd been clumsy, falling against the cabin to stay upright.

Now every muscle hurt. His skin hurt.

He staggered to the window and pushed back the blind. Relief surged when he saw Alessandra, her hair like a flag behind her, heading for the wood pile.

The snow had stopped, and the wood pile wasn't far, but it was growing dark, and shadows cast by the trees around them had an ominous feel.

She shouldn't be out there alone.

Had he slept the day away?

So much for being a heroic protector.

Worry sent him to his duffel. A minor bout of dizziness slowed him down, but he managed to get a pair of jeans on. He was pulling a T-shirt over his head when the door opened and sent a blast of chilled air across his bare feet.

Alessandra came inside, arms full of wood.

"You're up." He heard the same relief in her voice that he'd felt moments ago. Had she been worried about him?

"So I am." He was opening his mouth to apologize that she'd had to light the fire and tend it all day when she turned and knelt next to the pot-bellied stove. Her armful of wood clattered to the floor.

"I was beginning to think I was going to have to drive down the mountain in the dark on icy roads."

He frowned. Alessandra rarely drove herself anywhere— or she hadn't back when they'd been close. She always had a driver or a security guard behind the wheel. Why—?

"To take you to a hospital." She tossed the words over her shoulder, and he caught the glint of unshed tears in her eyes before she gave him her back.

His heart in his throat, he took a step closer.

She didn't seem to register his motion. She opened the stove door with a creak and fed in two chunks of split wood. She closed the door but remained where she was, kneeling on the floor with her shoulders hunched.

He couldn't help himself. He crossed the space between them and reached out to touch her shoulder.

"Allie, I'm sorry—"

He wasn't prepared for the hit when he glimpsed her teary eyes, wasn't prepared for her to awkwardly launch herself at him, to knock him on his butt on the floor.

She was in his arms, clinging tightly to him, and he didn't care that she'd swept him off his feet.

He held her as she breathed into the neck of his shirt. She wasn't crying, not that he could tell. She'd always been tough.

He should let her go, get her a tissue or something. But instead, he found himself rubbing her back in soothing strokes. Every moment he held her heightened the storm inside of him. He'd missed this. Missed her. A constant pain. As if a part of him was missing.

"I'm sorry I scared you," he murmured into her hair.

She drew in a shuddery breath and then her head tipped back, giving him a close up view of the concern in her wet eyes.

"Are you in pain? How much pain are you in?" She corrected herself. "And don't say I'm fine."

He couldn't help the curve of his lips at her petulant demand. He brushed one long strand of her hair behind her ear. "I don't hurt anywhere."

It was true. Even the throbbing of his wound had dulled. Give him a full night's rest and he'd be back at full speed.

Her gaze skimmed his face. What was she looking for? He was telling the truth.

Suddenly, she was leaning toward him. Her mouth brushed his and all thought fled.

Alessandra was kissing him.

And it was glorious. Like coming home. Like fireworks on a Fourth of July. Like perfection.

One of her hands threaded into the hair at his nape.

His hands curled around her waist. He couldn't get enough of her. His wife. His.

The primal thought broke through. He gentled his mouth and then pulled away from the kiss.

She wasn't his. Not anymore.

What were they doing? When she walked away from him in a few days, it was going to decimate his heart. Again.

But he still couldn't quite make himself let her go completely. He pressed his jaw against her temple as she panted, trying to catch her breath.

We probably shouldn't have done that. He bit back the words that would only hurt them both.

"I'm sorry I scared you," he said again.

She drew away. He let her go.

Though they were sitting a foot apart on the floor in front of the stove, his arms felt empty. His soul felt empty.

"Maybe we shouldn't have come here alone."

Her words battered him. If he'd planned better, if he'd had a team instead of stubbornly insisting it be only him...

"Maybe you're right."

He hadn't been enough to rescue Maggie. The thought slipped into his consciousness. A memory, a hazy one, of being half-frozen and holding Alessandra. He'd said *I should've found her. I should've been the one.*

This was the true cost of his stubbornness, insisting that isolation was the only way. There was nowhere to hide when the painful past they shared jumped out in the open between them.

It had happened so long ago. But the pain was still there, eating him up. That pain felt new again, slicing him open inside. Making him bleed. Was it the same for her? She didn't deserve that. Maybe being here was a chance for them to get this out in the open.

"When Maggie got grabbed—"

Her soft gasp interrupted him.

His hand crossed the chasm between them, curled around hers. And she let him.

"I tried to find her. I thought I was close but—" He shook his head. He'd found nothing. An abandoned warehouse that had been a dead end. No connection to the actual kidnapper.

She squeezed his hand, bringing him out of that terrifying place he'd gone to in his mind.

"That wasn't your job. Not yours alone," she said when he opened his mouth to protest. "You were a frightened father."

He'd been terrified. He knew what evil men could do, had

seen it firsthand during his time with the SEALs. Maggie had been helpless.

"I should've seen something. Done more."

She let go of him, and he felt the loss of her touch keenly. She turned her face away, but not before he saw a silver tear slip down her cheek.

"It wasn't your fault. It was mine." Her voice was choked. "I'm the reason Maggie was taken."

———

ALESSANDRA WASN'T TOUCHING GIDEON, but she felt him go dangerously still.

"How do you figure that?"

Her husband was one of the smartest men she knew. Maybe he wanted her to spell it out for him.

"The girls were in attendance at that event at my request." Putting it into words was painful. She couldn't look at him, so she tilted her face to one side.

"That wasn't your fault."

"Of course it was."

"How could you have known the girls would be targeted?"

Gideon wasn't a cruel man. She couldn't understand why he was playing dumb. She didn't expect forgiveness or absolution —but she hadn't expected him to make her say it aloud like this.

She inhaled and exhaled, her breath shaky. She was trying to make her words less so.

She couldn't stop another tear, then another, from slipping down her cheeks. She brushed them away quickly.

"Allie—"

Gideon sounded strangled.

She wished he would stop calling her that. He hadn't addressed her so informally in years. It reminded her of nights spent in the ranch house bed, in a house that'd been in

Gideon's family for generations. Gideon had liked to sleep with her tucked right up against him, his arm a warm weight around her. He'd whisper, "G'night, Allie," right before he fell asleep.

Now, it just hurt.

She wiped her face again, still unable to look at him. "We both know I'm to blame. That's why you pulled away." It was the only reason that made sense, all these years later.

"What?" His voice was flat, still with that dangerous undertone.

She glanced at him and then away. "You stayed away."

"Maggie needed me." There was a softening, a resignation to his voice when he said their daughter's name. And then a coolness slipped through. "And you didn't."

The words were an unexpected blow, one that rattled her, stole her breath.

"Of course, I needed you."

When he didn't reply, she glanced at him. He had turned his cheek so he was in profile to her. A muscle jumped in his jaw and his brows were drawn like a thundercloud.

He shook his head slightly. "I can't do this." He stood up, grimacing.

Was it his gunshot wound? Was he in pain?

She stood up too, desire warring within her. She wanted to touch him again, feel for herself that he was alive and well. But there was also fear. He was putting distance between them again. It felt safer to leave it be.

But was it safe to feel alone all the time? To miss him so deeply that she sometimes couldn't eat? Couldn't sleep?

"What can't you do?" she demanded.

His eyes flashed at her before he turned away. "That ice princess bit doesn't work on me. Never has."

"Gideon, don't walk away from me. From this." She dared to reach out and stop him with a hand on his arm. Beneath her touch, he was tense. "Why do you think I didn't need you?"

"Because you had him. Arnault." Another man might've spoken the words explosively. But Gideon had never shouted. When he was most angry, he got quiet.

She felt the reverberation of his near-whispered words, as if they'd been a bomb detonating between them.

Her hand fell away from his arm.

"Ronald?" Her own anger spiked. "Please tell me you don't believe the drivel those gossip rags write."

"It isn't what they write," he said bitterly. "It's how Arnault looks at you in the photos. Like a sappy, lovestruck fool."

She felt as if he'd slapped her.

"I have never been unfaithful to you." The words trembled, like her body, from the force of her anger. "Is this really what's kept us apart all these years? Paparazzi photos? You should've just asked me—"

"I didn't need to." Now he exploded, a little, one hand flying out from his side.

She flinched. He ran his hand through his hair.

"I flew to Glorvaird for your birthday." He exhaled, a bitter sound. "It was supposed to be a surprise. You can't imagine how difficult it was to leave Maggie. She was still so vulnerable. She'd only started speaking again." He paced to the window and stared out. "I bypassed everybody in the palace, coming to see you. And when I arrived at your private chambers, he was there. You were in this embrace..." He shook his head, as if he could wipe the memory. "I'd seen a few photos of you together. I already knew how he felt about you. But the look on your face..."

He clamped his mouth shut, but she'd heard enough. What he'd seen had devastated him.

How could she fix this? How did she tend a wound so deep and so old?

New tears fell, these for the pain Gideon had gone through, for the years they'd lost.

"I have never been unfaithful to you," she whispered. "I

swear it. I gave you my heart. Not anyone else."

"Honey, I saw..." She heard the resignation in his tone.

Shook her head. "I can't even remember what we were working on. A proposal for the royal council, maybe? I'd been terribly distracted. My family was falling apart. I never told Ronald. Eloise was the only one who knew. He worked seventy-two hours straight and rewrote the proposal. Maybe you saw gratefulness on my expression. I was grateful. He saved that proposal when I was too heartbroken to do right for my country." She wiped her face again. "There's only ever been friendship between us."

She wished she would have known. All this time... all the wasted years between them. Maybe they could've been spared some of the pain and loneliness.

He stared at her, and she willed him to see she was telling the truth. She'd given Gideon her heart. No one else.

He blew out a loud breath, startling her. Rubbed both hands down his face."I don't know what to think right now."

She wanted him to reach for her. To hold her again, kiss her like he had not that long ago.

"By the time I hit the tarmac back in Texas, it was like what had happened was confirmation of what I already knew. Maggie needed me—in Texas. The ranch needed me. And you were tied to Glorvaird." *Still are.*

He didn't say the last part out loud, but she knew he must be thinking it. She had a deadline to get back to. A proposal to finish. Her country needed her. She had a duty.

Thirty years ago, they'd believed they could do it all. She could work for the crown, uphold the family legacy. And Gideon could manage the Triple H with help from Carrie and Trey.

But those parts of their lives had pulled them in opposite directions. Still were.And she didn't know how to change that. Whether or not it could be changed.

She would always be a princess. Glorvaird needed her.

And Gideon would always feel the pull to Texas, running the ranch and the charity.

She ached from wanting to be close to him again, but he didn't cross the space that separated them.

And neither did she.

"Maybe we should get some rest," he offered. "Tonight's been... a lot."

He was right. Of course he was.

But she hated the distance between them as they passed each other, brushing teeth and changing clothes in the bathroom, lying silently in the dark.

She was drifting off to sleep when she came awake with a realization.

He'd never actually said he believed her.

It took her much longer to fall asleep after that.

Chapter Five

"ARE YOU WARM ENOUGH?"

Alessandra glanced up from watching the sidewalk pass beneath her feet. Gideon was beside her, handsome in jeans and a dark coat over his T-shirt.

She was the only one who knew he'd strapped a shoulder holster beneath his clothing.

"I'm plenty warm." The air chilled her cheeks and neck, but she was bundled up. It was a few minutes before twilight, and the snow had moved off several days ago.

They'd come off the mountain to get supplies, to this quaint, tiny town with a Main Street that reminded her of an American sitcom from the nineteen-fifties. The brick-and-glass buildings were so different from the historical architecture in Glorvaird. And she loved it. There was even a small park ahead, in the town square.

"This way." Gideon guided her with a touch at the small of her back, but she balked at the shadowy indoor stairway between two storefronts.

Gideon was glancing both ways, reading the street around them, and didn't seem to notice.

When he moved forward, she reluctantly went with him.

His arm came around her waist, as if they were teenagers who couldn't keep their hands off each other.

"Sorry to be overbearing," he murmured.

"You're not."

Things had been... strange between them these past few days. They hadn't spoken of Ronald again, but there'd been an openness, a hopefulness in the quiet moments spent together in the cabin.

Or maybe that was all on her side.

She didn't think so. Not when she caught the occasional thoughtful glance Gideon directed at her.

She'd been the one caught staring at his lips when she'd been curled up on the tiny sofa, supposed to be reading through the documents for Ambassador Cain. He hadn't kissed her again, but she couldn't stop thinking about his kiss.

At the top of the stairs, Gideon reached past her to pull open a heavy, metal door. He shielded her with his body momentarily. Then light streamed around them.

A familiar scent hit her. Books. A library.

"Thought maybe you'd want to check your emails."

A part of her was happy to stay in the little bubble they'd lived in for the past four days. Without the outside world pulling her in all directions, she'd been reminded of the quiet protector her husband was. The man who worked tirelessly without expecting thanks.

She hadn't asked for her phone, not after that first day. And a part of her hesitated even now as she stepped inside the public library. Once she opened her emails, the real world would demand her time and attention.

Things would change.

She didn't want the world to intrude. She hadn't found a way to say what she needed to say yet, to clear the air fully with Gideon. Because she couldn't see a way forward.

If she admitted she still loved him... then what? They'd tried and failed to keep their marriage together when they both had duties to attend to on different continents.

But there was no putting it off. She sat down at one of the six public computers. The machine was old and shaped like a box. How long would it take to load a browser-based email program?

Gideon stood nearby, pretending to peruse a shelf of crime thrillers. She knew he was diligently watching.

Not that there was much to be wary of. The librarian had smiled at them from behind her desk near the door when they'd entered. There was maybe one other patron browsing in the stacks at the rear of the building.

Her assistant was worth her weight in gold, for only three emails had been flagged that needed Alessandra's attention. Two she was able to answer immediately. The third was from Eloise, asking for an update. Alessandra closed the browser window and cleared the cache without answering.

She should've finished the proposal by now. She could've found a courier for her handwritten notes on the document. She was letting her sister down—her country down—by mooning over her husband.

She couldn't continue like this.

She stood and went to Gideon. "I'm finished."

He took them a more circuitous way to the door, so that they passed by a bank of windows overlooking main street.

He was so determined to keep her safe.

"This way," he murmured on the street. They walked toward the park, but the SUV was down the street in the other direction. Where—?

She grew distracted as they passed the park entrance. A mother and teenage daughter sat with a picnic blanket, where they'd set up a big cardboard box. On the side of the box in thick, black marker strokes was written "Puppies for sale".

Two floppy ears and a snout covered in blond fur peeked above the edge of the box.

Alessandra glanced at Gideon, only to find him watching her. His eyes had gone soft, and the corner of his mouth was twitching.

"You'd better stop for a minute."

It was all the permission she needed.

"May I?" she asked the mother, who nodded.

She knelt on the blanket and reached inside the box where there were not one, but three puppies.

They were happy for the attention and clambered all over each other to try to get to her. She laughed when one got close enough to lick her chin.

A sneaky glance at Gideon showed he was watching her, smiling. Not keeping an eye on their surroundings at all.

"Did you—?" He couldn't have planned this.

"I saw the sign when we were driving through." Not planned, but he'd brought her down the street just so he could give her this moment.

The man knew her every weakness. Knew she could never resist a puppy.

For a moment, she let herself get caught in his smile, let herself imagine what it would be like to stand up and throw herself into a hug.

He'd catch her.

But she didn't. No one in this town knew who she was, but there was still decorum. When she stood up, she beamed at him. He seemed to steel himself, before he looked away.

Gideon might know everything about her, but he didn't know she was falling in love with him all over again.

"Time to go?" she asked.

He nodded.

They walked on the opposite side of the street this time. As they came out of the park, a teenager and her boyfriend were passing. The girl did a double-take, but then seemed to forget about them as she kept walking with her friend. Gideon had noticed, though he didn't seem bothered.

The setting sun shining off the mountain behind the buildings across the street distracted Alessandra. It was picturesque.

And then Gideon took her hand.

Her face flooded with heat. He didn't seem to notice as he nodded to the movie theater marquee. They were nearly underneath it.

He didn't wait for her to answer, but ducked inside, pulling her by the hand. The interior was dimly lit and smelled slightly musty—how old was this building?—but she didn't care.

Until he dropped her hand and slipped past her to check the door.

Her smile faded.

She'd thought—

She'd hoped—

Gideon came next to her, pointing toward a hallway that led alongside one wall. A red exit sign glowed.

"What's the matter?"

His low murmur reached her ears as she allowed herself to be hustled in that direction. "Nothing."

He stopped her when someone came out of the theater itself. An employee.

"Not nothing," she said.

He stood close in front of her. Watching her closely.

"I didn't mean to scare you. That girl started videoing. I couldn't be sure, but it looked like she was pointing her phone at us."

Of course, he'd been paying attention. Protecting her, even when she'd been distracted.

"What's wrong?" He was apparently paying close attention to her now.

"Nothing. It's fine."

He clearly didn't believe her. He waited patiently, his eyes demanding answers.

Embarrassed, she had to look over his shoulder to get the words out. "I thought it was real. That we had come in here to watch a movie."

"Like a date? Would you really want that?"

—————

LIKE A DATE? Would you really want that?

Alessandra's soft but certain, "Yes," twisted Gideon's stomach in a knot.

He checked over his shoulder. The lobby in this single-theater movie house was empty. The uniformed employee had disappeared for now.

Which meant Gideon was free to lean his elbow on the wall Alessandra had scooted next to and lean. Not too far into her personal space, but enough that she would be able to tell he was interested.

She tipped her head back to look into his face. Man, he'd missed her.

"Being with you these few days has been..." She trailed off and he braced for what might come. Difficult. Strange. Harrowing.

"A blessing." Her voice caught on the words. "I'd forgotten so many things. I've just... missed you."

"Me, too, Princess." He couldn't help himself. He stepped in and scooped her into a hug.

Holding her was the one thing that made sense. She fit in his arms. Her cheek laid right over his heart. She smelled like whatever custom-made shampoo she used and the sweetness that was all her.

He never wanted to let her go.

A commotion came from behind him. Voices.

"I think they came in here."

He had Alessandra moving with a hand at her back before whoever it was made it through the front door.

They ducked down the dark hallway toward what he hoped was a rear exit. Alessandra went tense in the darkness, her breathing hitched.

"I've got you," he whispered.

"Is it—?"

"It's not assassins. Some dumb teenager with a phone must've recognized you."

"If they get a video of you on social and it goes viral..."

He didn't have to finish the sentence. She already knew. A random small-town teenager could bring down a heap of trouble on them.

He found the exit door with his hand. Prayed it wouldn't set off some kind of alarm as he pushed it open.

It didn't. No lights flashed or siren rang out. Probably the teenagers who worked here used the door to sneak in a friend every now and then.

Out in the alley, he took his bearings. There was a single lane running behind the buildings on this side of main street. No cars parked back here and a clear view to the end of the block on both sides. No foot traffic.

Thank God for small towns.

Alessandra took the gray scarf she'd had wrapped around her neck and tucked her hair up under it, did some magic until it was tied around her head like she was a movie star in an old-fashioned film.

"That ain't gonna work," he commented lightly. "Now everyone's just going to focus on your pretty face."

She rolled her eyes, but he got the blush he was trying for.

She tucked in closer to his side and he let his arm wrap around her shoulder. He wasn't too worried. This alley would put them out right across the street from where he'd parked the SUV.

But if she wanted an excuse to be close to him... well, he wasn't going to complain.

He hustled her into the car, the dark tinted windows a measure of safety, when he spotted the teen girl cruising the street, looking in all directions. The boy she'd been with was trailing behind her, looking miffed.

"Time to vacate this area," he said as he turned on the engine.

Alessandra didn't look up from buckling her seat belt. "Whatever you think."

She was going along without protesting?

"It might be a long ride."

She looked at him, and he felt the force of her gaze in his soul. "Good."

That knot in his gut twisted tighter.

He pulled out into traffic, making his way out of town and back down the mountain. She settled in, curling one leg beneath her and pulling a thick sheaf of papers out of the leather satchel she'd tucked in the floorboard earlier.

They'd both taken precautions and brought all their stuff out of the cabin. Not that they had much.

He snuck glances at her as he drove. She pored over what must be the big proposal she'd been so worried about when they'd first come up the mountain. She tapped her pen on the page. Then scribbled something. Clamped the end of the pen between her teeth.

Every once in awhile, she glanced over at him. The warmth in her eyes hadn't been there on day one.

After almost an hour, she put away her papers, tucked her head against her bent elbow, and drifted off.

She was so beautiful that he had to remind himself to keep his eyes on the road.

He wasn't kidding himself that everything between them was hunky dory now. There were still things that had been left unsaid.

She'd claimed there was nothing between her and Arnault, but Gideon had seen plenty of photos and video of the other man in the same room with Alessandra. Maybe she was innocent, but the man cared about her deeply. Was maybe even in love with her.

And Gideon was supposed to just let her walk back into a committee meeting where she'd sit right next to him? He'd once read an interview where Arnault had disparaged Gideon, though in the most polite terms imaginable. *The Princess's husband was not available for this meeting. He has his own interests overseas.*

Gideon hated the guy.

But Alessandra claimed he was a friend.

He didn't know whether he could be okay with that.

Besides, he had a life in Texas. A family legacy spanning generations. He'd spent the past fifteen years on the ranch building a new herd, growing the infrastructure for the Triple H. He didn't know if he was fit to live in the royal palace anymore.

Or if Alessandra would want that.

Things had changed between them, sure. He wanted his family back. His wife back. But just because she'd warmed up to him a little, would she be happy sitting in a movie theater next to him? That didn't mean she wanted all of it. The good and the bad.

He didn't have any answers by the time he stopped driving.

It was well after dark. The fact that no one had known their destination, except for the palace staff and security he'd notified, meant the tarmac was empty save a security car and the private plane, with its steps extended.

Gideon sighed.

He got out of the car and rounded the front, opened Alessandra's door gently. He didn't want to frighten her.

"Wake up, honey." He brushed the back of her hand with his thumb and she came to with a little sound, half hum and half purr.

She didn't even know where they were, but she smiled at him so beautifully it was like a kick in the gut.

"I like it when you call me honey," she murmured.

She reached for him, and he was very aware that this might be their last moments alone together.

He curled his hand around her jaw and claimed her with his kiss. She met him sweetly, her nose brushing his cheek when she turned her head for a better angle.

He heard a voice from far away. The last thing he needed was for her to be embarrassed. So he pulled away, both of them breathing hard.

I love you. The words remained trapped behind his breastbone. He had the worst timing ever.

She brushed aside her hair that had fallen in her eyes. She seemed alert now, looking to their surroundings.

"Are we—? Gideon, what's going on?"

He gestured to the private plane. "It's time to go home."

Chapter Six

I DON'T WANT TO GO WITHOUT YOU.

Alessandra had spoken the words before she'd exited the SUV.

At that moment, Gideon's heart had leapt, knocking against his sternum.

But hours later, he was sitting on a fancy leather seat on that private plane staring out the window at the ocean below.

Alone.

He hadn't been surprised in the least when she'd been whisked away by an aide and quickly surrounded by an advisor and a stylist. Two security guys sat near the front of the plane, at ease for the moment.

Gideon had been plied with food and drink by the attendant and left to himself.

They were getting close now. Glorvaird was waiting for Alessandra. She'd slip back into her old life, and he would…?

What had he thought? That by stepping on this plane he was making some big gesture? The threat wasn't over. Someone was out there, possibly even on the ground in Glorvaird by now. Alessandra was determined to proceed with her meeting with Ambassador Cain. Gideon wasn't needed as a bodyguard. And they hadn't made any declarations.

Through the space between two seats, he could see her blonde hair cascading past her shoulders.

If she'd wanted him to stay for her, wouldn't she have spared a few minutes in the hours they'd been on the plane to come and talk to him?

Maybe this was his answer.

He felt the change in altitude before he'd come to any decision. The easiest thing would be to hop on a commercial flight back home. A convoy of security would be waiting for Alessandra on the ground. They wouldn't make the mistake of taking this threat too lightly, not after what'd happened at Maggie's ball.

But just thinking about that made his stomach twist.

The plane touched down. He only had his duffel bag, the strap was quickly thrown over his shoulder.

Alessandra was closer to the door when the release was turned and the steps extended. He'd been right about the convoy. Through the window, he could see two black SUVs and several men in suits and dark sunglasses standing at attention.

Maybe it would be better to say his goodbyes here, where there was a modicum of privacy.

But by the time he'd gone out into the aisle, Alessandra was being escorted out the door by her security team.

His feet hit the tarmac and he breathed in deeply. How long had it been since he'd stepped foot here? He'd never forgotten the scent of ocean air, the rocky landscape beyond the airport buildings and a high fence.

She glanced over her shoulder and their gazes clashed. There was something in her expression, something vulnerable. Maybe this didn't have to be another end for them.

He followed her off the plane. The sun shone brightly, and he wished he hadn't forgotten his sunglasses in the SUV back in the States.

Alessandra was several paces ahead of him, between the two guards. He was familiar with this private section of the airport. Security was tight and it would be near-impossible for a threat to get through.

Still, he appreciated that the security guys were hustling her toward the safety of that SUV, with its bullet-proof glass.

Or was she the one hurrying?

Because standing next to the open door of the first SUV was Arnault, in a crisp suit, looking like a million bucks.

Gideon's stomach plunged.

Arnault was her welcoming committee? So much for *there's nothing between us.*

The guy was watching her approach with a starry-eyed expression, and Gideon suddenly couldn't stand it. He wasn't staying.

Couldn't.

He jogged a few steps as her escort came even with a handful of other security guys.

"Alessandra," he called out.

One of the big, bear-like figures stepped into his path and nearly bowled him over.

"Hang on, buddy." The kid couldn't have been older than Bea. He was clean-shaven and bulky-shouldered. Just looking at him made Gideon feel old. "You got a press badge or something? Why don't you give Her Highness a minute—"

Heat flashed into Gideon's face. It'd been years since he'd been mistaken for a commoner—back when he and Alessandra had first married.

"It's all right." Alessandra was right there, flanked by two burly guys. "Gideon is my husband. No badge required."

Of course the baby security officer was only doing his job. Someone he didn't recognize had stepped in front of the princess. How could Gideon fault him?

"I'm sorry, sir. Your Highness." Gideon saw the flash of the man's eyes from Alessandra to himself. He could practically feel the wheels in the guy's head turning. Wondering.

How did someone like Gideon, in his jeans and cowboy boots, belong with her?

He'd always felt like an imposter, standing beside her at royal functions.

Alessandra was staring at him, and he worked to neutralize his expression. He didn't even know what mess of emotions might've been showing on his face.

"Are you blushing?"

"We need to get you in the car."

Their words tumbled over each other. Gideon didn't answer her question as he stepped into place beside her, forcing the security guy to fall in behind.

"Staff informed me there are a couple of photographers with long-range lenses near the fence." She murmured the words without really moving her lips, in full-on princess mode. Perfectly coifed and serene. They were only yards away from the SUV and Arnault. Their last moments together and they couldn't even be private.

Emotion boiled up inside him. *Did you know he would be here? Are you happy to see him?*

He bit back the questions. He didn't even know if he had a right to ask them anymore.

What he wanted to do was take her hand. Right in front of Arnault and whoever had a camera out there. In front of the whole world. And whisk her away. Somewhere it'd be just the two of them. No royal duties. No ranch. Just Gideon and Allie.

Talk about pipe dreams.

"I wanted more time to talk," she murmured. They were within a few steps now.

Had she? He gave her the absolution he thought she wanted. "You've got a lot riding on this meeting. We both know how important it is."

It was true. For a lot of years, he'd been the sibling to be tasked with keeping his family's legacy alive. Alessandra's legacy was even bigger. She had a country depending on her.

He would never ask her to shirk her duty to the crown. It was a part of her. He'd known that before he'd gotten involved with her.

"I'll see you back at the palace," he said, though he didn't know whether or not that was true. Eloise and the palace staff held a lot of power of Alessandra's schedule. They might keep her so busy he couldn't get a minute in her presence.

She glanced from him to the first SUV. Or maybe Arnault. He saw her mouth move, but she was holding it in, whatever she wanted to say.

Fine.

"See ya, Allie." He didn't lean in and kiss her. Didn't take her hand, didn't make a single demand. He did his royal duty and got in the car.

And tried to shut off his imagination as to what kind of greeting she was getting from Arnault.

It was stupid to stay. He knew it.

But he couldn't get on a plane, not yet.

Giving up wasn't the Navy SEAL way.

———

ALESSANDRA SAT STIFFLY in the back of the SUV. There was one seat between her and Ronald, but it didn't feel like enough.

He'd started to greet her with a kiss on the cheek but Alessandra had stuck out her hand awkwardly between them, aware of Gideon. Was he watching them? Watching her?

Ronald had raised an expressive eyebrow, but she found she didn't care. She wanted Gideon to know there was nothing more between them than simple friendship.

As the car rounded a bend, she couldn't help turning her head in an attempt to glimpse the SUV behind. It was silly. She couldn't see Gideon through the tinted windows anyway.

"Is everything all right?" Ronald asked.

She realized he held a computer tablet in the space between them, a passage from the proposal highlighted.

No. She closed her mouth over the initial response that wanted to escape.

She wasn't all right. Things were still uncertain between her and Gideon. They'd cleared the air of some of the hurts between them, but nothing had been resolved. Not really.

Now she smiled tightly. "I have some unfinished business with my husband."

Something shifted in Ronald's eyes. An expression there and gone so quickly... but one that made Alessandra wonder whether Gideon had been right. Surely Ronald didn't have romantic feelings for her. He'd never breathed a word.

There was something stiff about his smile. "You've been married a long time. He must understand what the crown demands of you."

He changed the subject, smoothly moving to show her the changes suggested after her administrative assistant had faxed over her penned-in edits from the plane.

But she couldn't focus on his words or the tablet. Instead, she found herself staring out the window.

He must understand.

Gideon had always understood the demands on her time. Wasn't he the one who had been playing on the floor with Maggie and Tirith when Alessandra had been late to celebrate his birthday? The girls had obviously had an elaborate celebration in mind, the room had been covered in streamers and balloons. The girls had screamed for her when she'd arrived. He'd glossed over the fact that she'd been in meetings all day across the border in their neighboring country.

She could still remember the tired lines around his eyes. Bea had been a toddler, demanding and needy. And yet Gideon had come to her and held her close, kissed her cheeks as the girls watched. He'd told her she was the only gift he ever wanted.

In those early years, they'd agreed that they didn't want

nannies for their daughters, not if they could help it. Gideon had spent many exhausting days watching the girls, caring for them, while Alessandra did her duty for the crown. Often, he'd stood by her side at some gala or evening event. She was the only one who'd known how tired he was.

And then when Maggie had been so broken after the kidnapping, Gideon was the one who'd spent years of his life helping her heal. Alessandra was ashamed to admit now that she'd used her work for the crown to hide her own grief and fears and inadequacies.

She hadn't been strong enough to help Maggie. He had.

And he'd never asked for anything different. He'd never asked her to drop an event, even when the girls were sick with the flu and he hadn't slept in two days.

He understood the crown's demands. And he'd always put Alessandra and the girls first.

He was doing it again, even now.

He'd been shot. Given up a week of his time to protect her. She knew he would lay down his life for her.

And she'd gotten in the car with Ronald to work on this proposal. It was important work. It would impact her people and their lives.

But what about her life? What about Gideon's?

Hadn't he given up enough?

She felt an irrational fear that the second SUV would peel off and head back toward the airport. That Gideon would be gone before she had a chance to speak to him again.

Ronald must've given up on having her attention, because he'd gone silent. Finally, they arrived at the castle. She was out of the car before her bodyguard could open the door.

Gideon exited his car and frowned at her for that. Didn't she know better?

But before she had a chance to go to him, to talk to him, an aide was at her side, pointing her toward the arched entrance. And Eloise, who was waiting just inside.

There was no refusing the Queen. The Queen rarely

sought her out. They were both busy with their respective duties.

Alessandra barely had a chance to send an apologetic glance over her shoulder. Gideon's expression was shuttered, closed off. And then another aide stepped between them, and she lost sight of him.

Eloise jumped into an in-depth discussion of the proposal, one that Alessandra didn't dare drift away from. Her sister was demanding and impatient. And ultimately the ruler and protector of their kingdom.

Time passed as aides took rapid notes on their computers. Supper was brought in.

By the time Alessandra excused herself, it had grown late.

That didn't matter. She needed to see Gideon. But when she retired to her apartments within the castle, he was nowhere to be found.

Chapter Seven

Thirty-six hours after arriving in Glorvaird, Gideon was sequestered in a hotel room in a neighboring country.

The room was Alessandra's suite, and he passed through the living room into the bedroom. He pulled back the curtain just a bit. The window was ten stories high and had a view of the parking area, staffed by a valet, below.

It was a high-end hotel. The very hotel, in fact, where Alessandra and Ambassador Cain would meet to sign their finalized proposal in front of a bunch of television cameras.

Gideon didn't like the way this felt.

Maybe he should've gone home. Back to Texas.

"Dad? Did we get disconnected?"

Maggie's voice came from the cell phone he had pressed to his ear.

"I'm here, Mags. I heard you. Scarlette wants to sell off some of the cattle."

His niece—Carrie's daughter—and her husband co-ran the daily operations of the ranch now. They handled things when Maggie was called away to Glorvaird.

He let the curtain twitch back into place.

"Scarlette's got a good head on her shoulders."

Better than him. He felt foolish, being here.

He wasn't at this hotel in any official capacity. Not a part of the security team. And Alessandra sure as shootin' didn't know he was here.

He understood that Eloise had demanded her attention when they'd first arrived. But it'd been radio silence since.

No text, no phone call. She hadn't asked him to stay.

His wife couldn't have made it any clearer that she didn't want to see him.

So what was he doing here?

Nursing a broken heart, that's what.

"Dad? You okay?"

Had he made a noise? Maybe he'd sighed, like the sap he was. "I'm fine."

He strode back into the suite's sitting room. He'd notified the security team about his presence, but Alessandra didn't know he planned to meet her here.

There was no window in this room and the lack of a visual to the outside bothered him. There was no balcony. No secondary escape route,. Which of the crown's security dunces had booked this room?

When he opened the door to the public hallway, he got the stink-eye from one of the two security guys outside. The hotel had claimed they'd blocked off access to this floor, but that was easy enough to overcome.

Gideon shut the door again, brain working.

"Why don't you just tell Mom you love her?"

Maggie's words through the phone line shocked him into stillness in the middle of a horrible hotel rug.

"What?"

Impatience blasted him through her sigh. "That's why you took off with her. Trying to protect her. Why you're in Glorvaird now."

He wasn't in Glorvaird, but he didn't say that. Maggie was too astute for her own good.

He stood frozen, emotion battering him. He'd kept busy since the interrupted ball so that he didn't have to face it. But Maggie wasn't letting him off the hook.

He closed his eyes and pressed a thumb and forefinger into his eye sockets. It didn't help.

"I've always loved your mom." There was a relief in saying it. Admitting it to himself.

"When's the last time you said that to her?" Maggie asked.

He'd almost blurted it out in that little cabin, when she'd saved him from hypothermia. He was supposed to be the one rescuing her. She'd turned his life upside-down, from the very beginning. Made him realize what was truly important.

It had broken him, when they'd grown apart.

"Dad?"

He shook his head. His voice emerged rough. "I don't know, peanut."

"What do you really want?"

Her words galvanized him to go to the narrow desk on one wall and pull his laptop out of the leather carrying case. What he wanted right this second was for Alessandra to be safe. He'd managed to get it out of one of the old security guards he'd worked with before that she was due to arrive within the hour. He could spend that time memorizing an escape route. Just in case.

Because his gut was telling him something was wrong.

"If you want Mom back, you need to tell her how you really feel. Don't hold back."

He blinked away a hot layer of tears, quickly here and gone. His daughter knew him. He didn't admit to his feelings easily. Never had. Had that stubbornness cost him years with Alessandra? Probably.

But Maggie might be onto something.

"It might not be that easy," he said as the schematics for the hotel popped up in his email inbox. "There are things that could keep us apart."

"So eliminate them." Maggie had always been the most

practical of his daughters. And the most bloodthirsty. She loved a good revenge movie.

For a moment, he imagined getting Arnault out of his way in the most creative of ways. There was a visceral giddiness to the thought. But he blinked it away.

"One of those obstacles is your aunt," he said.

Maggie made a noise of understanding.

They both knew the strength of Alessandra's loyalty to the crown and the duties Eloise assigned her. He didn't think she'd ever walk away. It was part of who she was.

He personally thought Eloise took advantage of that. And Eloise knew that he thought it. It was part of why she didn't like him.

But it didn't mean the obstacle was insurmountable.

"The ranch can survive without you," Maggie said quietly. "You've put years of your life into it. If you want to stay in Glorvaird... I guess it comes down to the same question. What do you really want?"

His daughter might be a cowgirl, but she was also a royal, through and through. She could hold her own against any politician.

"When did you get to be the one dispensing advice?" he asked. If his voice was a little rough, he hoped she wouldn't notice through the cell phone connection.

She'd grown up when he wasn't watching. Fallen in love. He liked her husband well enough, even if he was a city slicker who barely knew how to ride. He treated Maggie right, and that was all that mattered.

"I just want you to be happy, Dad."

Now he had to blink a couple of times to get rid of that heat in his eyes. "Right back atcha, peanut."

She told him she loved him and rang off.

And he was left to stare at the hotel floor plans.

I just want you to be happy.

That's how he felt about Alessandra. If she was happy without him in her life, maybe the right thing was to walk away. Go back to the way things had been for the past fifteen years. Keep his broken heart to himself.

But he couldn't make the choice for her, could he? He was going to have to find some iota of courage and tell her how he felt. Find out whether she was really done with him.

Over the past week they'd spent together, he'd thought he felt their relationship opening back up again.

But once she'd stepped foot in Glorvaird, she'd gone silent.

Maybe that was his answer.

But he was a stubborn cowboy. Had been his whole life. He was going to make her say it to his face.

But first, he had to make sure she survived the night.

―――――

"YOU LOOK DIFFERENT," Bea said.

The video connection on Alessandra's phone flickered momentarily and then stabilized. She was riding in the back of a black Town Car, this one reinforced so it was as secure as possible. She was alone in the backseat—the first time she'd been alone since she'd awakened this morning. One bodyguard drove, while another sat beside him in the passenger seat.

"My stylist hasn't changed," she told her daughter.

She looked past the image on the phone to the proposal still in her lap. The final version. She was meant to meet with the ambassador in an hour. They were only minutes from the hotel.

"That's not what I meant. Mother—do you need to go?"

She felt a faint flush rise under her skin as Bea called her on her distraction. She locked her eyes on the screen.

"I can talk for a few more minutes. What did you mean?"

"There are fewer lines around your mouth," her daughter said with a smirk. "Have you been smiling more?"

Alessandra felt her cheeks pull into a too-false smile even as she answered her daughter. "I smile."

Bea lifted an eyebrow.

"I smile." This time her voice held a note of petulance.

In the front seat, one of the guards shifted and Alessandra straightened in her seat automatically, self-conscious.

"I was afraid you and Dad would argue the entire time."

"We did."

But the memory that popped into Alessandra's head wasn't from those tense first few hours. It was Gideon watching her as she'd knelt over a basket of puppies and giggled like a young schoolgirl.

"You're smiling now," Bea pointed out helpfully.

Alessandra strove to control her expression. She didn't know what was wrong. She'd struggled to contain her emotions all day. She'd nearly snapped at a poor staffer who'd done nothing but moved a bit too slowly when Alessandra had hoped to have a few minutes to locate her husband.

"Are you seeing Dad tonight?"

Alessandra's gaze flicked to the front of the car and back to the phone. "I don't know. I'll be at this trade meeting for hours. I haven't been able to get in touch with him."

She'd called once. He hadn't answered, and she hadn't left a voicemail. It had seemed too impersonal after everything they'd weathered the past week.

He might even be at the airport right now.

The thought of Gideon leaving, walking away again, brought tears pricking her eyes. She gave her daughter her profile as she tried to collect herself.

"I've been busy since we touched down yesterday." It was a flimsy excuse, and they both knew it.

"You're a princess of Glorvaird," Bea said quietly. "You're in control of your own diary."

It was true. And it was courageous of her daughter to call her out on it. There was an element of bowing to Eloise's wishes. And a whisper of her Father's voice echoing in her memory, demanding she put aside all else for the crown.

But that wasn't all of it.

"I'm frightened," she admitted in a whisper, "that we've hurt each other one too many times."

Gideon hadn't shown his face after Ronald had been waiting at the airport. Last night after Eloise had finally been finished with her, Alessandra had pored over paparazzi photos for hours.

Gideon was right. Ronald often put her in a more compromising position than was true. Leaning in closer than a friend. Watching her with a certain look on his face. Had he done it on purpose? She wanted to give him the benefit of the doubt. Perhaps some of the photos looked how they did because of a camera angle.

But perhaps there was a portion of blame to be borne by herself, too. She'd chosen to go to lunch or out for coffee after their official meetings were over. A part of her had craved the attention. Her own husband didn't want her, but Ronald always listened. Was there to share a meal.

She'd done Gideon wrong. And she hadn't apologized, not really. She'd told him the truth, that there was only friendship between them, that she'd never betrayed Gideon's trust. But she'd also made excuses instead of addressing the hurt her husband had admitted to.

"Did you ever think maybe Dad's scared, too?"

A tiny laugh hiccuped out of her. "Your father? He's never scared."

Even as she said the words, she remembered a long-ago time, waking up from a hazy, poison-induced coma. Gideon had been at her side, and he had been deathly frightened. Of losing her.

Had he just become better at hiding his fears over the years?

They'd both learned to hide from each other.

And they'd suffered for it.

Even now, the urge to put things off rose inside her. It would be easy to simply fall back into old routines. Go back to the way things were.

"I don't want to be estranged any longer." The words were out before she'd fully thought them through. But once she'd spoken, she felt the rightness of them.

She wanted Gideon back in her life. She wanted the closeness they'd once had.

She knew it would be a fight, but it would be worth it.

"I'll call you soon," she promised her daughter before they rang off. Then she realized they'd been idling at the curb for long minutes.

"Just waiting for the interior security team to give us the all clear," one of the guards responded when she asked what was going on.

It gave her time to dial Gideon's number. She would ask him not to leave. To give her a chance to see him.

She would beg, if that's what it took.

But his phone went to voicemail.

She stared at the shadowy building that stretched up to the sky. It was beautiful and gothic and historical. Gideon would say there weren't enough lights. Too many shadows, too many places to hide.

It sent a shiver of unease through her.

She had her security team, but the reminder wasn't as comforting as it would've been with her husband by her side.

Even through the assassination attempt at Maggie's ball, she hadn't been afraid. Not really. She'd known Gideon wouldn't let any harm come to her.

He'd always put her first.

She had to do her duty. Sign this proposal in front of a bunch of cameras. But that was it. After that, she would find Gideon. Hire a private detective if he didn't go back to the ranch.

She needed him.

Chapter Eight

Something was wrong.

It was there in the tense silence of the three bodyguards escorting her to the hotel room to wait. They would convene in the conference room within the hour.

Alessandra jumped when someone slammed a door nearby.

The bodyguard on her right reached beneath his suit jacket for his weapon.

That wasn't good.

There was the room. Weren't there supposed to be two guards outside?

Prickles ran up the back of her neck. What would Gideon advise her to do?

"Call for backup," she ordered the man on her right. There'd been several new hires in the past months, and she didn't know his name.

Her heart raced. Her palms dampened.

And then the door to her suite opened.

She gasped as a tall form filled the doorway.

"Gideon." She breathed his name.

Gideon was here. He would—

He took in the three guards with one of his thundercloud frowns.

"Do you trust me?" he murmured.

There was no question. "Of course."

He didn't pull her into the room, but stepped into the hall, taking her arm and pulling her away from the suite, in the same direction they'd been walking.

"Hale!" One of the security guards wasn't happy about it.

"She'll be a sitting duck in that room. There's no other exit." He let his words encompass the entire team, who had no choice but to stay at her side when she kept walking.

They approached a corner where the hallway split into a T. Gideon held back as one of the guards moved forward to check both directions.

At the momentary pause, Alessandra reached down to remove one of her three-inch heels. She swayed as Gideon's hand came underneath her arm to steady her. She switched feet and took off the other shoe.

"Where are the guards from the hallway?" she shot the commanding question at the bodyguard to her left, François, who was the lead today, and Gideon shot her an appreciative look.

The man shook his head as she clutched her shoes in one hand, leaving the other free.

The bodyguard in front of them motioned them forward.

Alessandra's stomach twisted. Something still felt wrong—

Gideon ushered her forward. Just as they cleared the corner and turned right, a door thunked closed somewhere down the hallway they'd just come from.

The guard behind her peeled away at a look from François. Gideon pushed her into a run.

"This floor is supposed to be completely empty," he whispered fiercely.

"Where's the backup?" she demanded of François.

Another appreciative glance from Gideon. She didn't

have time to soak in his praise that she'd asked for rein-forcements.

They reached the end of the hallway as sounds of a scuffle then a pop like a muffled gunshot sounded.

Terror smothered her in an instant. Her brain wanted to spiral back to the moments at the gala, or further, to thirty years ago when an assassin had nearly killed her.

Gideon seemed to know it, and his arm came around her waist. He steadied her and put himself between her and whatever was happening behind them at the same time. There was only one doorway at this end of the building. A stairwell.

The bodyguard ahead yanked it open and went inside with gun drawn.

"It's clear—"

He didn't even get the word out before Gideon pushed her inside.

The stairwell was well-lit, white fluorescent lights buzzing overhead. Was that good or bad?

"Down," Gideon said decisively.

One of the guards stayed behind at the door, which meant that only one remained with Gideon and Alessandra.

She started down the stairs between the two men. She had a stitch in her side from the short run and now the stairs. Her husband wasn't even breathing hard. But she hadn't forgotten he was injured.

"Your side," she panted.

"Ssh."

She sent him a scathing look. He grinned at her, though she saw the worry behind his easy expression.

He was trying to keep her from spiraling into that place of fear and frozenness.

"I'm fine," he mouthed when they reached the next landing.

She didn't know whether to believe him, didn't have a choice as he motioned the guard to keep going.

They'd started on the tenth floor. Surely this stairwell wasn't the best place to be—

A shot rang out from above them.

She flinched even as Gideon pushed her into a ducking position near the wall and covered her body with his own.

She half-stumbled, half-ran down the next flight of stairs.

Another shot rang out. Gideon dove for the exit that would lead them out onto the fifth floor.

She scurried through, trying not to make any noise. She hadn't dared look. Had the gunman been on the tenth floor? Had he somehow seen them exit?

The hallway was empty except for a young mother and her toddler at the far end, who looked startled to see them.

"Police are at the lobby level," François said. "They're locking down the hotel."

But the gunman was still behind them.

Gideon looked into her eyes. "Can you run some more?"

"Of course." She might wish she'd hired a better personal trainer, but she would.

He flew down the hallway, propelling her with him. François was at their heels.

He stopped at the elevator, mashed the button.

Gideon never chose an elevator. He'd once claimed you could never know who was waiting when the door opened.

Were things this desperate?

The doors opened, the car was miraculously empty.

Gideon pointed to some kind of card reader on the panel as they stepped inside. "Scan your pass." He aimed his words at François.

The guard took a key card from an inner pocket. Her security team had been granted access to every space in the hotel. The guard stepped off the elevator as Gideon pushed the button for a basement floor. Why there?

The doors closed, and they were alone.

"What are you even doing here?" she asked, still breathing hard, clutching the elevator railing with one hand.

Her husband had the grace to look slightly sheepish. Was he blushing beneath his tan?

"Please don't tell me you only came to protect me."

Not that she was ungrateful for his protection right now. If he hadn't followed his instinct and gotten her away from that hotel room, she would've been stuck inside—possibly facing—the barrel of a gun.

And then his expression changed to determined. "We've got some unfinished business between us, don't we?"

Her heart leaped. "There are a lot of things I need to tell you."

The elevator's motion started to slow. Gideon glanced at the numbers flashing on the wall display. "Tell me when we're safe."

"No."

She surprised him. Surprised herself.

"I'm not waiting to tell you I still love you."

He only had a beat to stare at her in surprise before the doors opened on a long utilitarian hallway. Not a space open to the public.

Gideon went right back into soldier mode. He escorted her off the elevator then nodded to the first set of doors, a swinging double door.

She followed him inside to a busy kitchen.

And a whole heap of security guards filing in from the opposite side.

Pure relief that made her burst into tears.

———

GIDEON WATCHED as Alessandra lost control of her emotions in a spectacular way. His wife usually had iron control over herself. The fact that they were in public made it even more surprising.

He was aware that the attacker could still be out there, but when she turned into his arms, he scooped her in close.

He turned his shoulder to shield her from anyone who might use their phone as a camera. She took a hitching breath and shuddered.

I love you.

His heart was pounding, but not from the danger. Not when Alessandra had just told him the words he longed to hear.

He and his wife were surrounded by royal guards almost instantly. He recognized Roberto, a man only a few years younger than himself, with whom he'd worked closely years ago. The man tapped his cheek, drawing Gideon's attention to the earpiece.

"They've apprehended him. He claims he was working alone, but we'll sweep the hotel. Local police are en route."

A lone gunman. Gideon felt some of his tension drain away.

Alessandra was still trembling in his arms, though she'd composed herself and now swept one hand across her cheeks.

"I imagine you still want to meet with the ambassador," he said quietly.

She glanced up, the tip of her nose still red. She was so close. All he had to do was lean forward, close those few inches...

But he didn't. This was real life. Alessandra was still a member of the royal family, and now a TV camera had entered the room. Some reporter must've gotten wind of the guards' movements and followed them.

Two guards were already ushering the cameraman and reporter out, but Gideon knew better than to make a spectacle. Even though he dearly wanted to.

Alessandra took a half-step back, and he let his hands fall away.

"Is it safe?" she asked, her words encompassing both him and the guard.

"We're sweeping the conference room floor first. The

ambassador is already here, and his security team is frantic to ensure his safety."

"I'd like to sign today," Alessandra said. "This is too important to delay."

He'd known she would say that.

As the guard faded back, she glanced up at Gideon almost shyly. "I worried you'd gone to the airport."

His heart leaped. Worried was good. "No airport."

"No. Because...?"

"Because there are things I need to say."

She was looking at him with such a hopeful, warm look that he wanted to sweep her in his arms and kiss her.

And of course, an aide chose that moment to interrupt. "Your Highness, they're ready for you."

Duty called.

It was only a matter of minutes before Alessandra was ushered into a large conference room. He remained at her side, mostly because of how tightly she was gripping his hand. Inside the room, a dais showed where she would stand, along with the ambassador. There were fewer photographers and reporters than he'd expected. And a larger security force, the men in dark suits outnumbering the press.

He attempted to let go of Alessandra's hand as she neared the stage, to fade back and stand against the wall, out of the limelight.

She turned to him. And didn't let go.

"Come up there with me."

He shook his head. "My place—"

"Is right next to me."

Maybe she was still frightened.

"Not because of any threats." Or maybe she'd read his mind. "Because I need you beside me."

His heart thumped hard. "What about—" He cut himself off as he glanced to the stage. There wasn't room on that little platform for both him and Arnault.

Except Arnault was nowhere in sight.

"There's a lot I need to talk to you about," she murmured. "He isn't here. And he won't be. I want it to be you, standing beside me."

Eloise wouldn't be happy. But Gideon was done arguing. If Alessandra was going to fight for them, he was too.

He wasn't dressed for the event. Alessandra and the ambassador wore tailored pantsuits, and he was dressed in jeans and a T-shirt. Ruining the photo opp. But Alessandra didn't seem to care.

She introduced him to the ambassador, who shook his hand and took his measure with a gaze. Cameras flashed.

Gideon stood back a bit as they signed the document. He was proud of his wife and the work she did. He could feel it oozing from his pores.

In his pocket, his phone buzzed. He resisted the urge to check it. This spectacle wouldn't last much longer. The guards for both the ambassador and Alessandra were antsy. They wanted both high-profile marks out of the public eye after the thwarted attack.

It was only a matter of minutes before he and Alessandra were ushered out through an underground parking garage and into the back of a limo with darkly tinted windows.

To his surprise, she asked for privacy. Slid the divider up that would separate them from the driver.

But she was dialing her phone.

He used the moment to dig his own phone out of his pocket. Tirith had texted him.

You're standing up with Mother!

While he was holding the phone, it buzzed with another text. Bea. *I expect to hear details.*

He loved his daughters.

Alessandra had the phone pressed to her ear. "I need to speak to her."

She glanced at him with a trembling smile.

His curiosity was piqued.

"Eloise, I'm pulling back on my duties."

His heart went into his throat as he registered her words.

"Valentin can take some of the committee work. My marriage deserves more of me than I've been able to give. I'll have Clara clear some time for us to sit down and talk through what that will look like."

He was shaking his head as she rang off, disbelief rampant.

"You didn't have to do that," he said.

She tossed the phone on the cushion beside her. "Yes, I did." She motioned to his phone with a curious look on her face. He tilted the phone so she could see Bea's text.

"Tirith texted too. Sounds like the girls are hoping for reconciliation."

"That's what I'm hoping for as well."

The vulnerable words cost her. He saw it in the downward tilt of her chin, the clench of her hand in her lap.

It was his turn to be vulnerable. "I should've run after you a long time ago. Left the ranch behind and moved here permanently. But if I'm not too late, that's what I plan to do now."

Beautiful hope was shining from her tear-filled eyes.

He did what felt natural and slid his arm around her shoulders. With his other hand, he brushed some hair out of her eyes. Swallowed hard. "I've been so stupid. I should've told you every day how much I love you. I never stopped, even though I lost the words. You'll never know how sorry I am for that."

One tear slipped free and rolled down her cheek. He brushed it away.

"I'm sorry too," she whispered. "I love you. I never stopped either."

Joy and warmth flowed up inside him, filling every crack.

He leaned in and kissed her, and it was just the same as always—like coming home. Like everything he'd always wanted.

Chapter Nine

Alessandra zipped the simple white sheath dress before taking a settling breath and looking in the full-length mirror.

Her hair had been pulled back in a French twist. Her makeup was natural, the way Gideon preferred. The tiniest nerves buzzing along beneath her skin didn't show.

"Mother?" A knock at the door. Tirith.

"Come in, dear." Oof. Her voice was shaking, just the slightest bit. She took another settling breath.

Tirith slipped inside the room. The secluded cottage was sequestered in the Glorvaird foothills, private, and as beautiful as a wild rose garden. Alessandra and Gideon had rented the entire space, creating a haven for their family for this momentous weekend.

"Are you nervous?" Tirith wore a teal calf-length dress that accentuated her figure.

"No." Alessandra ignored the butterflies tickling her stomach at the denial. "Why should I be?"

She and Gideon had been together nearly every moment of every day since that terrifying week almost a year ago.

Gideon had stayed with her in Glorvaird, turning over the

ranch operations to Maggie and Scarlette. Alessandra had taken a step back in the number of commitments she accepted at Eloise's behest.

They shared meals together. Slept in the same room. Traveled together.

She'd only been this incandescently happy in the early days of their marriage.

"Why should I be?" she muttered to the mirror, lest Tirith see that she actually was.

"You shouldn't." Tirith came to stand close behind her, offering a quick hug and then stepping back slightly, still visible in the mirror's reflection. "You love Dad. And he loves you."

He told her so every day. When she woke up to find him watching her from his pillow, sleepy and content. When they slow danced together without music on the balcony outside her rooms in the castle. In little notes left in her briefcase, and through his touch when he kissed her.

"And today was your idea." Tirith offered the reminder with a faint smirk that quickly turned into her lips pressing into a white line. She inhaled through her nose as Alessandra whirled in concern. Her daughter had gone a familiar faint shade of green.

"I wondered why there were saltine crackers and ginger candies left in such a sweet display on my dresser when we checked in." She pointed Tirith to the long, low dresser along one wall. Her daughter hurried over and wasted no time in unwrapping one of the candies and popping it into her mouth.

A few moments and a few deep breaths later, Tirith had regained a bit of color.

Alessandra raised her brows. "Something you want to tell me?"

Tirith shook her head slightly. "No. Edward and I agreed that we weren't going to tell anyone this weekend. We want this time to be about you and Dad."

What a sweet sentiment.

She crossed the room to hug her daughter gently. "Congratulations. What does Edward think?"

"He's over the moon," Tirith admitted, the words slightly muffled in her mother's shoulder. "I can't believe the staff delivered my things to your room."

Alessandra felt the prick of tears as she stepped back, though she still held on to Tirith's shoulders. "I'm so very proud of you."

Of course, that was the moment that Gideon chose to knock on the door and then step inside. "You about ready?"

He took in her closeness with Tirith in a glance and a smile kicked up one corner of his mouth.

"I just need my earrings." Alessandra let go of Tirith, who discreetly moved to the dresser and slipped several candies into an invisible pocket in her dress.

From the nightstand, Alessandra saw their daughter kiss Gideon's cheek on her way out the door.

Alessandra slipped one earring in, then the other, feeling Gideon's gaze on her the entire time.

"I should've sent Maggie after you."

She cocked one eyebrow. "If you compare me to cattle to be rounded up..."

She left the threat hanging, a smile slipping free.

His eyes were warm as she approached. "Nah. Maybe a docile little sheep."

She laughed in surprise. He caught her waist in his hands. "Careful. You look so delicious that if you come any closer, I won't want to let you go."

She blushed. It shouldn't have been possible, not at her age. "Gideon."

His eyes sparked. "It's true. And you've got a room full of people waiting for you."

That was a slight exaggeration. She'd asked for their girls to be here, along with their husbands. Bea was seeing someone, and it was serious. The young man had asked for an audience with Alessandra and Gideon only a week ago to seek their blessing to propose to Bea. He'd been invited too.

An intimate ceremony. A renewing of their vows with the people they loved best.

"You ready?" Gideon asked.

They'd been through the fire, and she'd almost lost him, this dear man she loved. The ceremony today was an affirmation of every promise she'd made in their wedding ceremony years ago.

She still chose him.

And she was ready for what life would bring, with him at her side.

"Let's go."

Christmas Homecoming

Heart of Gold

SUTTER'S HOLLOW SERIES
(CONTEMPORARY ROMANCE)

His Small-Town Girl

Secondhand Cowboy

The Cowgirl Next Door

COWBOY FAIRYTALES SERIES
(CONTEMPORARY FAIRYTALE ROMANCE)

Once Upon a Cowboy

Cowboy Charming

The Toad Prince

The Beastly Princess

The Lost Princess

Kissing Kelsey

Courting Carrie

Stealing Sarah

Keeping Kayla

Melting Megan

The Other Princess

The Prince's Matchmaker

The True Princess

His Forever Princess

HOMETOWN SWEETHEARTS SERIES (CONTEMPORARY ROMANCE)

Kissed by a Cowboy

Love Letters from Cowboy

Mistletoe Cowboy

The Bull Rider

The Brother

The Prodigal

Cowgirl for Keeps

Jingle Bell Cowgirl

Heart of a Cowgirl

3 Days with a Cowboy

Prodigal Cowgirl

Soldier Under the Mistletoe

The Nanny's Christmas Wish

The Rancher's Unexpected Gift

Someone Old

Someone New

Someone Borrowed

Someone Blue (newsletter subscribers only)

Ten Dates

Next Door Santa

Always a Bridesmaid

Love Lessons

NOT IN A SERIES

Wagon Train Sweetheart (historical romance)